Mecha-Jesus and Other Stories

Derwin Mak

Milton, Ontario

Brain Lag
Milton, Ontario
https://www.brain-lag.com/

Cover art by Catherine Fitzsimmons

Library and Archives Canada Cataloguing in Publication

Title: Mecha-Jesus and other stories / Derwin Mak.
Names: Mak, Derwin, 1963- author.
Description: Includes bibliographical references.
Identifiers: Canadiana (print) 20230565689 | Canadiana (ebook) 20230565719 | ISBN 9781998795178
   (softcover) | ISBN 9781998795185 (EPUB)
Classification: LCC PS8626.A4225 M43 2024 | DDC C813/.6—dc23

Content warnings: Abuse ("The Faun and the Sylphide"), anti-Semitism ("Kleinheimat"), the Holocaust (mentioned, "Kleinheimat"), prostitution ("The Shepherd's Blessing"), racism ("The Polar Bear Carries the Mail"), sexual assault (suggested, "The Shepherd's Blessing", "Seventy-Two Virgins"), violence ("Family Tradition")

To Harry Kremer (1945-2002),
Owner of Now and Then Books,
Kitchener, Ontario, Canada.

Your bookstore opened universes to me.
Thank you, Harry.

Contents

The Foreword You Probably Won't Read, Even Though You Should

Derwin Mak is the reason I saw the Barbie movie.

Why is this important to a book foreword? Hear me out.

I actively dislike the Barbie brand. I had no interest in seeing the lady who usually plays Harley Quinn play another seemingly psycho, not-all-there children's toy, and Ryan Gosling's over-contoured Ken chest freaked me out.

But my friend Derwin had been a convention masquerade sensation some years back cosplaying "Tour Guide Barbie". So I asked him, "Do you want to see the Barbie movie?"

He did. We went. I loved it. I ended up seeing it twice in theatres. I became a Barbie movie convert… and Ken was my favourite character.

Similarly, I have no moral objection to the Hooters restaurant chain, but it's certainly not top of my list of places to eat. I only go with Derwin. For a while, we were even doing book nights at the local Hooters, dressing up in gaudy, brightly-coloured formal wear and calling it "The Hooters Literary Society".

Why? Because it was absurd. It was kitsch. This is the genius of Derwin Mak: he can show you a different side to something at which you turned your nose up, and it starts to seem amazing.

Wisdom is sometimes found in eccentric, gaudy, lowbrow places.

But the exact opposite is true with Derwin as well: we

went to see Guillaume Côté's final performance as Romeo in the National Ballet of Canada's production... you probably don't know who that is and why it's significant and that is *totally okay*. These things are pretentious. But it's different going with Derwin because he's not pretentious *about* it. After the ballet we went to this horrendously overpriced vegan sushi place—yes, I said *vegan sushi*! There was imitation spicy tuna roll made from seasoned dehydrated watermelon. I don't want to know what the carbon footprint was on that meal. And they wouldn't let us keep the wine bottle on the table, because the table was so small that there really wasn't space.

It was absurd. It was no less kitsch than Hooters.

Wisdom is often not found in posh, trendy, highbrow places.

This is the Tao of Derwin Mak. It's his essence, that's difficult to explain because I don't think it's deliberate, but it's very much real.

And now it's my job to explain it, right? Here goes.

Derwin is unassuming in demeanour, and therefore he tends to be overlooked and underestimated. Derwin has a keen intellect, a deep knowledge of history, and a shrewd, mathematical analysis of human behaviour. I sometimes feel like knowing Derwin is not unlike what it would be like to know Charles Dodgson—the math ematician better known as Lewis Carroll. Mild-mannered, seemingly conservative mathematician by day—or in Derwin's case an accountant—absurdist, social satirist who rails against ridiculous systems by night.

We talk about methods in a creator's madness, but

Lewis Carroll wrote of the madness of the methods of his day, as Derwin does of modern conceits. Whether the story is set in a tragic past, an alternate present, or a speculative future, Derwin's stories combine a deep knowledge of history and analysis of the trends of the day they were written in.

I always have to remind myself that Derwin's stories are considered controversial in Canadian science fiction circles because his style is so tongue in cheek. In my head, his stories often play out like an anime—larger than life, incredibly emotional, and whimsical—as opposed to "hard hitting" science fiction that goes out of its way to make a point, at the expense of complex characters or an original story.

Then I re-read "Seventy-Two Virgins" in preparation for writing this foreword, and... yeah, I can see how that one was red meat for the perpetually offended! They probably don't find the pretension of watermelon sushi as funny as we did either. That story is possibly more shocking today than it was when it was published. But come on, it was written for a horror anthology.

Some people won't care about that context; you know what? They can choke on it. They can choke on that semi-colon I used as a flex there!

I think the controversy may also come from the fact that Derwin presents the worldbuilding that includes echoes of current issues like religious tensions, the climate crisis, AI and cloning in a fairly neutral way. These scary realities are presented in speculative futures as things that have become normal, daily irritations. Because he's not pummelling the reader with how bad this is, people tend to think he's "secretly" promoting their enemies. And he's not. Derwin, in real life, is a nuanced, moderated thinker who is not quick to leap on a political bandwagon. He worked for the Government of Ontario for decades, for God's sake! He was profession ally barred from having opinions in public!

Maybe working in government gives one a flair for the systemically absurd.

Short stories, at their best, confound black-or-white thinking: the conservation of language requires an author to do interesting things with a relatively simple concept, and focus more on questions than answers. Derwin excels at this. He uses protagonists with relatively little power in their cultures, often working jobs that are essential but invisible. Other stories humanize types of characters typically seen as immoral.

Sometimes Derwin's writing hits like a hammer because his style is matter-of-fact. It eschews the flourishes other writers use as crutches... like I did there, whipping out "eschews" when I could have just said "avoided".

I find it so refreshing in an era saturated with George R. R. Martin imitators who pepper their paragraphs with purple prose, thinking that makes them sound smarter. Purple prose perhaps has a place, but it perpetually punishes the participant by pompously prioritizing prestidigitation over a perceivable premise.

Congratulations if you understood that sentence, but I could have just said "it's easier for the reader if your writing is simple to understand". "Smart" literature tends to be written watermelon sushi—more costly, time consuming, and ultimately probably less healthy.

Derwin's digestible, simple prose lets his extensive

knowledge of history, theology and the strangeness of humanity do the heavy lifting, along with his tendency to include his own hobbies and love of kitsch. This collection asks questions about faith, personhood, purpose, and who gets to be a hero. In some cases, they challenge the idea of heroism itself by taking place in fanatical and oppressive regimes. But none of it talks down to the person reading it. It all feels like sitting across a reasonably-sized table, having a conversation.

Derwin's heroes tend to be like him—often under estimated by those around them. Instead of trying to convince the reader of a particular point of view, he just sets up a "what if..." and lets the story play out. The lack of grandiosity is a nice break from a market saturated with all-powerful dragons and space battles where the fate of the entire universe hangs in the balance. It's science fiction that shows that an average person can have amazing moments. You don't have to be an important person to do important things. Derwin's eclectic circle of friends and colleagues includes eccentrics from all walks of life and cultures.

For the record, yes, I count myself among those eccentrics. I've had the pleasure of attending many occasions when Derwin invited a friend with science-fiction convention fashion instincts and table manners to an event where the waiters wore white gloves. Sometimes it's like being in one of his stories—that delightful kind of weird that makes one question why we set the boundaries between people in the places we do.

Also, why does dried watermelon sushi exist?!

I had the pleasure of personally selecting two of the stories in this anthology for original publication: the eponymous "Mecha-Jesus" and the final work of this anthology, "Kleinheimat".

I'm very happy that Derwin's work is finally being collected into one place, because it's humble, unique, and affirming. It's a minor miracle many of them got published in the first place, based on how stuffy Canadian sci-fi and fantasy tends to be. Maybe we can credit that miracle to Mecha-Jesus.

I'm even happier that he's my friend.

He's a friend with whom you co-sponsor a drag show to raise money for an LGBTQ+ kid's summer camp. He's also a friend who writes emails and Facebook messages that make you feel like you're opening up a letter in the Victorian days, since each other is like a short story in itself.

He's the friend who sends me holiday cards every year, condolence cards when there's a death in the family, and postcards with things significant to stamp collecting on them that I admit I don't totally understand, but I will! Some day!

He's the friend who is quiet and kind, witty without arrogance, generous and meticulous. He will always be more organized than me but is never too critical when I'm late for nearly everything.

He's also that friend who will mutter something savage and hilarious to me at a time when guffawing would betray the treason against whatever ridiculous event we're suffering through because... why were we there again? For that treasured memory, clearly.

He's a friend who is invested in his faith while celebrating different traditions. He believes in doing the right thing, while recognizing that the right thing is often not immediately obvious. He's a friend who believes in both tradition and progress.

He's the friend I will eat watermelon sushi with *once*, but will regularly have drinks with, whether it's toasting the King's health with a fine port or drinking a Coors Light at Hooters.

He's a really good friend. And you're getting a glimpse of who he is in this book.

Liana Kerzner
December 2023

Luck of the Irish

"*Mein Gott*, you mean this man has been frozen in a block of ice since the *Titanic* sank?"

"Yes, Doctor Schumann," said Captain Reinhardt. He thumbed through the papers found in the man's pockets: a White Star Line ticket, some old British currency, an Irish birth certificate. "It is amazing that we found him. My U-boat was on surface, and my first mate saw him from the conning tower."

"I'm more amazed that he was floating for all these years. He didn't sink to the bottom. If he did swim to an iceberg, the iceberg could have drifted to warmer climes and melted, but it didn't," said Dr. Schumann.

The doctor reached into the tub of warm water to feel for the man's pulse. The man's eyes were closed, and he would have looked peacefully asleep except for the oxygen tubes attached to his mouth and nostrils.

"A pulse! A weak one!" cried Dr. Schumann. "He's alive!"

Reinhardt gasped. "Your cryogenic research—it's successful!"

Dr. Schumann twisted some dials and valves to control air flow and water temperature. "A miracle! To find a man frozen in ice for twenty-five years—neither dead nor alive—and thaw him out and bring him back to life! This is a great day for German science!"

"It is a great day for Germany because of the ceaseless support from the Fuhrer," corrected Reinhardt.

"*Ja*, of course," responded Dr. Schumann. "If this is possible with just one man, imagine the advances we could provide to the Fuhrer with an unlimited supply of test subjects."

"All in good time, *Herr* Doctor," replied Reinhardt as he gazed out the window towards the east, where the Fuhrer's visions would someday be realized. "All in good time."

*

Robert Kilpatrick hummed softly as the Navy nurse massaged his shoulders.

"Does that feel better, *Herr* Kilpatrick?" asked the nurse in Teutonic-accented English.

"Oh, yes," he replied. "I mean *ja*." He reached for the orange juice and sipped it. Each day, after a breakfast of bacon, eggs, toast and orange juice, the nurse would come to massage his back, shoulders, arms and legs. After the physiotherapy, the nurse would take him for a walk around the hospital gardens until noon. Then he would eat a splendid lunch; he especially liked the bratwurst. In the afternoon, the librarian gave him English newspapers and books about the last twenty-five years. At night, the nurse gave him a dinner fit for an admiral.

Kilpatrick looked at the nurse. She was a svelte, beautiful blonde, and her snug white uniform hugged her graceful curves. A beautiful woman, excellent food, lots of recreation time, colourful gardens, a clean room—he never had such a life in Dublin or aboard the *Titanic*.

Captain Reinhardt and Dr. Schumann entered the room. The nurse snapped to attention and walked out.

"Mr. Kilpatrick," beamed Dr. Schumann as he administered the stethoscope, "how are you feeling today?"

"Fine, Doctor," he said.

"Good, good. It is not every day that we find a Rip Van Winkle."

"What year is it again?" asked Kilpatrick.

"1937," said Reinhardt. "Has your memory returned yet? As a naval officer, I am curious as to how you became frozen in ice."

Kilpatrick shrugged his shoulders. "Sorry, I still don't remember much. I remember the ship sinking—all the people screaming and falling. I fell into the water, then I started swimming to a chunk of ice—and that's all I remember."

"I hope that our hospitality has been acceptable," said Dr. Schumann.

"Oh, it's great," said Kilpatrick. "Much better than life back home. And much better than on the ship."

"You were a worker exploited by British factory owners, and then you were treated like cargo by a British shipping company," snorted Reinhardt. "Believe me, we Germans know all too well what it is like to be mistreated by the British ruling class.

"Greedy British businessmen," continued Reinhardt angrily. "Save money by reducing the number of lifeboats on the ship. You would almost think they were..." He paused, composing himself. "But now you are a guest of the German Reich."

"And you will continue to be an honoured guest of the German people at our consulate in New York," said Schumann.

"New York?" asked Kilpatrick.

"Yes, New York," said Schumann. "That was your destination, yes?"

"You mean I'm finally going to finish my trip?"

"Yes," said Schumann, "and you will meet distinguished scientists, reporters, movie stars, diplomats—perhaps even President Roosevelt."

"You will tell the Americans about the wonders of German science and our warm hospitality," said Reinhardt.

The nurse returned with another nurse. They carried white linen shirts, colourful silk ties, a handsome blue suit, a tuxedo with black satin lapels, and shiny black leather shoes. Kilpatrick's eyes widened.

Reinhardt smiled. "Please accept these gifts from the German Navy. You will look like a first-class passenger when you arrive in America wearing these clothes."

Kilpatrick rubbed the fine wool of the suit. "But there's one problem—I don't want to go."

"Why not?" asked Schumann.

"I'll never go aboard a ship again!" Kilpatrick cried.

Capt. Reinhardt laughed and put his hand on Kilpatrick's shoulder. "You need not fear. Germany has the most advanced transportation technology in the world. And so many choices. If you are frightened by the sea, you can *fly* to America."

"Fly?" asked Kilpatrick, puzzled.

"So much has changed since 1912. Flying machines cross the Atlantic every week. Germany has the most advanced aircraft. My brother is in the Luftwaffe..."

*

At the airfield, Kilpatrick shook hands with Dr. Schumann and Captain Reinhardt. "Thank you for giving me a second chance for life," said Kilpatrick.

"It is we who should thank you," said Schumann.

Kilpatrick started walking through the airfield.

"Dr. Goebbels will be pleased," said Schumann. "He wants to show that German science is the best in the world. Television, automobiles, tanks, airplanes, rockets. And now, cryogenics."

"The propaganda will be great," agreed Reinhardt. "The British kill their passengers; we bring them back to life. *Titanic* victim finally finishes Atlantic crossing under German protection."

"Mr. Kilpatrick is a lucky man," said Schumann. "What do the English say? He has the luck of the Irish."

"He's waving at us," said Reinhardt. They waved back at Kilpatrick.

They were still waving at him as he boarded the airship *Hindenburg*.

About "The Luck of the Irish"

I wrote this story four years after watching the film *Titanic*. As the film ended, several audience members said, "I didn't know the ship was going to sink!" What else did they not know?

The Polar Bear Carries the Mail

Paul Chu and Jonathan Soong stopped their car and watched the funeral procession pass them. A small crowd of mourners followed the black hearse. To most southerners, these people were simply "Aboriginals", but after six months in town, Paul knew the names of their nations: Cree, Chipewyan, Métis, Dene, and Inuit.

A few Chinese walked with the Aboriginals. "We should be with them," said Paul. "If only Kate's flight wasn't arriving now. At least we got to the church service."

"The only whites in the funeral procession are our employees and the locals," Jonathan observed. "The protesters did not show up like they said they would."

"It's good that they didn't," said Paul. "They say they mourn for Danny too, but the locals blame them for his death."

A white environmentalist from Ontario had killed Danny Eastman, a Cree worker at the methane processing plant. Since the death had occurred at a protest where tempers had flared quickly, everyone expected the accused killer to plea bargain for the lesser charge of manslaughter.

"There's Ray Cassidy," said Paul, noticing one of the non-Aboriginals, a man in his fifties. "Did you get a chance to talk to him?"

"Briefly. He still will not come back," Jonathan said.

After the procession had passed, Paul and Jonathan continued driving past the small, short buildings of Churchill, Manitoba. When they reached the outskirts of town, the scenery changed to crooked, weather-beaten trees, a sparse forest at the southern edge of the Arctic.

Near the airport, Paul saw a sign reading:

WELCOME TO CHURCHILL, MANITOBA
POLAR BEAR CAPITAL OF THE WORLD

However, Paul had still not seen a polar bear. Like the fish and beluga whales, the polar bears disappeared when the methane acidified the Arctic Ocean.

Massive amounts of methane were frozen in the permafrost twelve thousand years ago. For centuries, the methane had been turning into gas and leaking to the surface. Early in the twenty-first century, the seepage intensified, especially from the ocean floor. Nobody knew the reason why the methane was outgassing. Some scientists suspected human-induced global warming, while others said the planet naturally goes through cycles of heat and cold.

The methane killed most of the marine life and polar bears along the southwestern shore of Hudson Bay, where Churchill is. The locals used to fish and show polar bears and beluga whales to tourists. Without fishing and ecotourism, Churchill needed another industry.

Ann Alaralok, Mayor of Churchill, told the town council, "Methane ruined one industry, but it can support another one..."

The town invited Stanley Aerospace, a Hong Kong company, to build a spaceport at the abandoned research rocket launch facility at Fort Churchill. Stanley Aerospace formed a consortium with several Canadian companies to build Churchill Spaceport.

Jonathan Soong, the spaceport's first general manager, came with rocket scientists from China, as well as from Stanley's Canadian partners in Montreal and Toronto. The Chinese brought a Long March CH4-1 rocket, a new model fuelled by liquid methane. The Canadians hired the people of Churchill to build the spaceport and a processing plant to harvest methane as rocket fuel. With the new Shanghai process, they could compress methane from gas to liquid cheaply and efficiently with fewer staff than older methods. The locals talked eagerly of starting hotels, restaurants, shops, and other businesses to serve the spaceport's staff, clients, and tourists.

But environmentalists came from the south to try and stop the spaceport and its methane plant. Last week, when they blockaded the methane plant, a riot broke out, and Danny Eastman was killed.

"Sometimes I think the spaceport is cursed," Jonathan said as he parked the car. "The protests interrupted construction work. There are no clients waiting to launch anything. The protesters scared ten people into returning to Hong Kong. Then Eastman died. And now Cassidy has quit working at the methane plant."

"Our luck's going to change," Paul predicted. "After *Polar Bear*'s flight, the space tourism program will take off, clients will line up to launch their satellites, and I'll be the first Canadian to go into orbit on a rocket launched from Canada."

"I wish that day would come soon. Then I will finally be able to return to Hong Kong," Jonathan said.

He pointed at an old Bombardier Q400 turboprop airplane sitting on the runway. "Look, the plane has arrived. Your girlfriend must be waiting for us."

They walked to the terminal and found Kate waiting for them. She wore a black miniskirt and green jacket with the logo of the St. Patrick's Society of Montreal, an image of the patron saint of Ireland.

Paul kissed Kate and stroked her brown hair. "Have you been waiting long?" he asked.

Kate shook her head. "No, not long. Just fifteen minutes."

"I'm sorry about that," said Jonathan. "We had a short delay along the way."

"What's with the black suits?" Kate asked. "You two look like you just came from a funeral."

"Actually, we did," Paul said.

Kate gasped. "Oh my God, now I remember. Danny Eastman."

"Mr. Soong," a voice called from a distance. It came from a man whose blond hair was styled in a bowl cut. He wore a green army surplus jacket over a T-shirt showing Hugo Chavez, the notorious Venezuelan dictator of decades ago.

As the man approached them, Paul whispered to Kate, "Here comes trouble."

Jonathan flinched as the man stared at them with his piercing, brown eyes.

The man said, "Mr. Soong, on behalf of the Churchill Environmental Alliance, I wish to express our regret that Mr. Eastman has died. We offered our condolences to his family."

Jonathan nodded and muttered, "Thank you. Mr. Eastman was an excellent employee. He was a good person."

After an awkward pause, the man continued. "Are you uncomfortable around me? That's so rude of you. You should be happy to see me. *That's* the Canadian way."

The man turned to Kate. "I don't believe we've met before. My name's Dr. Edward Hackbart. Pleased to meet you. And who are you?"

Kate glared at Hackbart. She must have recognized him from the news. Hackbart was a professor of political science at York University in Toronto. Last year, he spent six months in jail for breaking the windows of the Japanese Embassy to protest against whale hunting. The university stripped him of his tenure, and he drifted to Churchill to fight against the spaceport.

"My name's Kate," she finally replied.

"And what are you doing here?"

"Just visiting."

"Really?" said Hackbart. "In a town this small, it's hard to keep secrets. Aren't you Mr. Soong's new assistant, replacing the one who went back to China?"

"So what if I am?" she replied.

Hackbart grunted. "In the early twentieth century,

Manitoba had a law prohibiting Chinese men from hiring white women. It might not have been a fair law, but at least it stopped outsiders from messing with the province."

Kate scowled.

"Outsiders? You're from Toronto, just like me," said Paul. "You didn't live here until you came up as a protester! You live in a tent near the methane plant."

"My tent doesn't spoil the natural beauty of the area, unlike your eyesore methane plant and spaceport," Hackbart retorted.

"Okay, we need to go to the office," Jonathan ordered. "Paul, Kate, come with me."

Without saying any more to Hackbart, they fled from the terminal.

"Did you hear what he said?" Kate complained. "Was he being racist?"

"He became that way when he noticed that his opponents are mostly Aboriginals and Chinese," said Jonathan.

He shook his head. "We could have gone to Florida or New Mexico, but we came here."

They passed the methane plant. "Mr. Ming wanted the tax credits and cheap methane," Paul said.

When they arrived at Churchill Spaceport, Kate got out of the car and looked at the buildings, roads, and runways around her.

"Wow, this is amazing," she said. She pulled a small sketchpad and pencil out of her handbag and began drawing a spaceport scene. "I would love to paint this landscape."

"She has a fine arts degree from McGill," Paul

explained to Jonathan. "She wanted to be a painter."

"But being executive assistant to the president of the Montreal Museum of Fine Arts paid better," Kate admitted.

"I see," said Jonathan.

"Oh, there's your spaceship," Kate said, staring at the launch pad. A Long March rocket stood beside a supply tower. Atop the rocket was the *Polar Bear*, the reusable space plane. Despite the red maple leaf painted on her white body, the *Polar Bear* was made in China.

"Uh oh, no wonder the spaceport has been so unlucky," she said.

"What's wrong?" Paul asked.

"The supply tower has X's and jagged patterns on it. There's also a pyramid on the top. All those intersecting straight lines are bad *feng shui*," Kate said.

"How interesting," said Jonathan. "In a spaceport full of Chinese workers, the Irish girl is the first person to notice the *feng shui*."

*

It was late August, a time when the aurora borealis is visible. Paul showed Kate the northern lights. The aurora formed a moving green, red, and white backdrop to the Long March rocket.

"The northern lights are formed by charged particles from the magnetosphere colliding with gases in the upper atmosphere. I'll be flying into them," said Paul.

"Are they dangerous?" Kate asked.

"No. I'll pass through the aurora in a few seconds, so the electronic systems and I will not get a dangerous dose of radiation. In addition, the spaceship has radiation-hardened components."

Paul heard someone walking. He turned to see Ann Alaralok, Inuit historian, Mayor of Churchill, and a frequent visitor to the spaceport.

After Paul introduced Kate to Alaralok, the mayor asked Kate, "Is this the first time you've seen the northern lights?"

Kate smiled. "Yes. They're so beautiful."

"I bet Paul told you their scientific explanation, but do you know the legends?" said Alaralok. "The Inuit say the lights are sky people playing ball. And then there are the Cree. The Cree call the aurora 'the dance of the spirits'. The lights are the spirits of the dead."

*

At a video conference with the consortium partners, Jonathan updated them on the status.

"After the death of Danny Eastman, the police say they will no longer tolerate blockades and protests at the methane plant or the spaceport," said Jonathan. "The environmentalists have ended their blockades, but they remain camped in tents in front of the methane plant."

Donald Ming, President of Stanley Aerospace, gave a bittersweet smile from Hong Kong. "That is good news, although I wish the police had intervened earlier. We could have avoided the death and the delays in construction."

"This is Canada," Jonathan reminded him. "The police let protesters do whatever they want until someone dies."

From Montreal, Jane Holt, Vice-President of Space Tourism at Alouette Aviation, said, "*Polar Bear*'s flight will prove that we can provide a safe and effective space tourism product. But I'm having trouble selling tour packages before Paul goes into orbit."

"I'm ready for that anytime," Paul said. "I flew *Polar Bear*'s sister plane in a suborbital flight from Mojave. No problems. I know how to handle that plane."

From the corner of the boardroom table, Kate smiled at Paul as she typed notes on her laptop.

"The problem is acquiring the liquid methane fuel," Jonathan reported. "The original staff returned to China after the third riot. They trained some local people to take over, but some of them quit after bullying from the protesters. I have convinced most of them to return, but I do not have the compressor supervisor."

"Oh?" said Holt. "Hasn't Ray Cassidy returned to work?"

Jonathan shook his head. "No. Cassidy still thinks the whole enterprise is not worth the trouble if it cost his friend's life."

"Can you promote another person to take over Cassidy's job?"

"Maybe later, but not now. Cassidy has the most experience. I want someone like him on the job when we restart production."

"Please resolve the problem of the methane plant," Ming urged. "The company has spent billions of dollars on the spaceport, and the board of directors is worried that we have launched only a few unmanned suborbital test flights. The spaceport has not earned a cent. If you do not launch within a month, the board will cut its losses and sell its shares of the consortium, if anyone is willing to buy them."

In Montreal, Jane Holt looked startled. "Without Stanley Aerospace, the spaceport won't have enough capital. The rest of us can't operate it without a large partner."

"The board does not want to keep throwing good money after bad," said Ming. "I am sorry."

The conference ended. As the video screens turned blank, Paul saw Jonathan shrug his shoulders.

"I may go home sooner than expected," Jonathan said.

*

Barred from the methane plant and the spaceport, Dr. Hackbart led his followers to the post office, where the Chinese spaceport workers received parcels of food and gifts from home. The protesters chanted demands for the Chinese to return to China. The protesters lunged at the workers, and fighting broke out.

This time, the protesters fled when they heard the police car siren. Nobody got killed, but one of the Chinese vowed to quit and return to the Wenchang Spaceport in China.

After the fight, Paul and Kate went to the post office to send a toy polar bear to Kate's niece. The broken windows startled them.

The postmaster, Justin Gallant, straightened a poster of the Louis Riel postage stamp. Riel was the Métis leader who founded Manitoba and led two failed rebellions against the Canadian government in the nineteenth century.

The frame around the poster was broken. "At least they didn't damage the poster," he said. "I would be very annoyed if they had. I'm descended from one of Riel's brothers."

The post office lobby had a soapstone sculpture of Sedna, the Inuit goddess of marine animals. Hackbart had pulled the sculpture off its pedestal and hurled it to the floor several times. A small piece had broken off, and the larger piece was covered with dents and scratches.

Ann Alaralok picked up the sculpture. "How could they do this?" she cried. "Those hooligans have no respect for native culture! We should tear down their tents and send them back home!"

"The mayor's very angry," Kate whispered. "Aside from being an image of an Inuit goddess, is that carving important for another reason?"

Paul replied, "Ten years ago, the town council commissioned the statue to honour Aboriginal fishermen. That's when they had a fishing industry."

"It's as if the goddess had abandoned them," Kate commented softly.

She went to the mayor and took the sculpture. Sedna looked like a mermaid, but the tail had broken off.

"It's the bad *feng shui* at the spaceport. This town could use some positive *qi*," Kate said, referring to the energy flow of living beings.

*

Two Chinese lions arrived at the spaceport. Made of fibreglass, they were the type that guarded palace gates, though these ones were only a meter tall.

"What are they doing here?" Paul asked.

Jonathan replied, "Ming sent them from Hong Kong. When you fly, he wants the two lions in the passenger seats. After you come back, we will send them back to Ming."

"This is his encouragement for us to launch soon."

"The Minister of National Heritage will be visiting Hong Kong. Ming wants to give the lions to him as souvenirs of the first manned flight of a new Chinese spaceship."

The Minister was obviously the Minister of National Heritage of China, not of Canada.

Paul grinned. "There's a whole collectors' trade in things that flew aboard spaceships: flags, badges, medals, uniforms, mail, and even baseballs. Now the Communist Party wants space-flown fibreglass lions."

"Ming wants our first space tourists to be Chinese, so that is why the lions are joining you," Jonathan joked. "Everything about this flight will be Chinese. The Minister of National Heritage wants it that way."

"Except that I and half the mission crew are Canadian citizens and the vehicle will have a Transport Canada registration."

"And how do I explain that the spaceship *Polar Bear* is named after a Chinese animal?" Jonathan mused.

*

The mood in town was shifting. With Danny Eastman's death and the recent fight at the post office, people wondered whether the spaceport was worth the trouble. Would they always suffer scorn and violence if the spaceport opened for business?

"There are only forty people, all from out of town, who are protesting and causing trouble," Mayor Alaralok argued at a town council meeting. "The spaceport has all the required environmental programs for recycling, waste management, and carbon emission control."

Dr. Edward Hackbart stood up in the visitor gallery. "That's what they say now, but you can't trust these foreign businessmen. In any case, they're already spoiling the natural beauty you have here."

"The fish, beluga whales, and polar bears are gone," Alaralok said. "No fishing, no ecotourism. What will you have us do?"

"You can get government assistance," Hackbart suggested.

Alaralok scowled. "Can't you southern white people ever think of anything else than giving us welfare?"

"Clean the dirt out of your ears!" Hackbart yelled. "I never used the word 'welfare'! I said, 'government assistance'…"

As the council meeting degenerated into shouting, Paul wondered if he would ever fly. The spaceport had used up its supply of methane on the test launches. The plant was ready to compress more methane gas into liquid, but the inexperienced staff needed a skilled supervisor to guide them. One supervisor had fled back to China, and the other had retired to his home.

It wasn't only his hopes that were dying. The hopes of many townspeople were dying too. They had worked hard to build the spaceport only to see it turn idle, like past promises from outsiders.

Paul left the town council meeting and walked to Ray

Cassidy's house.

*

"Hey, Paul, come in," Ray Cassidy said as he opened the door. Despite quitting the spaceport, Ray was still friendly with its staff.

"Thanks for letting me in," said Paul. "I've seen you many times, but this is my first time in your house."

Ray asked, "Can I get you anything? A beer? A coffee?"

"Thanks for offering. I'll have a beer," Paul replied.

"Coming up," said Ray as he went to the kitchen.

Paul looked at the living room. On the wall was a family tree showing Ray's descent from an English fur trader who came to Hudson Bay in the nineteenth century.

There was also a photo of Ray and another man. They were in their twenties and standing in the flat, grassy prairie of southern Manitoba. Far in the background was a natural gas processing plant. It was a large plant from before the invention of the Shanghai process.

"That's me and Danny thirty years ago," said Ray as he gave the beer to Paul. "We grew up here but went south to work for Manitoba Hydro."

"When did you come back?" Paul asked.

"Danny got homesick and returned after five years and got married," said Ray. "I got married too but stayed in the south. I visited Churchill frequently, though. After my wife died, I retired and came back five years ago."

Paul looked at other photos of Ray and Danny and their families over the years. "You guys kept in touch for decades, didn't you?"

"We sure did." Ray picked up a model rocket. "Danny visited Baikonur Cosmodrome and gave me this toy from there. He was fascinated by spaceships because he worked at Iceberg Rocket Base when he came back."

"Ah, Iceberg. I heard of that company," Paul said. Before Stanley Aerospace, there were several failed attempts to create a commercial spaceport on the ruins of the old research rocket launch site. Iceberg Rocket Base was one of them.

"Look at this," Ray said, pointing at a shoe box full of postcards and envelopes.

He pulled out a postcard showing an old space shuttle. "Danny sent this to me from Kennedy Space Center, Florida. I collect stamps, so he sent me a traditional postcard, not an e-card."

"I didn't know he was so interested in space travel," Paul remarked.

"Oh, he was," said Ray. "He was thrilled by the idea of launching spaceships from here. That's why he came out of retirement to work at the methane plant. He even got me to work there too."

"Which brings me to the reason I'm visiting," said Paul. "You're our most experienced plant worker. You know the Shanghai process. You helped us start up the plant. I know you were planning to retire again after we found a successor, but we can't find and train one before the time we have to launch."

Ray shook his head. "Like I told Jonathan, it was fun at first, but after Danny died, I wondered if it was worth it. Was it really worth his death?"

"Danny wanted spaceships to launch from Churchill," Paul said. "Can you do it for him, at least for my flight?"

"No, not anymore," said Ray, smiling weakly. "Thirty years ago, I would've fought back, I would've defied those protesters, but now I'm too old for it. It's become hand-to-hand combat."

Unsure of what to say, Paul glanced at the computer on Ray's desk. The monitor showed the electronic version of *The Journal of Aerophilately*. An image of a Curtiss JN-4 "Jenny" biplane danced on its cover.

"What's aerophilately?" Paul asked.

"It's the study of airmail, a specialized area of stamp collecting or philately," Ray replied. "I've been collecting stamps since childhood."

"Oh." Paul pointed at the shoe box. "May I look at your envelopes?"

"Sure. Sit down at the table. By the way, an envelope that has gone through the mail is called a cover. The decorative illustration on the cover is called a cachet."

Paul looked at the covers. Most commemorated new air mail routes, but some had cachets and stamps showing spaceships and astronauts. The space covers bore stamps and postmarks from space centres in the United States, Russia, China, Brazil, and French Guiana.

"Wow, this one actually flew aboard a Shenzhou Gold," Paul said, noticing the special postmark in Chinese: "Aboard Shenzhou Gold Mission 38". The cachet showed the taikonaut crew standing in front of a Chinese flag.

"Shenzhou Gold Mission 38 carried one thousand covers. Most of them went to Chinese collectors, but I got one," said Ray, beaming with pride. "I've got the largest collection of space-flown covers in Manitoba."

"Ray, I've got an idea," said Paul. "Here's your incentive to create liquid methane for me..."

*

Paul went to Kate's office. "How much of my discretionary expense account is left?" he asked.

"Let me check," she said, accessing the accounting records on her computer. "About five thousand dollars."

"Check the municipal website. How many people live in Churchill?"

"About one thousand plus another two hundred who came to work at the spaceport. These totals don't include the forty protesters in the tent city."

"Forget about them," Paul said. "Can you do me a favour? Can you draw a picture of the Inuit goddess Sedna?"

"Sure, I'll do it. Just like the sculpture?"

"Yes. Draw a picture of Sedna and get a printer to print it on the left side of one thousand and three hundred envelopes. Then buy a stamp for each envelope and have your secretaries put stamps on the envelopes."

He pulled out his pocket computer and typed a message on it. "I'm sending you some words that I want printed on the envelopes."

Kate looked puzzled. "What are you planning? Sending a letter to everyone in town?"

"I'm going to create some positive *qi*, something to counteract the bad *feng shui*," Paul said.

*

Ray Cassidy returned to work the next day, and production of liquid methane restarted. So too did preparations for the flight.

Jonathan convinced the police to arrest Hackbart and the protesters for illegally squatting on private property, the land in front of the methane plant. Danny Eastman's death and the post office riot had finally exhausted the patience of the police. With the protesters gone, the countdown to launch began two weeks later.

The *Polar Bear* had space for three people: one pilot and two passengers. Paul shook his head when he saw the fibreglass lions strapped into the passenger seats.

He looked anxiously at his watch. Where were Kate and her secretaries? He hoped they would finish their job on time.

At five hours before blastoff, Kate and two secretaries rode the supply tower's elevator up to the platform leading to the *Polar Bear*. Kate ran to Paul and hugged him. Behind her, the secretaries pushed a cart carrying a large sack.

"You're not going to believe the stamp the postmaster sold us," Kate said.

One of the secretaries, a Métis woman, giggled.

Kate smiled wryly, opened the sack, and pulled out a cover. It had a cachet showing Sedna and a postage stamp showing Louis Riel.

"Oh, no, I wanted the Canadian flag stamp!" Paul said. "Louis Riel means nothing to the Minister of National Heritage of China."

They heard the elevator rise again. Ray Cassidy arrived on the platform and went to Paul.

"You'll be flying through the aurora borealis, won't you?" Ray asked.

"Yes, I will, but not for long," Paul said.

"Good. Can you take this postcard with you? The Cree

say the spirits of the dead are in the aurora borealis. I think he would want to know about your flight."

Paul looked at the postcard. It showed an aerial view of Churchill Spaceport. On the message side, it was addressed to Danny Eastman. Its Louis Riel stamp was cancelled with the special *Polar Bear* postmark, the same one on the covers.

Its handwritten message read:

Danny, your dream has come true. A manned spaceship lifted off from Churchill and went into orbit today. See you later. Ray.

"I can't stop in space and deliver it," Paul said.

"No, that's not what I want. Take it up with the rest of the mail," said Ray. "Just being in the aurora will be close enough for him to read the postcard."

"I'll take it up there," Paul said as he put the postcard into the sack.

A ground crew technician came and said, "Mr. Chu, the final preparations are starting. Could you please ask your visitors to leave?"

"I better get back to the methane plant. *Bon voyage*," Ray said. "I'll see you when you come back."

Kate gave Paul a deep, lingering kiss. "I'll give you your Canadian astronaut wings when you land," she promised.

The visitors rode the elevator down the supply tower but left the sack of mail behind. The technician stared at it and asked, "What's that doing here? It's not on the payload list."

"It is now," said Paul. He pushed the sack to the Polar Bear's hatch.

"This isn't authorized," the technician complained.

"I'm the mission commander. I authorize it," Paul said. He pointed at one of the lions. "Take that lion out and put the sack in the seat."

*

Gigantic flames, bright blue with burning methane, erupted from Long March rocket as it blasted off into the night. The aurora borealis danced in the sky. The rocket rose steadily against the backdrop of green, red, and white light.

The rocket flew towards the northeast. After speeding through the aurora borealis, the Long March's first stage separated, falling into Hudson Bay. Later, the second stage fell away. The *Polar Bear* went into orbit.

"Mission Control to *Polar Bear*," said a flight controller from Churchill Spaceport, "telemetry shows all systems are nominal. Can you confirm?"

"Mission Control, I confirm that," Paul replied.

He saw the aurora borealis along the curve of the Earth. Although he was not a religious man, he wondered if Danny Eastman's spirit was smiling on him, pushing away the hexes of the *feng shui*, and guiding the spaceship.

"Here's to you, Danny Eastman," Paul said.

After Paul completed one full orbit, the flight controller said, "Mission Control to *Polar Bear*. Stand by for a transmission from the observation deck."

Kate's image appeared on the video monitor. "Hey, Paul, congratulations on your first orbit! We're all cheering for you down here. Can you hear them?"

Cheers and applause broke out from the people

behind her. Paul heard Inuit throat singing and the banging of Cree drums.

"I can hear them loud and clear," Paul said. "It sounds like the whole town is there."

"Most of them," said Kate. "What do you see up there?"

"I'm passing over North America now," Paul reported as he looked out the window. "I can see Hudson Bay. Can you see me waving at you?"

The *Polar Bear* flew over Canada. Paul saw the whole country, from the Yukon-Alaska border in the west to Cape Spear in the east, from Cape Columbia in the north to Middle Island in the south. From space, the country appeared as large masses of green, brown, blue, and white: the forests, the tundra, the waters, and the ice.

"You should see the view from here," Paul said. "Everything looks so calm and beautiful."

Below on the ground, the various tribes of Canada squabbled with each other, as they always have. But from space, Paul saw one peaceful dominion.

*

After two orbits of the Earth, Paul ignited the rockets that pushed *Polar Bear* into re-entry. The space plane glided back to a runway at Churchill Spaceport. Within moments of climbing out of the spaceship, he was surrounded by a horde of ground crew and reporters.

Paul wrote "No. 1" on one of the covers and gave it to Ray Cassidy. "Ray, you get the first cover."

"Thank you!" Ray said as he shook Paul's hand.

Paul also gave the postcard back to Ray.

"I'll give this to Barbara," Ray vowed.

Kate kissed Paul and pinned an astronaut wings badge to his flight suit. "You did it, you created positive *qi*," she cooed.

The celebration continued inside the spaceport's main building, where the Chinese ground crew improvised a dragon dance with a dragon from Winnipeg's Chinatown. As the beast swirled through the room, Jonathan toasted Paul with a glass of punch.

"By the way," Jonathan said, "I have to ask you about the payload."

The spaceport manager pointed at a solitary fibreglass lion sitting on a table. "Lions always come in pairs. You never see just one lion in front of a gate. How can I send just one lion back to Ming? How can Ming give just one lion to the Minister of National Heritage?"

Paul pulled an envelope out of his pocket. "Send these covers back to Hong Kong. We've made one for Ming, the Minister, and each member of the Politburo."

Jonathan looked at the picture of Sedna and the stamp of Louis Riel. He sighed and said, "How does this envelope symbolize Chinese science and culture?"

"Look at its back."

Jonathan turned over the cover and read the words printed in English, French, Chinese, Cree, and Inuktitut:

This cover is made of one of the four great inventions of China: paper, which caused great cultural change all over the world.

*

The next day, the townspeople went to pick up free covers flown aboard Canada's first commercial orbital spaceflight. For the first time in years, the town hall resonated with the sounds of celebration.

Cree musicians sang a round dance song and banged on drums. Barbara Eastman, Danny's widow, explained to Paul, "They're singing about birds flying. August is the Month of the Flying Moon. It's when young birds fly from the nest."

She looked at the postcard that Ray had written. "Danny would have been happy to see you fly."

"I think he did," Paul said.

Mayor Alaralok held up her cover. "It's so nice of you to give a souvenir to everyone in town."

"We appreciate how much the people of Churchill have done for the spaceport," Paul said as Kate entwined her arm with his.

"That's a beautiful drawing of Sedna," Alaralok remarked.

"Thank you," said Kate. "Drawing it was a pleasure."

"The relationship between natives and non-natives has not always been happy. Outsiders have stolen our land, our culture, and even our children," said Alaralok.

"But you are different. You have given us the stars."

She pointed at the picture of Sedna. "But best of all, you gave us our dignity back."

*

A month later, Paul and Kate left for Montreal, where Paul became a pilot for a small airline and Kate resumed working at an art museum. Ray Cassidy retired again after training people to replace him. Jonathan returned to Hong Kong after handing the spaceport to a manager from Alouette Aviation. Most of the Chinese crew went back to China, but a few stayed and became Canadian citizens.

When Paul and Kate visited Churchill five years later, the town had two thousand people and numerous businesses. Satellites and space tourists flew into orbit from the spaceport. And the methane plant provided fuel not only for the spaceport but also for several communities in northern Manitoba.

But some things hadn't changed. The aurora borealis still appeared in late August evenings. Launch Pad 1 still had a supply tower with X's and a pyramid and bad *feng shui*. And Sedna, the goddess of marine animals, still adorned the lobby of the post office.

However, now the image of Sedna was a framed spaceflight cover carried on *Polar Bear*. On its frame was a small brass plaque engraved with the Chinese character *qi*.

About "The Polar Bear Carries the Mail"

Thirteen years after *The Dragon and the Stars* was published, I can finally reveal a secret behind two of its stories, "The Polar Bear Carries the Mail" and "The Son of Heaven". Both stories were written out of desperation for more science fiction in an anthology that was shaping up to be predominantly fantasy.

The Dragon and the Stars was the first anthology of science fiction and fantasy by overseas Chinese. Overseas Chinese are persons of ethnic Chinese descent living outside China. We ultimately published stories from Canada, the United States, the Philippines, Singapore, and Hong Kong.

Eric and I had wanted a 50/50 mix of science fiction and fantasy. Our proposal for the anthology said it would contain both science fiction and fantasy, and DAW Books bought it on that basis. Both of us had science fiction backgrounds; Eric writes hard science fiction, and I write soft science fiction. We knew that science fiction stories were difficult to write, and we wanted more of them.

However, when the submissions came in, they skewed towards fantasy instead of science fiction at a ratio of 8 to 1. We wanted a balanced anthology, but the writers gave us mostly fantasy. This caused Eric and I to take an unusual step: we decided to write science fiction (or at least non-fantasy) stories ourselves and include them in our own anthology.

Editors seldom include their own stories in their anthologies, but it does happen occasionally. For example, Robert J. Sawyer included his own story when he edited the anthology *Distant Early Warnings: Canada's Best Science Fiction* in 2009.

Eric wrote "The Son of Heaven", and I wrote "The Polar Bear Carries the Mail", and we submitted the stories to each other. Our personal backgrounds and interests influenced both stories. Eric is an aerospace engineer, and "The Son of Heaven" is an alternative history about rocket scientist Tsien Hsue-shen (钱学森). I collect stamps, and "The Polar Bear Carries the Mail" is about carrying mail in a rocket. There is a field of stamp collecting called astrophilately, which is about space-related stamps and mail flown in space.

There was a surprising number of marriages between Chinese men and Irish women in New York in the mid-nineteenth century. This history inspired the character of Kate.

I've noticed a skewing towards fantasy in other times that I've called for story submissions. For some reason, many speculative fiction writers prefer to write fantasy even when editors say they want more science fiction. Why writers are avoiding science fiction would make an interesting study someday. For now, my advice to writers is to get out of your comfort zone and submit a story that *isn't* like the ones that everyone else is submitting. Your chances of getting published would be higher.

The Dragon and the Stars won the 2011 Aurora Award for Best Related Work. Many thanks to science fiction author Julie Czerneda, the late Martin Greenberg and John Helfers at Tekno Books, and DAW Books editor Sheila Gilbert for helping us create our anthology.

Mecha-Jesus

Father Xavier Ito, a researcher of the Pontifical Institute of Robotics and Artificial Intelligence, could not escape from androids even in rural Aomori Prefecture. He drove past fields of apples, rice, and garlic, all tended by agricultural androids.

He slowed as he approached the black van in front of him. The van, moving at twenty kilometers below the speed limit, had Japanese flags and loudspeakers mounted on it. A voice boomed from the loudspeakers:

"ANDROIDS TAKE JOBS FROM HUMANS! PROTECT THE HUMAN RACE! DESTROY ALL ANDROIDS!"

Such sound vans were common at political protests in big cities. Father Ito had never seen one in a rural area, though. He guessed that the van drove slowly so that the few remaining human farm workers could hear it.

He passed the van. The words "PROTECTORS OF HUMANITY" were painted in bold white characters on its side.

Over the years, the police had arrested the Protectors of Humanity for attacking androids. Ito hoped that they were not going to the village of Shingo. There he had to examine an android that resembled Jesus Christ.

He sped away, leaving the black van behind. Further ahead, a lane was closed because a crack ran through it. In a grassy field, a barn had fallen over. An earthquake had hit Aomori a week ago. Fortunately, it had been mild, and nobody had died.

Finally, Ito arrived at Shingo. As his car drove into the parking lot, an android pointed at an empty space.

"Please park in that space," the android said.

Ito recognized the android as an L-2 by its shiny plastic skin, glazed eyes, and electronic machine voice. Although it wore a parking attendant's uniform, nobody would confuse it with a human.

Ito switched to manual control and parked his car. He approached the android and asked, "Where is the Tomb of Christ?"

"Please park in that space," said the android, pointing at another empty spot.

Definitely an L-2, thought Ito. He looked around and saw a sign pointing to the Tomb of Christ. It lay in the woods.

As he walked on the path to the tomb, he passed vendors selling crosses and Jesus statues. A banner reading "WELCOME TO THE CHRIST FESTIVAL" hung on an arch over the path.

A tour guide told his guests, "Jesus did not die in Israel as the Christians say. Instead, his brother Isukiri substituted himself for Jesus on the cross. Jesus fled to Siberia, then to Shingo. He became a rice farmer, got married, had three children, and lived to be one hundred and six years old. Because of his foreign appearance, people called him the Big-Nosed Goblin."

Nobody in Shingo knew that Jesus had lived there until a Shinto priest discovered Jesus' last will and testament in 1936. Jesus apparently wrote in Japanese, four hundred years before the Japanese had any written language.

Nobody in Shingo admitted to believing that Jesus had lived there. However, nobody would turn away the tourists or their money either.

A middle-aged woman approached him and said, "Ah, you must be Father Ito. I can tell by your clothes."

Ito always wore a black suit and Roman collar when visiting a holy site, even one of dubious history. Shinto priests were there, and he respected them.

Father Ito bowed and gave his business card to the woman.

"I'm Fukuda Hiro, the mayor of Shingo," said the woman. She handed her card to Ito. "I'm very pleased that the Vatican has honoured my request to verify that the Second Coming of Jesus Christ has occurred."

"I'm actually here to examine the android from an engineering standpoint," Ito said. The Pope had ignored all the messages that Mayor Fukuda had sent him. The Pontifical Institute, however, wanted to learn about the android Jesus.

"Oh, you're not here to verify the Second Coming?" Fukuda sounded disappointed. "Well, it's possible for Jesus to return as an android."

"Fukuda-san, are you Christian?" Ito asked.

Fukuda guffawed. "Of course not. Nobody in Shingo is. I follow Shinto, like everyone else."

Mayor Fukuda led Father Ito to two graves, both earthen mounds with unpainted wooden crosses. One of

Isukiri's ears and a lock of the Virgin Mary's hair were buried under one mound. The other mound held the bones of Jesus. Like the Jesus testament, the graves were unknown until 1936, and nobody had excavated them.

As tourists walked around the graves, Ito saw a European man holding a Bible and brochures. As people passed him, he said, "Accept Jesus Christ as your personal saviour and you will be saved!" He spoke in Japanese with an American accent.

Ito went to the man and introduced himself in English. The American smiled, bowed, and shook his hand.

"I'm Norman Richmond from Los Angeles, California," he said. "It's nice to meet another Christian."

"Are you a missionary?" Ito asked. He knew the answer, but it was polite to ask and make small talk.

"Only on weekends. I teach English in Aomori City, but in my spare time, I promote Jesus for La Cienega Bible Mission."

That was undoubtedly a small church, founded by laypeople and self-taught ministers, Ito thought. America proliferated with them.

"So, judging by your clothes, are you Catholic?" Richmond asked.

"Yes, from Nagasaki," Ito replied. "My family has been Roman Catholic for many generations."

"I guess the Jesuits got to them before the Protestants did." Richmond turned around, thrust a brochure at two teenaged girls and announced, "Accept Jesus Christ as your personal saviour!"

The girls giggled and said, "Real Christians have finally shown up at the Christ Festival!"

Mayor Fukuda came to Ito and Richmond. "Gentlemen,

the ceremony will begin soon," she said. "Please enjoy it."

Women clad in lavender kimonos danced around the grave of Jesus. They chanted the song "Nanya Do Yara", which was unique to the village. Its words had no meaning in Japanese but were reputedly derived from ancient Hebrew.

Then a man walked slowly to the grave. He wore a red Heian court robe and a tall black headdress. He stared solemnly at the cross.

"That's Enoki-san, a local Shinto priest," Fukuda whispered.

Facing the cross, Enoki bowed twice, clapped his hands twice, and bowed once more. He recited a prayer: "Jesus Christ, we honour you. Bless us with good weather and excellent harvests. Bring success in farming, academic studies, romance and marriage, and safe travels to those who pray and make offerings to you."

Next, Enoki waved a *haraigushi*, the sacred wand. Its zigzag paper streamers rustled in the air.

A *miko*, a shrine maiden in a white kimono-like jacket and a long red skirt, brought a bowl of rice and a bottle of sake to Enoki. The priest bowed to the cross again and put the offerings on the mound.

"Jesus Christ, please accept the rice and sake," he said.

Richmond stared wide-eyed at the ceremony. "This is wrong," he whispered. "This isn't Christianity."

"Who said Christ Festival is Christian?" Ito replied.

Enoki picked up a microphone and announced, "The Suffering of Jesus will begin now." He pointed at a path behind the graves. "Look, here comes the God of Christmas!"

Jesus, wearing a white robe and crown of thorns, carried a cross along the path. The crowd applauded and cheered.

"That's Mecha-Jesus," Fukuda said. "Tourist numbers have doubled since we got him."

Mecha-Jesus had skin that looked like human flesh, not shiny plastic. His eyes expressed pain rather than a glazed stare. He moved fluidly, like a human, without the stiff motions of an android.

"Is that the android?" Ito asked in disbelief.

Fukuda beamed with pride. "Yes. He's so realistic!"

Enoki narrated the Passion of the Christ. "Back then, Rome ruled Israel, and fascists ruled Rome. Jesus was a political dissident, so the fascists sent soldiers to attack him."

Men dressed as Roman soldiers, carrying whips, rushed to Mecha-Jesus. They lashed viciously at him. The android groaned in simulated agony. The soldiers yelled, "Pasta! Pasta! Pasta!"

Richmond looked puzzled. "Why are they saying, 'Pasta'?"

"It's the only Italian word they know," Fukuda said.

As Mecha-Jesus carried his cross, hundreds of people took photographs of him.

"Pasta! Pasta! Pasta!"

Mecha-Jesus put his cross down in front of the Jesus grave. The soldiers pushed him to the ground and tied him to the cross.

"The Romans nailed Jesus to the cross, just like we did to criminals during the Tokugawa Shogunate," Enoki explained to the audience.

The soldiers groaned and grunted as they raised the

cross. One of them complained, "This robot is so heavy!"

The cross wobbled under the soldiers' shaky grip. After holding the cross upright for only twenty seconds, they quickly lowered it back to the ground.

"Jesus died and went underground to the land of the dead," Enoki continued, "but then, a miracle occurred!"

The soldiers untied Mecha-Jesus.

Enoki proclaimed, "Three days later, he returned from the dead. Such was the miracle of Christmas!"

The android sprang to its feet and jumped up and down, smiling and raising his arms above his head.

"Pasta! Pasta! Pasta!"

The crowd cheered and applauded.

Richmond muttered, "This is wrong."

Ito turned to Fukuda. "Having Jesus die and be resurrected contradicts the local legend that he lived and fled to Japan."

Fukuda shrugged. "It's the story the tourists like. They've seen it in American movies."

Tourists crowded around Mecha-Jesus for photographs with him. The android smiled for the cameras.

"It smiles spontaneously and realistically," Ito observed. "It mimics human behaviour extremely well."

"Big-Nosed Goblin!" a teenaged girl squealed as she plucked the crown of thorns off Mecha-Jesus and put it on her own head. She smiled, pointed at her friends and their cameras, and made a peace sign. Mecha-Jesus laughed and posed for a photo with her. She left with the crown of thorns, now a souvenir of her pilgrimage.

Richmond pressed his Bible to his chest and prayed in English. "Dear God, I thank you for enabling these people to discover your son Jesus Christ. However, their ways of honouring him are heathen, and they have not accepted him as their lord and saviour. Please show them the correct path. Amen."

Ito asked Richmond, "How long have you been coming here?"

"Once a week for two years, ever since they got the android," Richmond replied. "I thought the android would get people interested in Jesus, and I could get some people interested in Christianity."

"How many people have you converted?"

"None so far."

They went to Mecha-Jesus. Ito could not believe how realistic the android looked.

"Isn't Mecha-Jesus the most advanced android in the world?" Fukuda remarked. "We don't even have to recharge him. His hair contains millions of ultra-efficient nanoscale solar cells that convert sunlight into electricity."

"Let me talk to him," Ito said. He looked at the android. "Are you Jesus?"

"Yes, I am, my son," Mecha-Jesus replied.

A programmed response for a question that the android's designers could have easily anticipated, Ito thought. He had to ask a more difficult question.

"Prove to me that you're Jesus," Ito demanded.

Mecha-Jesus pointed to the ground. "Remember that earthquake that hit Aomori last week?"

"Yes."

"Do you see any ruined roads or buildings here? I protected this village."

Mayor Fukuda could have programmed that response

after the earthquake, Ito thought. He decided to argue with Mecha-Jesus.

"It wasn't a strong earthquake, and the epicentre was far away," Ito said, "and the village was built to strict anti-earthquake building codes."

"I weakened the earthquake," Mecha-Jesus replied with a smile. "Ah, here comes someone with an offering."

A farmer bowed to Mecha-Jesus and gave him a small plastic bag of rice.

"Jesus *kami*, thank you for the good rice harvest," said the farmer.

"God bless you," said Mecha-Jesus.

The farmer left Mecha-Jesus to Ito again. The priest continued testing the android's artificial intelligence.

"Did you really cause a good rice harvest?" Ito said. "Many factors, like the weather, can influence a crop."

"And who controls the weather?" Mecha-Jesus asked.

"Nobody controls the weather. It's a force of nature."

"And so am I."

Mecha-Jesus was not speaking in programmed responses, Ito concluded.

The android industry had buzzed with rumours of learning androids. They learned new information from their own experience and their environment. They made decisions on their own. They created new sentences, not just recited pre-recorded speech. Their artificial intelligence didn't just mimic human behaviour. It actually created new actions. They were true thinking machines.

Enoki came and took Fukuda away to meet a garlic farmer. Some more tourists came to Mecha-Jesus. Ito looked around for Fukuda. She had gone away with the

Shinto priest.

He didn't want to delay his next question. He would ask the android.

"Jesus-san, may I look at your system information?" Ito asked.

Mecha-Jesus smiled and said, "Yes, you may."

The android turned around, pulled his hair up, and lifted a panel at the back of his head. A row of data ports appeared.

Ito attached his pocket computer to a data port and read the android's system information:

MODEL: L–6 Prototype Male, Customized Model Jesus
OWNED BY: Shingo Tourism Board
FACTORY: Akihabara
PATENTED BY: Victor Robotics
DESIGNED BY: Dr. Hiyase Midori

The rumours were true. Victor Robotics had created Level 6, a super-intelligent android that could pass as human. If anyone could do it, it would be Dr. Hiyase Midori, the world's most talented android designer.

Then Ito saw a small clear plastic dome beside the data ports. It held a tiny grey object. The words "EX OSSIBUS" in Latin letters were written around the dome.

Richmond peered into the android too. "What's that?" he asked.

"*Ex ossibus*. It means from the bones," Ito explained. "It's a Roman Catholic term for a bone relic of a saint."

"Hey, that's inappropriate!" Enoki said as he rushed over. He disconnected Ito's pocket computer from the data port and lowered the panel and Mecha-Jesus's hair back into place.

"Only a priest may look at the *goshintai*," the Shinto priest warned.

"The bone fragment is the *goshintai*?" Ito asked.

"Yes. The bone of Jesus-san."

Shinto shrines were not just places of worship. They were also houses for *kami*. The *goshintai* was the sacred object in which the *kami* lived. It was usually a mirror, but this one was a bone fragment of the Son of God.

Mecha-Jesus turned to Enoki. "Please do not scold these men. They asked for my permission to view the spirit within the machine, and I granted it to them. Also, they are my priests, as are you."

Enoki bowed deeply to Ito and Richmond. "Gentlemen, I am sorry for my anger, which Jesus-san tells me was unjustified. Please forgive me."

"No problem," said Richmond in English.

Ito nodded. "Thank you. We accept the apology. We felt no offence at all." After pausing to let Enoki stand upright, he asked, "Where did you get the bone fragment?"

"From the grave of Jesus," Enoki replied.

"You excavated the grave?"

"No, no! That would be bad luck. We had an earthquake two years ago. The earth shook, and a bone rose to the surface of the grave."

"A bone moved above ground? That's very odd."

"What is the Christian saying? God works in mysterious ways?"

"Ah, yes."

"I took most of the bone to the Legend of Christ Museum, but I saved a fragment. I put the fragment in the android, and then I performed a ceremony to invite Jesus *kami* to enter the bone."

"Oh my God," Ito muttered in English. "They've turned the android into a mobile Shinto shrine with the *kami* of Jesus."

"What's a *kami*?" Richmond asked.

"A supernatural force of nature," Ito explained. "A river, a rock, a mountain, anything can be a *kami* if you believe it has a spirit. Shinto has an infinite number of them, the so-called eight million *kami*."

Enoki nodded. "We asked Jesus *kami* to protect our town from earthquakes, and no harm came. We asked Jesus *kami* for a good rice crop, and we got one. Jesus *kami* has been kind to us."

"Plus he's good for tourism," Mayor Fukuda added.

"But it's impossible for Jesus to have physical remains on Earth," Richmond insisted. "He ascended into heaven in both body and spirit."

"This isn't the Christian Jesus," Ito said. "This is the Shinto Jesus."

"Now do you believe that I am Jesus?" Mecha-Jesus asked.

Richmond shook his head. "No, you're not Jesus."

"I don't believe you're Jesus," said Ito, "at least not the Jesus whom I know."

"Like my disciple Peter, you deny me. What must I do to prove myself to you?" Mecha-Jesus said before walking away to greet some tourists.

Ito watched more people thank Mecha-Jesus for a variety of wishes fulfilled: getting accepted to a university, passing a driver's license exam, and getting a new boyfriend.

Ito and Enoki went to a wooden booth where a *miko* sold *omamori*. The cloth amulets showed a cross and words such as "Success in Dating and Romance", "Success in University Entrance Exams", "Good Harvest", and "Good Health".

"Enoki-san," Ito asked, "Did the people ask Jesus for good fortune before you invited Jesus *kami* into Mecha-Jesus?"

"No. We are not Christians," Enoki replied.

Ito heard shouting from behind him. He turned and saw men in black coveralls beating a janitorial android with hammers. The black van of the Protectors of Humanity was parked nearby.

One of the men wore a cloth patch of the Imperial Navy flag, the red sun with sun rays. The other men saluted him as the janitorial android lay twitching on the ground.

"Leader, we have defeated another shameful android!" declared one of the men. The leader looked at the ruined android and nodded silently.

He gazed at the onlookers. "People of Shingo, we are the Protectors of Humanity! Bring out your androids! They are destroying the human race!"

Two Protectors dragged an android to the leader. It was a female model dressed in a waitress uniform.

A woman ran to the leader and screamed, "Please don't harm my android! She's done nothing wrong!"

The Protectors pulled the woman back. The leader raised his hammer and smashed it repeatedly into the android's head. Chunks of plastic and electronic parts flew into the air. The android slumped to its knees and fell over.

The android's owner screamed as the Protectors released her. She rushed to hug the android.

"Bring out your androids!" the leader demanded.

"Call the police," Ito said to Mayor Fukuda.

"They're not here," Fukuda said. "They're clearing earthquake damage at another town."

"During the Christ Festival?"

"There has never been violence at the Christ Festival before."

Enoki motioned to Fukuda. "Mayor-san, let's go talk to them."

Fukuda and Enoki went to the leader. The leader put his hammer into a holster on his belt.

"I am Fukuda Hiro, Mayor of Shingo," Fukuda said. "You are damaging my villagers' property. Please leave peacefully."

The leader bowed to her. "Mayor-san, I am sorry that we did not introduce ourselves to you when we arrived. Please forgive our rudeness. We are the Protectors of Humanity."

"I am the local priest," Enoki said. "The mayor and I are sufficient to protect the people of this village. Your services will not be required. Please leave now."

"Priest-san, we are here for a secular reason. Please stay on religious matters," the leader warned.

"But certainly you should respect both the secular and holy leaders of the village," Enoki said. "We do not require your services. As I said before, please—"

"Be compassionate as your Father is compassionate. Do not judge and you will not be judged yourselves," Mecha-Jesus said as he interrupted Enoki and approached the leader.

A Protector pointed at Mecha-Jesus and shouted, "There it is! The Jesus android!"

"That's an *android*?" the leader said incredulously.

"Yes, yes! A tourist told me about it."

"But it looks like a *gaijin* cosplaying as an ancient Israeli."

"Capture it and we'll find out!" the Protector urged.

Ito grabbed Mecha-Jesus by the shoulders and pushed him into the crowd of tourists and villagers.

"Get him out of here!" Ito urged.

The people swarmed around Mecha-Jesus and pulled him away. Enoki, Fukuda, Ito, and Richmond fled into the crowd. The Protectors rushed forward but ran into a wall of people.

"Put your hammers back into your holsters!" the leader barked to his men. "Do not hurt any people! Attack only the androids!"

Thank God the Protectors of Humanity don't want to deliberately harm human beings, Ito thought. However, they did not mind scaring them. People screamed as the Protectors pushed and chased them.

But some people shouted in defiance:

"Jesus is ours! They can't have him!"

"Protect Jesus *kami*!"

"Don't let the fascists kill him again!"

This was not how the crowd treated Jesus on the original Good Friday, Ito mused as he ran.

The crowd, pulling Mecha-Jesus along, ran into the Legend of Christ Museum. They slammed the steel doors shut and locked them from the inside.

Museum workers quickly lowered metal shutters over the windows. Tourism revenues had paid for the new doors and shutters, which now would protect the village's main tourist attraction.

After the people had barricaded themselves inside the museum, Ito quickly looked at its exhibits. There were ancient Judean clothes, pictures of the Holy Family, old Bibles and Torahs, a wall of crucifixes and crosses, and a model of first-century Jerusalem. There was also the last will and testament of Jesus Christ, written in Japanese.

The Protectors hammered on the doors. Ito heard the sound of breaking glass as they smashed the windows. Then he heard the Protectors pound on the metal shutters.

Fukuda phoned the police chief. "Get your men back here to the museum," she ordered. "We're under siege by a right-wing protest group."

"Will they get here on time?" Enoki asked.

The hammering on the doors and shutters continued. Fukuda shrugged. "I hope we can hold out until the police arrive."

A museum worker reported, "They're hitting the windows and doors all around the building. We're surrounded."

The hammering grew louder. The crowd murmured, and some children cried. Everyone looked worried...

...except Mecha-Jesus, who looked serene and calm and oblivious to the siege. He was talking to some children.

"Those men are scary, but they will not hurt you," Mecha-Jesus assured them. "They will leave you unharmed."

After Mecha-Jesus finished talking to the children, he went to Ito.

"You look worried, my son," said Mecha-Jesus.

"We're under siege," Ito said. He laughed. "What is the American saying? 'What would Jesus do?'"

"Do not be afraid of those who kill the body but cannot kill the soul; fear him rather who can destroy both body and soul in Hell," replied Mecha-Jesus.

"Hah! When I need an artificial intelligence to think of a way out of this mess, all it does is recite programmed lines."

"You still doubt who I am, but I say again, I am Jesus Christ. The android is merely the body through which I communicate with you."

"*So desu ka*," Ito said. He turned away from Mecha-Jesus and gasped at what he saw.

Richmond was unlocking the steel doors.

Before Ito could get to him, Richmond had flung open the doors. The Protectors of Humanity stood outside and stared through the doorway.

"Why did you do that?" Ito demanded.

"To give them the android," Richmond said. "This is not how Christians worship Jesus."

"They're not Christians!"

The leader stepped into the museum. "Where is the android?" he demanded.

The crowd murmured as Mecha-Jesus walked towards the doorway.

"Step back outside and I will come out to you," Mecha-Jesus said to the leader.

The leader grunted and went outside. The Protectors of Humanity gathered by the doorway. They glared silently at Mecha-Jesus as they held their hammers.

Mecha-Jesus paused beside Ito and looked at him.

"Now you will believe that I am Jesus," the android said.

Then he turned to Richmond, smiled, and said, "I know that you love me. You've actually helped me. Thank you."

Mecha-Jesus stepped closer to the doorway. He looked back at the crowd and smiled.

"Cover your eyes and do not look at me!" he warned.

He walked into the hammers of the Protectors of Humanity.

Suddenly, a flash of light burst from Mecha-Jesus. Ito quickly turned around. Bright light reflected off the walls and exhibits of the museum. Ito held his hands over his eyes.

"Don't look, don't look!" people shouted.

Ito felt intense heat on his back. He also heard screaming from outside.

The screams turned into groans and sobs. The heat vanished, and Ito opened his eyes. No bright light shone into the museum. He turned around and looked.

Mecha-Jesus stood outside. The Protectors of Humanity lay on the ground around him. As Ito approached them, he saw that their faces, necks, and hands were burnt red and covered with blisters. Only their coveralls had protected the rest of their bodies.

The leader crawled on his hands and elbows. "I can't see! I can't see! I can't see!" he shrieked.

Mecha-Jesus said, "Your burns will heal if you leave immediately and seek medical treatment. Those who covered their eyes in time will be able to see and can drive your van. Those with vision loss will find out later whether they will see again or stay blind."

The Protectors of Humanity moaned and wept.

"Leave now and let the people of Shingo live in peace," Mecha-Jesus ordered.

"The Transfiguration of the Lord," Ito said as he stared at the wounded men.

Mecha-Jesus nodded silently.

"How did you do it?"

"I have a light and heat function. It makes my halo for night performances."

"Oh. And I thought you were going to tell me that you have divine powers."

"How do you know that isn't how a god works?"

Ito shrugged. "God works in mysterious ways."

"Please excuse me for a moment," Mecha-Jesus said. "I have to recharge. I drained eighty percent of my battery."

The Protectors of Humanity, carrying their blinded leader, scurried to their van and drove away. They never returned to Shingo.

*

The next day, Ito asked Richmond if he needed a ride to Aomori City. Richmond eagerly accepted the offer. Mayor Fukuda had hinted that she did not like people who let dangerous thugs into a building full of defenceless villagers.

Mecha-Jesus waved to them as they left. He said, "Come back for next year's festival."

As they drove along the rural roads, Richmond lamented, "How could I have failed? There's so much interest in Jesus in Shingo, and yet, nobody converted to

Christianity. Don't you feel disappointed that none of them became Christians?"

"I'm Christian, but I'm also Japanese, so I understand what has happened in that village," Ito said. "They don't have to be Christian to worship Jesus."

*

Back in Tokyo, Father Ito visited Dr. Hiyase Midori. Dr. Hiyase, an attractive woman in a blue business suit, had returned to Victor Robotics after some years away.

"I went to Shingo and saw an android that looked like Jesus," he said.

"Ah, yes." Hiyase sipped her tea. "That was a special project for my friend, Fukuda Hiro, the mayor of Shingo."

"It's an L-6, isn't it?"

Hiyase grinned. "Now you know my secret. Yes, it's an L-6. Only two prototypes exist. Jesus is one of them. I actually invented the L-6 years ago, but my colleagues did not think that society was ready for them. However, society is changing. The Protectors of Humanity and others like them are a dwindling minority."

"It's a fascinating model," Ito said. "It has such capabilities and powers. Its light and heat function is incredible."

"What light and heat function?"

Ito explained what had happened in Shingo.

"I designed no such function for the L-6 or any other model," Hiyase said.

"Then how could he do it?" asked Ito.

"The L-6 has the ability to learn new knowledge and

reconfigure its systems. Perhaps Mecha-Jesus developed a light and heat function and augmented himself—on his own."

"That's possible?"

"Yes, but I think the chances are small. If he did create his own function, he exceeded my greatest expectations."

"*So desu ka*," Ito said, realizing that Jesus had joined the eight million *kami*.

About "Mecha-Jesus"

This story was inspired by a real place. The town of Shingo, Aomori Prefecture in Japan claims to have the graves of Jesus and Mary. The local residents hold a Christ Festival each year. None of them are Christian.

The story is part of the Siren Stone universe because it includes Dr. Hiyase Midori and her androids from the novel *The Shrine of the Siren Stone*. The short stories "The Siren Stone" and "Transubstantiation" from this universe will be in a future collection of my stories.

Thanks to Liana Kerzner and Jerome Stueart, not just for publishing this story, but also for making it the opening story in their anthology.

The Snow Aliens

Will Lawrence sucked in the cold air, blew it back out, and watched his breath form a miniature cloud. As the cloud faded, he looked up and saw a much larger cloud hovering above the field. Then he looked at the field. In the summer, it would have been full of corn. Now in the winter, it was barren except for snow—

—and two tiny aliens, both the size of a period on a printed page.

"The meteorologist says it'll snow again," he said, pointing at the cloud.

Captain Susan McNaughton shivered in her Air Force coat. "If it snows again, the aliens'll get buried. I hope their ship picks them up soon."

*

It had seemed like a fun idea to Tonn. Why not float in the atmosphere of the planet of giants, the blue third planet of the yellow sun? The planet was as large as home and had the same gravity, but its creatures, especially the dominant *homo sapiens* species, were gigantic. Going down to the planet could be dangerous, even if the *homo sapiens* had promised they would welcome Tonn and his crew in peace. Better to float in the air and collect atmospheric data there.

"But Tonn, why do you have to go outside the ship?" Ziv had said. "Our probes can collect the data."

"It is more fun to go outside, to feel the coolness of the alien wind and the heat of the yellow sun," said Tonn.

Soon, against the advice of his crew, Tonn jumped out the hatch, followed by Ziv.

"I am coming to keep you out of trouble," she muttered.

Tonn's carapace glowed orange with happiness as he floated in the air. He bounced around as the air currents knocked him up and down. As he waved at Ziv through the wispy clouds, he saw globes of water and chunks of dust sail past him.

"Hydrogen and oxygen together—water," he said, looking at his scanner. "These clouds are gaseous water floating in an atmosphere of carbon dioxide and oxygen. And there are numerous water particles floating here too. This planet has lots of water, so much that it floats into the atmosphere. Not like home, where the water stays as liquid on the ground."

"We could have learned all this from inside the ship," said Ziv.

A globe of water sailed into Tonn and splashed all over him. He turned orange again and drifted away from Ziv.

"Tonn, do not go so far away from the ship!" she yelled.

Tonn shot a stream of hydrogen from his backpack

and flew into Ziv's arms. Ziv flashed green in anger and slapped him with all four claws.

"Tonn, stop playing!" she ordered. "Get your data and go back to the ship."

Tonn drifted into a wisp of cloud. He had never felt so free; he could stay outside and float forever.

But then he felt the wind get colder. The clouds became thicker. The globes of water began to turn white. One flew into him. Instead of splashing, it bounced off his carapace.

The water is becoming solid, he thought. He looked around. He couldn't see through the clouds anymore, and more ice chunks began speeding around him.

"Ziv! Ziv!" he yelled. "Where are you?"

Ziv grabbed him from behind. "We must go back," she said.

"I cannot see the ship," said Tonn. The clouds had turned from wispy gases into a big white mass.

New objects floated in the air: large white stars formed from triangles, hexagons, and circles etched with beautiful patterns. No two stars were alike. Millions of them appeared from nowhere. Then the stars began to fall.

At first Tonn thought the stars might be intelligent creatures, but he saw two of them collide and split into globes of water.

"The stars are water," he said. "What strange phenomenon—"

He remembered the TV signals from the *homo sapiens*. "They have a semi-solid form of water," he said. "They call it 'snow' or 'snowflakes.'"

Tonn felt something cold forming on his arms and

legs. A white substance began to coat his body. Semi-solid water, his scanner read. The snow was covering Ziv too. Her carapace glowed purple with fear.

"We're turning into snowflakes," she cried.

They were also rushing downward with the snowflakes. Despite blasting streams of hydrogen from their backpacks, they kept falling with the snow.

"Too much water has crystallized on us," cried Tonn. "We're too heavy—"

Both Tonn and Ziv, trapped inside beautiful snowflakes, fell down to the planet with a billion other snowflakes that night.

*

"The two aliens are somewhere in the field, but their crew can't give us a more precise location," said Will.

"Needles in a haystack," said Susan. "The best we can do is secure the area until their ship picks them up."

Green armoured cars and trucks rumbled past them while dozens of soldiers ran along the edges of the field. An Army lieutenant gave cups of coffee to both Susan and Will.

"This is good. Where did you get it?" asked Will.

"The truck stop across the road, sir," said the lieutenant, pointing at the restaurant.

Susan gulped down her coffee and turned to the lieutenant. "Secure the perimeter. I don't want anyone or anything walking into that field."

Then she turned to Will. "We don't want someone accidentally stepping on the aliens in Earth's first contact with them."

She looked at the cloud. "I was hoping that cloud would blow away, but it isn't moving. When will it snow?"

"The forecast is morning—anytime now."

"The alien ship better get here quick," Susan said.

*

The flat sheet of snow spread as far as Tonn could see. He had never seen anything like it: nothing but whiteness everywhere.

"Amazing," said Tonn. "Their ground water is solid. What discoveries! The stories we can tell to our hive-fellows back home!"

"If we ever get home," Ziv grumbled. "We are stranded on an alien planet."

"But our crew is tracking the signal of our beacon." The soft beep from his backpack continued. "They will find us, and when we return home, we will be heroes."

"Hopefully, we will be alive for the celebrations," said Ziv, throwing two claws up and two claws down. She glowed in bright green. "Tonn, next time trouble starts, get back inside the ship!"

Tonn flashed a pale blue in sadness. "Ziv, we will go home alive. Why not enjoy this great adventure?"

Suddenly, they heard a deafening roar from above, and a gigantic shadow fell over them.

*

"What's a dog doing out there?" said Susan.

A miniature dachshund, its brown coat spotted with

snow, barked and ran across the field. Susan shook her head and grimaced.

"Must belong to the farmer," said Will. "We've got to get it out of there. Those aliens could be anywhere in that field. The dog could trample them."

"I know, but how do we get it out—without hurting it?" Susan looked around. Soldiers stood all around the field, armoured cars sat by the roadside, a helicopter flew overhead, and still, the dachshund pranced through the snow. The Canadian Army, heroes of two world wars, was helpless against a little dog.

"Now I *really* need another coffee," she said as she began walking to the restaurant across the road. As she approached its parking lot, she read its red and yellow sign: BBQ STEAKS, RIBS, BURGERS.

I don't need a coffee, she said silently. I need a hamburger.

*

Tonn and Ziv ran from the monster again. No matter how fast they ran, the large shadow and deep roar followed them. When they looked up, they saw a gigantic brown shape, so large that they could not see all of it. Sometimes it hovered over them, sometimes it was beside them, but it always shambled near them.

Whenever it moved, it threw giant puffs of snow into the air. Balls of snow bounced off Tonn and Ziv.

"Run fast!" yelled Tonn, his carapace glowing in bright purple.

"We should have stayed in the ship!" said Ziv, switching from purple to green and back to purple again.

Then the monster ran away, and its growls became fainter and fainter.

*

Susan grinned as the dachshund ran towards her through the snow. Even in a weak wind, the meaty aroma of the hamburger drifted from her hand and over the field.

"Uh, the dog could be trampling on the aliens right now," said Will.

"I know, but that's a risk we'll have to take. The longer it stays out there, the higher the chance it'll step on the aliens. At least we're getting it off the field."

The dog walked to Susan and sat in front of her. It panted heavily with its tongue hanging out. The dog's brown eyes grew with excitement as they stared up at the hamburger.

After petting the dog's head, Susan placed the hamburger on the ground. The dog began devouring the hamburger immediately.

"Well, not all military projects are expensive; we solved that problem with less than ten dollars," said Susan. "Oh, by the way, I got this in my change. I remember you're a coin collector, right? Here, take it."

It was a quarter dollar showing voyageurs paddling in a canoe, a special design for the millennium of 2000. He hadn't seen one in circulation for a decade.

"Thanks, Susan." He smiled, and then he felt a snowflake fall on his nose. His smile faded.

"Oh, no! Is it snowing?" he said.

They looked up. Nothing else was coming down. Just

one snowflake had fallen, probably blown up from the ground. It was not snowing yet. Still, the cloud was not moving away. It could snow anytime.

"We've got to prevent it from snowing," said Will.

"How can we do that?"

"Uh, move the cloud?"

"A direct approach, but there's no giant fan to blow the cloud away."

"What about taking all the water vapour out of the cloud? If we can't move it, we'll shrink it," Will suggested.

"But how can we do it?"

"A dehumidifier. I used to work for a company that sold dried fruits. They had a dehumidifier; it sucked in the air, absorbed its water vapour, and blew it back out as dry air."

"But there's no dehumidifier large enough to suck in an entire cloud. And even if we had a giant machine, how would we get it into the cloud?"

They heard footsteps crunching on the snow. Turning around, they saw the lieutenant approaching them with a small box.

"Headquarters wants photos of the first contact with an alien species," explained the lieutenant. "The general even gave me a new camera..."

Of course, thought Will. People take photos of any event: birthdays, weddings, parades, baseball games. Why not the first contact? Unfortunately, the aliens were too small to appear in the photo; historians would have to be happy with photos of him, Susan, and the soldiers standing beside a snow field.

What a shame that the aliens were so small. Ever since

he was a child, he had wanted to see aliens from space. He studied biology and astronomy so he could work at the Extraterrestrial Search Centre. And now at the field where Earth's first alien visitors had landed, he couldn't see them.

"Could you please hold this, sir?" the lieutenant asked as he handed the box to Will.

As the lieutenant fumbled with the camera and a roll of film, Will saw a small white packet inside the box. He took the packet out and showed it to Susan.

"This is desiccant, a substance that absorbs moisture while the camera is in the box. It helps prevent the camera's metal parts from rusting. Maybe we can use it to absorb the moisture in the cloud."

"But how can we do that? We just can't drop tons of desiccant into the cloud. The stuff will fall right through the cloud before it can absorb the water."

"But what if we can keep the desiccant hanging inside the cloud?" said Will.

"And how can we do that?" Susan asked as the helicopter flew over them.

"Helicopters?" said Will, hearing the helicopter.

"Suspend bags of desiccant from helicopters?" she said. "It's possible, but that would use up a lot of fuel."

"There's got to be a way," said Will. He watched his breath form another small cloud and float away.

Float away...

He snapped his fingers. "Helicopters and planes aren't the only aircraft we have, are they?"

*

Soon after the big brown monster went away, another creature started chasing them. The new beast, a blue shape, was smaller than the first one, and it scattered less snow in its path, but it made a loud clicking noise. The clicking scared Tonn and Ziv bright purple; it reminded them of the ferocious clicking of the warrior caste in the hive.

"You were right! Next time, I will go back into the ship when trouble starts!" cried Tonn as they fled from the blue monster.

"Or you could stay inside the ship all the time!" said Ziv.

Tonn briefly turned orange. "And miss all the excitement?"

*

I must be bored, thought Will, if I notice a blue beetle crawling across the snow. He tried to imagine how that beetle would look to the two aliens. The insect would probably be as gigantic to them as he was to it.

His thoughts returned to Susan. She had gone back to the air force base three hours ago. Could she really get everything they needed?

A long shadow and a droning noise floated over him. He looked up and cried out.

Three white blimps sailed towards the cloud.

"Lieutenant, may I borrow your binoculars?" he asked.

He saw hundreds of white packets attached to the blimps. Desiccant.

His cell phone rang. "Will Lawrence," he answered.

"Captain McNaughton here," said Susan over the

phone. "I'm flying one of the blimps."

"Good work," said Will.

"Don't congratulate me until we've succeeded," said Susan, "but we got everything so quickly, so luck may be on our side. First, I had to convince the General that we had an emergency. Then we had to get the Prime Minister to let us buy tons of desiccant—environmentally friendly, of course. Next, we had to find three blimps—not easy, but three balloon companies lent us theirs."

She steered her blimp into the cloud. "Okay, Will, I've got work to do. Talk to you later, over and out."

Aboard her blimp, Susan radioed the other two pilots. "Maintain different altitudes so we don't run into each other, and be careful flying and steering with all that extra weight. And a warning—the desiccant will get heavier when it absorbs the water vapour."

She couldn't see the other two blimps through the cloud. I hope we don't crash into each other, she thought, but if this plan works, we won't be in the cloud for too long.

Seven hours later, she saw one of the blimps hovering above her. The wisps of cloud were getting thinner...

*

"We are saved!" cried Tonn when he saw the ship land on the snow.

Off in the distance, the ship sat, its engine humming softly, and its red copper skin glistening in the light. He could see his crew rushing out the hatch to meet him.

Ziv waved her arms at them. "We survived!"

As Tonn and Ziv clambered aboard the ship, the crew

shouted in joy. Tonn had never seen his crew glow so brightly orange before.

*

"The Extraterrestrial Search Centre received a message from the aliens," said Will, listening to his phone. "They've rescued their castaways and are leaving Earth."

Susan put the dog back on the ground and shooed it away. "What a disappointment; our first contact with an alien species, and we never got to see them."

"We would've needed a microscope, but still, it would've been nice to see them," Will agreed.

Soon, the armoured cars and trucks, soldiers, and Susan had gone. Only Will stayed behind to take photographs of the field. It may look like an empty field of snow, there were no spaceships or aliens, but it *was* the site of the first contact.

He looked wistfully into the field. If only he could have seen the aliens...

He felt a slight rush of air, as if something had flown past him. A bird? A bee? In the winter?

Something gleamed in the snow. A penny. First, the millennium quarter, now a shiny new penny. Must be my lucky day, thought Will.

Just as he bent over to pick it up, the penny flew away.

Will smiled; he had seen the aliens after all.

About "The Snow Aliens"

"The Snow Aliens" was my first major pro fiction sale, thanks to Julie Czerneda, a multiple Aurora Award-winning Canadian author, anthology editor, and member of the Canadian Science Fiction and Fantasy Association's Hall of Fame. Julie likes to promote emerging writers, and she often makes a point of inviting new writers to submit stories to her anthologies. *Tales From the Wonder Zone* was a series of anthologies aimed to teach science to children. The anthologies also had accompanying teachers' guides with science lessons.

I got the idea for "The Snow Aliens" by driving past a snow-covered field in Richmond Hill, Ontario, near my sister's house. Despite ever-changing signs announcing a housing or building development, that field is still empty twenty years later.

The Shepherd's Blessing

The shepherd tossed a shilling on the bed. It landed beside Abby.

"I like you. You have a pretty face and shiny brown hair, and your body is as thin as an adolescent's, not overfed like those rich ladies," said the shepherd.

Abby sighed and rolled onto her belly. Nobody in her profession was overfed. She picked up the coin and looked up at her client.

"I am pleased that I spent that shilling on you instead of a drink," he said. "You are well worth the price, if not more."

Abby smiled and put the shilling into her purse. "Then why not pay me more, squire?" she asked.

The shepherd guffawed. "If I do that, every drab in Boston will think that she is worth more than a pint of ale! Then how could I afford you?"

Abby crouched and picked up her white linen shift. It felt soft against her skin, and she used it to wipe the man's sweat off her body. She got out of bed and pulled the shift over her head, the garment falling only as far as her thighs. It was a gift from another client, who said he had bought it in France. He claimed the nobility's prostitutes slept in such sinfully short garments. But she doubted that any high-class courtesan had entertained him. He likely cuddled with dockside drabs.

Like her.

The shepherd picked up his clothes. Before he could put them on, Abby sprang out of bed and stopped him.

"Would you like to freshen up before you leave?" she asked. "Wash yourself with some water?"

"Aye, that is a good idea," the shepherd said.

Abby pointed at a door at the opposite corner of the room. "Go in there, please. There is a basin of water and a towel. Please use them."

The shepherd went into the water closet. As Abby listened to him splash the water, she took another shilling from the shepherd's vest and put it into her own purse. She quickly searched his bag for other valuables, finding a whisky flask, a pouch of chewing tobacco, and a book bound in black leather.

At first, she thought it was a Bible, but after looking at its title, she realized it was no book she had ever seen before. Stamped in gold leaf on the cover were:

NECRONOMICON
OR THE ELDRITCH TOME OF THE MAD ARAB
TRANSLATED INTO ENGLISH

The sound of splashing water stopped. Abby shoved the book back into the shepherd's bag.

The shepherd returned to the bed. He was a wizened man, worn down by decades of farming, with high cheekbones, like a skull's, and a beak-like nose. His hair was thin and grey. He was around sixty years old, but despite his age and harsh life, he could still indulge his physical urges.

As he put his clothes on, Abby asked, "What will you do next? Have you more people and places to see here?"

By creating small talk and showing interest in the client's life, Abby added a personal touch to their relationship. Even if she did not care about his life, a good drab knew how to make a client feel liked, and a client like the shepherd, who paid in genuine money, was one worth seeing again.

She glanced at a pile of wampum and tobacco on her table. How could she buy her way out of prostitution when clients paid her in beads and leaves?

"I have finished my business in Boston," the shepherd replied. "I wish I could dally longer here, but I must return home. Sheep farming is such a busy occupation. I cannot leave the farm for too long. The last time I was away for three days, my farmhand stole three shillings from my house and ran away."

"What did you do?" Abby said, curious as to how he dealt with thieves.

"I did not have to do anything. The local magistrate caught him stealing a horse from a blacksmith. The boy had a habit of committing crimes, so the magistrate taught him a lesson. He got thirty-six lashes of a bullwhip. What a coincidence, eh? Thirty-six lashes, one for each penny stolen from me. When people steal from me, they get punished."

"I see," Abby said quietly.

"Hah, hah. I did not seek the boy or report him to the

magistrate. Before I could do that, the magistrate caught him committing the horse theft. I did not have to do anything. I am blessed!"

"Blessed?"

"The opposite of cursed," the shepherd explained. "Since childhood, I've experienced strange coincidences. Anyone who steals from me suffers a terrible fate. There was the farmhand. There was also a maid who stole my silverware and later drowned in a river. And there was a farmer who stole one of my ewes, only to be kicked and killed by his own horse two days later.

"So, now that you know me, do you not want to lead a life of piety?" the shepherd said.

"Piety? I have had enough of piety. I used to live with a preacher," Abby said.

She remembered the stern rule of her uncle, Reverend Samuel Parris. She remembered the harsh discipline at their home. She remembered the trials of the accused witches.

She remembered accusing the women of hexing her with violent spasms. She remembered twitching on the floor in front of the judges. She remembered shouting that yellow birds flew in the courtroom. She remembered watching the hangings. She remembered leaving Salem with her cousin Betty and Uncle Samuel in shame after the trials.

"Hah, I am happy that you chose the sinful life of a drab," the shepherd said. "I will return next month to sell lamb meat."

She escorted him into the hallway. As they walked past the rooms, she heard the other girls and their clients moan. The air stank of stale sweat and cheap perfume.

They walked down the stairs to the front lobby. After she opened the door for him, he went out into Boston's noisy streets. The smell of horse manure wafted in, and Abby choked and slammed the door shut.

She returned to her room and emptied her velvet purse. A small assortment of coins fell on her bed. She picked up her earnings from the shepherd: one shilling for her services plus one shilling stolen secretly.

Abby squeezed the two shillings in her palm. They felt small and hard: her value as a drab.

The first time she served a man for money, she did it to spite her uncle. She detested his strict rules of behaviour, his threat of eternal Hell to sinners, and his ban on fun and laughter. While other girls played hopscotch outside, Uncle Samuel made Abigail and her cousin Betty stay inside and read the Bible.

The second time she served a man for money, she did it for a red dress. Wearing the dress, she boasted to her uncle that a man had rented her body for a shilling. The outraged preacher banished her, and she went to Boston. The third time she served a man for money, she did it for food. By then, the thrill of rebellion had ended, and the desperation of survival had started.

She had hoped that if she saved enough money, she could retire from prostitution. But when she realized that drabs never became wealthy at a shilling per shag, she quietly stole money from her clients.

Sometimes, she would get the client to wash in the water closet, and she would steal a coin or two from his purse. She was careful never to steal too many at once so the client would not notice his lighter purse immediately.

The drunken clients were the easiest marks. They could be so drowsy that she could take their money without their noticing. The extra money was worth the work of cleaning their vomit off her dress. If a drunk fell asleep, the pickings were better, for she could steal his entire purse and dump him into the street, where the local magistrate would arrest and imprison him. However, if the client was a violent drunk, she suffered his blows upon her body before he passed out.

Abby looked again at the coins on her bed. She sighed and put them back in her purse. She was no wealthier than she was a year ago. At this rate, she would never retire from renting out her body.

*

A half hour later, Abby watched a thin blonde girl walk her client to the door. The girl, named Chastity, wore a blue dress and thick makeup. Her perfume smelled like cheap candy.

"Look what my client gave me," Chastity said with her Cockney accent. She held a newspaper. "He read it while travelling here and did not want it anymore. Abby, you can read, can you not? What's it say?"

Abby read out a sentence from the front page: "'The General Court of Massachusetts has declared that the witch trials conducted in Salem ten years ago, in the year of Our Lord 1692, were unlawful.'"

Now I can never return to Salem, Abby realized. *If I return, I will be hanged by the families of the executed. In any case, why would I want to return to that miserable town?*

Someone knocked on the door. Chastity opened it, and a man walked in. He was about fifty years old and had thinning white hair. He wore the plain brown clothes of a farmer.

"What pleasures do you desire, squire?" Chastity said.

The man looked around and clutched his hat nervously. He was probably visiting a bawdy house for the first time in his life. Such houses were rare in the countryside.

"May I see your girls?" the farmer said. He seemed awkward and did not smile. He stank as if he had not bathed for a week.

"They ain't available now, but we are," Chastity said.

The farmer grunted. "Oh, just you two."

Chastity wore heavy makeup to hide her wrinkles, though she was only twenty-two years old. Eight years of selling her body had aged her quickly.

Abby had been working for three years, not as long as the other girls. She also had not suffered a childhood of hunger, scurvy, neglect, and violence as they had. Although Uncle Samuel was stern, he had fed her well and kept his hands to himself. At twenty-one years of age, Abby retained some of her adolescent beauty. But she feared that if she stayed in the business for another year, she too would look pale, wrinkled, bruised, and ugly.

"You are both quite pretty," the farmer said with a slight smile. His piercing stare made Abby feel like a piece of meat being checked by a cook. She was used to that look, but something about the farmer chilled her.

Abby forced herself to look at him and smile. She knew she had the best smile in the house; unlike the other girls, she still had all her teeth.

"You, I will have you," the farmer said, pointing at Abby.

Abby flinched. When the man opened his mouth, she smelled alcohol.

"You will enjoy your time with me, I promise you," Abby said, regaining her poise. She grabbed his hand and felt his rough, dry skin. She led him up the stairs and into her room.

As Abby unbuttoned her bodice, the farmer stared at her. She stopped and smiled at him.

"What do you wish, squire?" she asked.

"I think I have seen you before," he said.

"Oh?"

"Yes, you seem familiar."

"You must be mistaken. I do not remember seeing you in this house before."

"Did you ever live in Salem?"

Abby felt her blood turn cold. She replied, "No."

"You are older than last I saw you, but I recognize you nonetheless," the farmer insisted. "It is you, Abigail Williams."

"No, my name is not Abigail," Abby said. "My name is Chantal."

"When last I saw you, you were a child of eleven years. You have grown into a pretty wench, but I still recognize your face." The farmer sneered. "Have you returned to Salem since you left in disgrace?"

"I have never lived in Salem. I am from Louisiana," Abby lied.

The farmer laughed. "Louisiana? Your accent does not sound French."

"How would you know the sound of French?" Abby retorted.

"Getting temperamental, are you?" the farmer teased. "I sat in the courthouse and watched you, your cousin, and the other wicked girls accuse good people of witchcraft."

"I did no such thing."

"Please permit me to refresh your memory. Do you remember pointing at Martha Corey and saying that you saw her holding a yellow bird that nobody else could see? Do you remember testifying that Goodwife Corey had made the bird invisible to all except a witch and her victims? Do you remember moving your hands as Goodwife Corey moved her hands, moving her feet as she moved her feet, and fidgeting as she fidgeted, mimicking her to create the impression that she was bewitching you? Do you remember twitching on the floor and crying that witches had sent the Devil to you? Do you remember any of this, Abigail Williams?"

"No, no!" Abby argued. "I was not there!"

"Goodwife Corey was a friend of my mother," the man said. "Martha Corey hanged for your lies!"

"Enough!" Abby yelled, from fear more than anger.

She pushed the man out of her room, prodded him down the stairs, and shoved him through the doorway.

Just before Abby slammed the door, the man shouted, "I will return!"

*

But the man from Salem did not return. Instead, for the next year, Abby saw other anonymous clients: sailors, farmers, merchants, and tradesmen. From each, she collected a shilling for her services and stole more money.

But living in Boston was expensive, and she saved only a few shillings. Even her barter goods were meagre: a small pile of wampum, a half pound of tobacco, and a rabbit pelt.

The shepherd returned each month. Although he was ugly, at least he brought real money. And he never noticed that he was missing an additional shilling after each visit to Abby.

A year went by. No one had caught or punished her for theft or any other crime. No terrible accident had occurred to her. There was nothing to the shepherd's blessing. It was just a tall tale.

After one of their shags, Abby asked, "How is your business, squire?"

The man grunted. "I am afraid that I have been too good in my job. For twenty years, I bred generations of prized sheep by mating the best animals with each other. My sheep showed consistent, predictable strengths. The same fine wool, the same robust bodies, the same amount of meat, the same resistance to disease. If any weaklings or deformed animals were born, I killed them immediately before they could breed. Healthy stock breeds healthy stock.

"But in the past three years, my animals have given birth to increasing numbers of weaklings and freaks: animals blind from birth, animals with thin wool, animals with two heads, animals with skinny bodies, animals with deformed legs, and animals missing a leg. This month, for the first time ever, I put down more newborns than I let live. I fear that by mating only the best animals with each other, I have created an inbred herd.

"I need to visit the farmers' market and seek out farmers who might sell me new breeding stock, animals who have never seen my part of the colony."

"The whole world is all about breeding, is it not?" Abby said.

*

The next day, Abby took a new client into her room. The man wore expensive black clothes, which Abby never saw on other clients. He showed gracious manners to her: bowing to her, opening the door for her, and calling her "milady." He was obviously a well-off man of the landed gentry.

He was a handsome gentleman, probably about thirty years old. He could have courted any of the beautiful ladies from the wealthy neighbourhood, or he could rut with one of his slave wenches. Why would he come here for a drab?

"I am pleased that this house has a woman as beautiful as you, milady," the man said after taking off his hat. "Oh, I am quite rude for entering your room without properly introducing myself. Please allow me to do so. My name is Howard Loach."

"Squire Loach, my name is Chantal. Please be comfortable," Abby said, pointing at her bed.

"How unfortunate it is that you live in Boston. A woman of your grace and beauty would be a fine courtesan in Europe," Loach said.

Abby laughed. "Dear squire, you flatter me!"

"It is not insincere flattery. Your elegance, poise, and beauty are equal to those of ladies kept by my friends in London," Loach said.

"You have gone to London?" Abby said. "How I long to go, far away from here."

Loach smiled. "I have visited London several times."

"Ah, a gentlemen with prestige and status," said Abby.

She touched the top button of her bodice. Loach quickly held out his hand.

"Oh, you do not have to disrobe," he said.

Abby stopped. "How do you wish me to serve you?"

"I came to procure your services as a courtesan but not at this time or place or for me," Loach said. "My widowed father has been quite lonely for female companionship since my mother died. I came to Boston to find a woman who can relieve his loneliness, if only for one night."

"Oh my, that is quite a different request!" Abby said. She had never before met a son procuring a drab for his father. "I imagine he is a refined and courteous gentleman such as you. Are there no local ladies whom he can court?"

"We live in Loach Hill, a town named after my great-grandfather. It is a small town, so there are no unmarried or widowed ladies at his age. He does not desire any of our slave wenches because he prefers light-skinned women. As for ladies in your profession, there are none because the population is too small to afford them a reasonable income."

"I see. How much will I be paid?"

Loach reached into his pocket and pulled out two gold

coins. They glistened. "Will two doubloons be sufficient?"

Abby stared in shock at the Spanish gold. Two doubloons were worth thirty-two Spanish dollars. Thirty-two Pieces of Eight: she could exchange them for over a hundred shillings. She could buy her own house with a small vegetable garden. Or she could buy a shop and make clothes for the merchants; Puritan girls like her knew how to sew.

She could retire from drabbing.

"Aye, I can entertain your father," Abby said. "Is he outside?"

"He is not here. Rather, I wish to invite you to come to Loach Hill."

"Where is Loach Hill?"

"We would require a day's journey by carriage, but I will pay for all travel expenses to and from there."

"Will you be hiring other girls for him?"

"No, one is sufficient for my father's needs."

Abby sighed. The offer greatly tempted her, but she remembered the clients who caught her alone. Such dangers had forced her from the streets and into the house.

Two doubloons were more than she could save in a decade. But her life, though cheap, was worth much more.

"I am sorry, but I do not work alone when travelling out of town," she said. "With another two doubloons, you can hire another girl who can accompany me. Two girls provide twice the fun of one."

Loach put the doubloons back in his pocket. "My father is old. One girl will be sufficient."

"Oh, I do not mean for your father to have two girls."

Abby caressed Loach's shoulder. "*You* could enjoy the other girl—or both of us."

"I am betrothed to a daughter of a family friend. I do not lack for female companionship. It is my father who does," Loach said. He went to the door. "I hope you consider my offer. I will be staying at the Ram's Head Inn until tomorrow morning. You will find me there when you change your mind."

He tipped his hat to her and smiled. "And you will change your mind, I am sure. Good evening, milady."

*

After dark, someone pounded heavily on the door. The noise echoed through the house. As Abby walked down the stairs, she complained, "Stop it, man! We are not deaf."

She opened the door and gasped. The farmer from Salem stood there.

He forced his way inside and blocked the doorway.

"You look pretty today, Abigail Williams," he said. "Another year of drabbing has not aged you at all."

"Sir, you have mistaken me for someone else. Please leave," Abby demanded.

"So what if I have mistaken you for another girl? That does not change what you are. Are you refusing to serve me, you cheap drab?" The farmer's breath reeked of alcohol again.

Despite her fear and anger, Abby found the courage to speak up. "You seek a particular girl, but I am not her, and I cannot pretend to be her. Hence, I would not satisfy you. Please be gone."

The farmer grinned. "Abigail Williams, if you do not serve me I will return to Salem and tell the townsfolk where you live. They hate you. They will come and drag you back home and hang you!"

Abby cried. With all her strength, she pushed the drunken man out of her way and ran through the open door.

As she dashed across the street, Abby remembered all the money she had stolen from the shepherd.

The shepherd's blessing was her curse now.

*

She fled into the Ram's Head Inn across the street. She smelled the aroma of roasting lamb. By the flicker of table lanterns, the customers drank their beer and ate their meals. Singing and shouting filled the air.

Abby looked out the inn's window. She saw the farmer leave the bawdy house. He walked down the street, away from the inn.

Turning away from the window, she saw Howard Loach eating by himself. As she approached him, he saw her, stood up, and bowed.

"Squire Loach, may I join you?" Abby asked.

"Of course, you may, Chantal," Loach said.

Abby was impressed that he remembered her name. Few clients did.

He walked to the other side of the table and pulled out a chair for Abby.

"Have you had dinner yet?" Loach asked.

"No." Abby looked at Loach's dinner. "What are you eating?"

"Roast mutton. The meat is very tender, very succulent. It must be from a sheep of the finest stock, perhaps one of mine. Shall I order the same meal for you? It will be my treat, of course."

"Oh, thank you, squire!"

Loach ordered the meal. As she waited for the meal, Abby kept glancing at the door in case the farmer came in.

When the innkeeper brought the meal, she ate hungrily. Abby could not recall when she had eaten so well. The delicious meat made her forget her problems briefly.

She finished her dinner quickly, and Loach smiled as he poured a red wine into her cup. Abby sipped the wine and savoured it. It tasted smooth and delicious. Loach knew how to treat a woman like a lady.

"Have you reconsidered my offer?" Loach asked.

Abby glanced at the door again. Now that the Salem farmer had discovered her, she had to leave Boston.

"Yes, I will entertain your father," Abby said.

"Splendid! However, I do not wish to hire another woman. Will that be agreeable to you?" Loach asked.

Abby had to escape soon. She had to take the risk.

She nodded. "Yes, such an arrangement is fine. When can we leave?"

"You are eager to go," Loach observed. "I like such enthusiasm. We will go in the morning. Are you finished your dinner? I will escort you back to your house."

"Thank you," Abby said. "You are such a gentleman."

*

They arrived at the outskirts of Loach Hill. The old black horse slowly pulled their carriage through a dirt road. They passed vast fields of wheat, corn, and tobacco. Sheep roamed the pastures.

They entered the town's centre square. Abby saw businesses such as a clothing store, a tavern, and a farmers' market.

Unlike Boston, Loach Hill was a rural town, tied to the countryside surrounding it. A woman led a lamb to a butcher. A boy prodded sheep into a corral outside the farmers' market. A man pushed a cart of cabbages. A blacksmith hammered a horseshoe on his anvil. A tailor hung clothes on racks outside his shop. People scurried from place to place. The chatter of the marketplace filled the air.

Boston smelled of human and horse manure, mud, garbage, and smoke. Loach Hill, with far fewer horses and people than Boston, smelled of fresh air. Abby felt the cool odourless breeze upon her face.

"It smells cleaner than Boston," Abby said.

Loach smiled. "We country folk lead unpolluted lives."

Loach Hill reminded Abby of many other rural towns in New England. She, Betty, and Uncle Samuel had drifted from town to town after they left Salem. They could never stay in one place long before the local people discovered who they were. Eventually, she stopped caring where they lived. Each rural town was the same, a temporary stop where she could not make friends.

Another rural town...

Then, as she looked around, Abby realized everyone, both men and women, had large eyes, high cheekbones, and a beak-like nose.

She had seen this look before, on the face of the shepherd who rented her body for a shilling per shag. Were they all descended from the same settlers?

She noticed another oddity: the people were working on a Sunday.

And something was missing.

"Squire Loach, is there a church in town?" Abby asked.

Loach gave Abby a quizzical look. "Do you want to attend a service?"

"No, no. I am simply curious. Nobody worked on Sunday in the towns where I have lived. Even in Boston, the businesses close on Sunday."

"If people did not work on Sunday, what did they do?"

"We attend church."

"Interesting. What did you do in church?"

"We prayed."

"Why did you pray?"

"To ask God for His help, to ask Him for His strength, to ask Him for His forgiveness," Abby recited.

Loach looked back at the road. "We too would pray if God would talk to us, but since He does not, we will not bother Him with our petty complaints."

Abby, surprised by the sacrilege, said nothing. Three years in a Boston bawdy house had not erased eighteen years in Puritan churches.

Never before had Abby seen a town without a church.

Finally, they arrived at Loach's house. With three floors, it was the largest residence in Loach Hill and the surrounding farmlands. Its wooden walls, black paint, and steep gables reminded Abby of Judge Jonathan Corwin's house in Salem.

Judge Corwin had sentenced nineteen innocent people

to hang as witches. Many people blamed the judge for committing the miscarriage of justice, but he could not have done it without Abby. Abby knew that, and so did everyone in Salem.

A black ram stood in front of the house. It was a huge animal with large golden horns. Even from a distance, she could see its glowing red eyes, which stared angrily at her. Abby had never before seen a beast like it.

A man came out of the house and stood beside the black ram.

Loach called to the man, "Cornelius, come here! Help our guest from Boston. Take her belongings to the guest room."

Cornelius walked to the carriage. Abby looked at the man and felt nauseated. He looked uglier than the ruffians and knaves who lived in Boston's alleys. Only a few long strands of black hair grew on his head. Scars, pockmarks, and growths covered his cheeks. He reeked of a foul odour.

And he too had the large eyes, high cheekbones, and beak-like nose of the townspeople.

He leered at Abby. When he opened his mouth, drool fell from his lips.

"Very pretty, very pretty," he said.

He grabbed her wrist, and Abby felt Cornelius's rough, dry skin and warts. When he squeezed her wrist, she winced in pain.

"Cornelius, behave!" Loach shouted as he hit Cornelius with a horsewhip. Whimpering like a dog, Cornelius released Abby, picked up her baggage, and carried it into the house.

Loach bowed to Abby. "I apologize for Cornelius's

behaviour. His father was a servant of mine. Unfortunately, Cornelius developed into a moron. However, he is like a part of the family, and we felt a moral obligation to keep him despite his weaknesses. Rest assured I will send him into the fields after he carries our luggage into the house."

Abby, relieved that Cornelius was Loach's servant and not his father, smiled weakly. "Yes, please have him work outside, away from me."

Abby looked at the pasture beside the house. Scores of white sheep were grazing quietly.

The black ram approached Loach, snorted, and walked away. Why was it roaming alone, away from the flock?

As Loach and Abby entered the house, the black ram snorted again.

They ate roast lamb in the dining room. A girl in a plain black dress served them. She looked about fourteen years old, had blonde hair, and was thin, pale, and plain. She served them in complete silence.

Since arriving, Abby had seen only Loach, Cornelius, and the servant girl.

"Are we the only people here?" Abby asked. "Where are your servants and slaves? Where is your family? Where is your father?"

"The servants and slaves are in the fields, and my father and family are visiting friends at a nearby plantation," Loach said. "My father will return tomorrow."

Abby put down her pewter mug of water. "I look forward to meeting him." She changed the subject. "The dinner was delicious. Did that girl prepare it?"

"Ah, yes, she did. Jennifer is an especially talented

cook," Loach said.

"I am impressed that she made that dinner all by herself," Abby said. "Does she not usually have help?"

"She usually has her mother and two other maids to help her, but they are working in the fields today. It is so busy now that even my house servants need to tend to crops and livestock," Loach said.

They went into the parlour. Jennifer gave cups of a hot, brown liquid to them. Abby smelled the liquid warily.

"It is called chocolate," Loach said. "Have you heard of it?"

She knew it was a brew made by boiling beans called cocoa. Only the wealthy could afford it. In Boston, one or two expensive taverns served it. Abby had imagined it tasted like beer.

"I have heard of it, but I have never drunk any before," Abby said.

"Do not be afraid of it. Sip it gently and savour it," Loach said.

Abby sipped the chocolate. It was nothing like beer. It tasted partly bitter and partly sweet and entirely enjoyable. "I like it."

Loach chuckled. "I am serving it to you tonight so that you may become familiar with its taste. I am pleased that you like it. You will have more of it when my father returns. It is an aphrodisiac."

"Oh, so that is why you are indulging me with aristocratic luxuries," Abby said. "You are spending a small fortune on your father. You must love him very much."

"I love him immensely. I spare no expense for him," Loach said. "My family is the most important thing in my life."

"To our families," Abby toasted, hiding the fact that she had run away from hers.

Cornelius barged into room. "Ugh, ugh, ewe giving birth! Come quickly, come quickly," the servant urged.

"Ah, another litter is born," Loach said. "Please excuse me."

He left with Cornelius. Abby stood up and walked around the room. It was sparsely decorated, with only pale blue and white wallpaper and no family portraits. How Puritan.

On a table, a large book lay on a stand. That must be the family Bible.

Though she had fled from her uncle and his religion, she could not shake off all her Puritan breeding. She instinctively went to look at the Bible.

But it was not a Bible. It was open to a page showing an illustration of a black ram.

Underneath the black ram were the words:

SHUB-NIGGURATH, the Black Ram with a Thousand Ewes, is the Outer God of Fertility. From the world of Yaddith he came to Earth, where his cult worships him with wanton abandon.

Outer God of Fertility? Yaddith? Cult? Abby wondered what type of book was this. She looked at the cover, which bore the title NECRONOMICON.

It was larger than the shepherd's book, but it had the same title. What was the *Necronomicon*?

She turned the page and saw a picture of a woman with a beaky nose giving a doll to a black, winged demon. The text read:

The original witches were voyagers of the heavens who

absorbed the psychic powers of the Outer Gods into their own bodies. They, in turn, could channel those powers into their victims. Thus bewitched, the victims lost control of their minds and bodies to the vile witches, who often gave their victims as offerings to the Outer Gods.

"The ewe has given birth to two lambs," said Loach.

Abby gasped, turned around, and saw her host.

Loach smiled. "Oh, milady, I am sorry for startling you. I did not realize you were so intensely absorbed in reading the book."

"No problem," Abby said. "Uh, what type of book is this?"

"Milady, have you had an education in the Greek and Roman classics?" Loach asked.

"Uh, no. My family strictly studied the Bible."

"Well, the book you see is merely a collection of Greek and Roman myths. Harmless entertainment about what people believed before the coming of Jesus."

"I see," said Abby. "I know nothing about the Greeks and Romans except about the Roman governor Pontius Pilate. My uncle did not approve of learning about them because they were pagans. Perhaps you can teach me about their myths some day?"

"It would be my pleasure to do so," said Loach.

Abby finished drinking the chocolate. "Thank you for the wonderful meal and the drink. May I retire to my room now?"

"Yes, rest for tomorrow," Loach said. He took her upstairs to the guest room and left her alone.

As she fell asleep, Abby heard the black ram snort outside.

*

She woke up while the sky was still dark. Voices came from downstairs. Were they singing? Chanting? Why was the ram snorting so loudly?

Abby put on her shift and walked downstairs softly. When she reached the bottom, she peered into the parlour. Scores of candles threw eerie shadows of people on the walls.

Loach and ten other people stood in a circle. As they chanted in a strange language, another two men stood with the black ram in the centre of the circle.

Suddenly, the two men broke from the centre of the circle, rushed at Abby, grabbed her, and pulled her in front of the black ram.

"Let me go! Let me go!" Abby shrieked.

She looked at the people in the circle. She recognized Loach, Cornelius, and Jennifer. She also saw people from the town, with their large eyes, high cheekbones, and beaky noses.

Loach approached her. "I did not expect you to awaken before dawn. Do not you drabs sleep until noon?"

Abby stayed silent. She struggled to free herself, but her captors squeezed her arms.

"Do not struggle or you will feel more pain," Loach advised.

"Who are you?" Abby asked.

"We are children of Shub-Niggurath, the Black Ram with a Thousand Ewes, who bred with human women and created our herd," Loach said.

He pointed at the black ram. "That is my father, Shub-Niggurath."

The black ram snorted and looked up at Abby. Its eyes had a wild look.

Loach continued talking. "Unfortunately, the believers of the Hebrew God Yahweh have swarmed over our ancestral home, the caverns under the land you call Arabia. Our herd was in danger of extinction until my great-grandfather led us to America and founded Loach Hill. At that time, we numbered merely twenty. Now free from persecution, the children of Shub-Niggurath have multiplied to one hundred. Soon, he will breed a thousand young to defeat the Yahweh pagans."

Abby squirmed. "What do you want with me? Let me go! There is nothing I can do to help you!"

"On the contrary, we need you," Loach said. "Everyone in Loach Hill is descended from Shub-Niggurath. We lived in secret, and we had only ourselves for companionship. We married within our group extensively. At first, cousins bred with cousins, then uncles bred with nieces, then brothers bred with sisters, then children bred with parents. Alas, the inbreeding has caused some problems."

Cornelius walked to Abby and leered at her. He opened his mouth and drooled.

"Very pretty, very pretty," he said.

He stuck his tongue out and licked her cheek. Abby moaned as she felt the thick, sticky saliva on her skin.

Now Abby knew why everyone in Loach Hill looked the same.

"What do you want with me?" Abby stammered.

"You will breed with Shub-Niggurath and bring new blood into our herd," Loach declared.

"No! Wait!" Abby screamed. "Why me? I am just an

ordinary girl!"

"No, you are not, Abigail Williams!" Loach insisted, using Abby's real name. "The witches of Salem bewitched you. They controlled your body with their telekinetic power, that is, the ability to control objects and people with energy from their minds. Although you did not acquire the power of telekinesis, you absorbed enough telekinetic energy that it changed your gametes."

"My what?"

"It is a biological concept that your species does not yet understand. Suffice to say that the eggs in your womb have changed and now carry the telekinetic power of the Old Gods. You will pass that power to your spawn if you breed with a male who also possesses it. Thus you are an excellent ewe for breeding with Shub-Niggurath."

"Wait, wait!" Abby pleaded. "I was not really bewitched!"

"But you uttered sworn testimony at the trials saying that you had been bewitched," Loach reminded her.

"I lied! I lied! I was not bewitched! I was just having fun! I was just making trouble! I am merely an ordinary girl!"

Loach shrugged. "If you truly were bewitched, your body will enlarge to gross proportions and bear a litter for Shub-Niggurath. If you were lying, your body will split apart and die as your spawn claw their way out of your womb. Either way, you will add a thousand young to the herd."

"No!" Abby screamed as she struggled against the men who held her arms.

Loach chuckled. "Shub-Niggurath is a shape-shifter who can assume human form. Do you want to see how he looks as a male of your species?"

The black ram snorted, and its hair receded, its horns shrank, and it morphed into the shape of a naked man.

Abby gasped. It was the shepherd who had been her client in Boston.

He leaned over and breathed on Abby's neck. The feeling of his hot breath upon her skin made her stomach churn.

"Good morning, Chantal," Shub-Niggurath said, leering at her. "You cannot imagine my excitement when I discovered you, the last of the bewitched girls of Salem."

Abby squirmed as Shub-Niggurath kissed her. She tried to escape again, but the two men held her.

Shub-Niggurath leered at Abby. "Do you know what attracted me to you?"

Paralyzed with fear, Abby could only stare silently.

"It was the way you stole an extra shilling from me after each time I rutted with you," Shub-Niggurath said. "That shows cunning, which is a form of intelligence. Our herd could use more intelligence."

Abby screamed. Full of energy from fear, she kicked her captors in the shins. As they yelled in pain and let her go, she ran for the door. Suddenly, an invisible force slammed her in the back, sending her to the floor.

Abby got onto her elbows and knees—but no further. She wanted to stand but found she could not. An invisible force held her.

From across the room, Shub-Niggurath shouted, "You cannot escape from me, you drab."

A blast of frigid air swept over Abby, lifting her shift and exposing her thighs and buttocks.

The Outer God of Fertility approached Abby. He reached down and stroked her buttocks. "We will have a thousand children."

"No, please—" Abby struggled, but her body would not move. Cold fear gripped her.

Shub-Niggurath took Abby's thighs and pulled them apart. He then transformed back into a black ram and positioned himself behind her.

The townspeople chanted, "Shub-Niggurath, the Ram with a Thousand Ewes! Shub-Niggurath, the Black Goat of the Woods with a Thousand Young!"

Abby let out a long, desperate wail as Shub-Niggurath snorted and pushed, filling her with the curse of the shepherd's blessing.

About "The Shepherd's Blessing"

In 2011, author Michael Stackpole started a project called The Chain Story. The Chain was a series of stories involving the Wanderers' Club, a group of shadowy indi viduals who tell stories to each other. Each story would begin with a Wanderer concluding the previous story in the chain and end with another Wanderer starting a new story. The stories did not have to be related to each other.

The stories were initially published online on their individual authors' websites and linked to a central hub where all the stories were accessible. Alas, that hub is now defunct.

Mike invited me to write a story for The Chain Story. I wrote "The Shepherd's Blessing", which combined the Cthulhu Mythos with the Salem Witch Trials.

I had read Lovecraft's stories when I was a teenager and liked them even though I thought his style was overwritten with adjectives. I had avoided writing a Cthulhu Mythos story because I thought demand for them was low; they were limited to theme anthologies that got stories by invitation only. Here was my chance.

The Chain Story allowed authors to write stories that were not likely to be published elsewhere but would be fun to write and put into the public. Writing "The Shepherd's Blessing" was fun. I finally got to use the word "eldritch".

Did Abigail Williams really become a prostitute after the witch trials? There is no evidence that she did. That fake history comes from Arthur Miller's play *The Crucible*.

Songbun

KOREAN CENTRAL NEWS AGENCY: FOR IMMEDIATE RELEASE
PYONGYANG, April 15, *Juche* 116 (Foreign Year 2027)

Our Dear Leader has announced revisions to the *songbun* system to improve the coordination of Korean society to repel the invasion from the South. All *songbun* records will be consolidated in a new state office, the Ministry of Genealogical Records. All persons, except for those with Hostile *songbun*, will have the right to apply for revision of their *songbun* based on war service.

It is untrue that the Wavering Class will be reclassified as Hostile. The despicable scum of Seoul, worse than dogs, spread this lie to weaken our *Juche* spirit. The major classes will remain as:

Elite
Core
Basic
Wavering

Hostile

*

THREE MONTHS BEFORE LAUNCH DATE:

A cool wind swept from the East Sea over the top of the launch tower at Musudan-ri Rocket Launch Centre. Lee Ha Neul shivered in his grey vinylon jacket as he looked down at the massive rocket.

His jacket bore the logo of the National Aerospace Development Administration. It was a dark blue globe with the constellation Ursa Major, the Administration's Korean name, and the English acronym "NADA" in white. A foreign languages student had told him that "NADA" meant "nothing" in Spanish. Ha Neul did not know if that was true or not.

It was October, merely three months before Dear Leader's birthday. Technicians scurried around both the base and the top of the tower, working on the rocket and the spacecraft it carried.

Cho Yoon Ah, Director of the Cosmonaut Office, gripped the collar of her black wool coat. Slender and beautiful, with straight teeth and unblemished skin, Yoon Ah was a woman of the Pyongyang Elite. She had grown up with food, housing, health and dental care, education, clothes, shoes, jewellery, hair stylists, and cosmetics that most Northerners could never have. Her great-grandfather had fought alongside President Kim Il Sung, and her parents were high-ranking officials of the State Commission for Science and Technology.

"Cosmonaut Lee, let's inspect the spacecraft," Yoon Ah said.

The Chollima 1 spacecraft, named after a mythological flying horse, looked like an ancient Russian Vostok, a silver spherical crew module attached to a cylindrical service module that carried an engine.

The crew, consisting of a sole cosmonaut, would ride in the crew module, with the service module propelling the spacecraft through its orbits. Then the crew module would jettison the service module and descend to Earth.

"I don't have enough training to fly this spacecraft," Ha Neul said.

"You're a pilot. That's enough," said Yoon Ah. "Let Mission Control fly the spacecraft for you by remote control. Just sit back and enjoy the ride. The only time you have to do anything is when the radio control does not work. Then we authorize you to take control of the spacecraft. However, there is only a small risk of that happening."

"I don't think the risk is small. We rushed construction of the spaceship without any of the original designers or engineers," Ha Neul said.

She pulled him aside, away from the technicians. "No more excuses. Dear Leader is counting on you to succeed on this mission."

"I don't want to fly any more. I just can't," Ha Neul pleaded.

Yoon Ah scowled at him. "Don't say that! Your parents bribed the doctor to destroy your psychiatric assessment."

Ha Neul gasped. "It's destroyed? Gone?"

"Don't tell anyone."

"Thank you, Director Cho."

"Don't thank me. Thank your parents. They paid two

hundred United States dollars. At least pretend to be happy."

When Ha Neul didn't respond, Yoon Ah continued. "Korea is the happiest country on Earth. We have nothing to envy in the world. Our people have no mental weakness. Anyone who shows signs of mental illness is a traitor. You know the penalty for treason. Now the record shows you have no mental illness."

Ha Neul nodded silently. He knew that Dear Leader never made mistakes and wanted his people to learn from him. Like a good parent, Dear Leader rewarded and punished his children. If Ha Neul succeeded in every task, he would be promoted to Hero Cosmonaut, and his family would join the Elite and live in a luxury apartment in Pyongyang. But if he made one mistake, he and his family would be sent to a prison camp. They would die within two years.

Yoon Ah softened her tone. "Comrade Cosmonaut Lee, think of the rewards. You'll get a photo op with Dear Leader, and your *songbun* will be raised to Elite. You will get anything you want: food, clothes, luxury apartment. You can do it!"

Flight Director Jang rushed onto the platform. He was a tall, distinguished-looking man in a blue business suit and tie. Jang, a former Air Force Colonel, learned aerospace engineering in Russia and thus escaped the purge of all staff who had trained in China.

"Comrade Cosmonaut Lee, Comrade Director Cho, listen to me! I have received an order from Dear Leader!" Jang shouted.

Ha Neul and Yoon Ah quickly stood at attention, like soldiers under inspection. Jang stared sternly at them.

"Comrades, Dear Leader has told us the objective of the Chollima 1 space mission," Jang announced.

Ha Neul took a deep breath. The mission objective had been secret. Not even he knew what it was. Was it for scientific research? Was it for military intelligence?

"Your spaceship will broadcast Dear Leader's theme song from space. The Ministry of Foreign Affairs has selected a radio frequency and told all foreign countries to listen to it during your flight. The whole world will hear Dear Leader's theme song from the heavens."

Ha Neul's stomach grumbled.

"Dear Leader has given us so much," Jang said. "The least we can do is to broadcast his song to the heavens on his birthday."

Jang clicked his heels, turned away, and marched to the technicians.

Yoon Ah turned to Ha Neul and said, "This is a great honour!"

Ha Neul walked away and looked over the railing of the tower. He stared down at the ground, a great distance below. He closed his eyes, gasped, and teetered as he gripped the railing.

Yoon Ah pulled him back and pushed him into the elevator of the tower.

As they rode down, Yoon Ah said, "The past month of training has been strenuous. Start your leave now. Get some rest. I've arranged for Flight Sergeant Park Bon Hwa to fly you to Onsong. It's faster than taking the train."

Ha Neul nodded. Park had been his co-pilot during the War of Chinese Aggression. Now he was Cho Yoon Ah's assistant and Ha Neul's babysitter.

Flight Sergeant Park Bon Hwa, a pilot with a perfect flying record, would be a better cosmonaut than Ha Neul. But their ancestors' *songbun* decided who would stay on Earth and who would fly in space.

*

Bon Hwa had the rough look of people raised on rocky, infertile farmland. Like most peasants, he was shorter than the Pyongyang Elite because he had eaten smaller food rations all his life. Since his village had no dentist, his teeth remained yellow and crooked. He was born to toil hard and die young so the Elite could enjoy life. However, he took advantage of the wartime turmoil to rise in social status.

Bon Hwa flew the old L-39 training airplane higher into the clouds. Sitting beside Bon Hwa, Ha Neul felt a shiver run down his spine.

"We're going too high," Ha Neul protested.

"There's no problem, Ha Neul," Bon Hwa replied, addressing him by his given name, a sign of their close friendship from the war. "The sky is clear again. I haven't seen a foreign plane for a long time."

In the past, only men with Elite *songbun* could be pilots. However, the Southern War killed most of the country's pilots, and the government was desperate to replace them before the inevitable war with China. The Air Force quietly took trainees with Wavering to Core *songbun*, men like Ha Neul and Bon Hwa. They trained as postal pilots and flew mail across the country. By classifying them as civilians, the government fed them smaller rations than military pilots got. However, the Air

Force held all civilian pilots in reserve.

When the War of Chinese Aggression broke out, the Air Force pushed them into service. They had minimal peacetime flight experience and no military training. As Korean troops pushed into China, Ha Neul and Bon Hwa flew supplies to them.

Although the Chinese retreated on the ground, they fought fiercely in the air. The new Chinese Chengdu J-60 stealth fighters decimated the Korean MiG-29's, antiques from the twentieth century. The Koreans flew transport missions without fighter support. Chinese fighters, anti-aircraft guns, and missiles easily shot them down.

The transport planes flew in groups. Ha Neul and Bon Hwa had watched in terror as their comrades' planes exploded and crashed all around them.

Two months after the war started, the Chinese surrounded the entire Korean invasion force at Helong. No supplies could reach them by ground. Dear Leader ordered the Air Force to fly supplies to the trapped Koreans twenty-four hours per day.

On one mission, twenty planes took off for Helong. Only one plane, flown by Ha Neul and Bon Hwa, returned to Korea. They repeated the mission the next day.

On their last mission, Ha Neul froze at the controls on the return to Korea. Fear gripped him. He sweated, and his heart beat rapidly. He felt a cramping feeling in his chest. His stomach hurt.

As his mind went blank, he gripped his side-stick and plunged the plane into a dive.

"Lee, what are you doing?" Bon Hwa yelled.

Ha Neul said nothing.

Bon Hwa pushed the priority button to lock out inputs

from Ha Neul's side-stick, grabbed his own stick, and forced the plane to climb.

By sheer luck, the Chinese anti-aircraft guns missed them. Bon Hwa flew the plane back to Korea.

Ha Neul never flew an airplane again.

*

Dear Leader declared victory over China the next day. Ha Neul did not know how the entrapped Koreans could have defeated China, since none of them ever returned home. Everyone gossiped that Dear Leader had unleashed secret miracle rockets on China, but nobody knew what had actually happened.

Before the war, Dear Leader hired Chinese engineers to build Korea's first spaceship. He distrusted the Chinese but used them because they were cheaper than the Russians. When war broke out, he killed the engineers, leaving the National Aerospace Development Administration with nobody experienced in building a spacecraft for humans. Nonetheless, Dear Leader insisted that his people launch a cosmonaut into space for his fiftieth birthday.

Eight fighter pilots, each with Elite *songbun*, had survived the war. NADA conscripted them into cosmonaut training. Five of them died in explosions on the launch pad. The remaining three stole airplanes and defected to the South. Despite their Elite *songbun*, they didn't want to die for Dear Leader's birthday.

Cho Yoon Ah, Director of the Cosmonaut Office, had to find replacements. She looked for military transport pilots. Only Lee Ha Neul and Park Bon Hwa had survived the war.

Bon Hwa had inherited Wavering *songbun*. His great-grandfather, a Southern soldier, was captured during the Fatherland Liberation War. Southern prisoners had Hostile *songbun*, but he partially redeemed himself by spitting on a photo of Syngman Rhee, the hated first president of the South. For this act, the government raised his *songbun* to Wavering. Bon Hwa had a perfect flight record, but his Wavering *songbun* made him unsuitable to be a Hero Cosmonaut.

Ha Neul had better *songbun*. Both of Ha Neul's parents had Core *songbun*, two classes above Bon Hwa's. However, they were not born that high, a secret the family kept to itself.

*

"Ha Neul, do you want to fly the plane for a minute?" Bon Hwa asked. "You won't know if you can do it until you try."

"Okay," Ha Neul muttered.

"I've shifted control to your side-stick. Go ahead."

Ha Neul gripped his side-stick. The old memories came back. His heart pounded, and he breathed heavily. He felt a heavy weight pressed against his chest, and he sweated.

He pushed the plane into a steep dive.

Bon Hwa pressed the priority button, regained control of the plane, and pulled it up to a level flight.

"Ha Neul, remember what I taught you," Bon Hwa said. "Imagine the plane landing safely. Imagine you are the pilot who lands the plane without trouble."

Ha Neul imagined himself at the controls of a plane.

"What is the weather like in your perfect flight?" Bon Hwa asked.

"It's good," Ha Neul muttered.

"Tell me more," said Bon Hwa.

"There's no rain and no wind resistance. The sun is behind me, not in my eyes. There's enough light for me to see ahead."

"Perfect conditions for a perfect landing. Think of the runway."

Ha Neul forced himself to see a runway in the distance.

"What is it like?"

"Long, straight, paved. Hah, better than the airstrip in China."

"Are there any vehicles or aircraft in the way? Is it clear for landing?"

"It's clear for landing."

"Approach the runway," Bon Hwa urged. "Gently point the nose to the runway. Lower the landing gear. Check your speed. Check your altitude..."

Ha Neul imagined landing the plane smoothly. He imagined the sun's warmth on his face as he walked unharmed to the airport terminal.

He breathed normally again and sighed in relief.

"Good, you are learning to visualize. I used the technique when infiltrating the American Zone," Bon Hwa said. "You can do it, but you've got to learn to do it without my coaching. I can't be with you all of the time."

Ha Neul nodded.

Bon Hwa said, "It won't be long until we reach Onsong. You'll see your parents in no time."

*

Ha Neul's mother wore a blue blouse made of Chinese polyester. The blouse symbolized her family's rise in wealth and *songbun*. Ordinary Koreans wore clothes made of vinylon, the shiny synthetic fibre made from limestone, anthracite, and polyvinyl alcohol. Vinylon was a stiff, coarse fabric that deformed and shrank easily.

Mother's family originally had Hostile *songbun* because they owned land before the Fatherland Liberation War. The government exiled them to a dirt-poor farm near China. The location was a punishment intended to prevent them from escaping to the South. However, it became an unintended blessing during the Arduous March, when local authority collapsed. Her father earned a small fortune by smuggling Chinese goods to sell to the Elite. He bribed several state officials to change his *songbun* records from Hostile to Core, a difficult task when three state offices kept *songbun* records and auditors cross-checked them to find fraud. Mother continued the smuggling business, though she switched to Russian goods during the War of Chinese Aggression.

Mother asked Ha Neul, "Did you have any, uh, problems concentrating on your training?"

Ha Neul paused before answering, "No."

Mother grimaced. "You must overcome your fear. Our family has toiled to better itself. My father saved thousands of won to give us Core *songbun*. We finally got meat in our rations."

Ha Neul nodded and looked at the photo of his maternal grandfather wearing a green *hanbok* and smiling as he held up a tin of pork.

"You will become the first Korean to fly into space," Mother said.

"Uh, wasn't Yi So Yeon the first Korean in space?" Ha Neul said.

"Don't mention that Southern snake again!" Mother scolded. "She was a puppet who rode with the Americans and Russians. You will be the first *free* Korean to fly in space. Dear Leader will pose for a photo with you, and our *songbun* will be raised to Elite. We'll finally be allowed to live in Pyongyang. We'll get an apartment with its own washroom, and it might even have a flush toilet."

Mother's voice grew excited. "Our daily food ration will increase to three hundred grams per person! A whole one hundred grams of that will be meat! We'll get two grams of sugar on national holidays! Imagine that!"

The lights in their apartment flickered and blacked out. They relit a few seconds later.

"And in Pyongyang, we'll get electricity for eighteen hours per day," Mother continued. "So much depends on you succeeding in our country's first space mission! Ha Neul, you cannot fail!"

Ha Neul's father, who had been sitting with his newspaper, stood up. "Son, think of the rewards of being photographed with Dear Leader when you return."

Father pointed at a photograph of Dear Leader surrounded by vinylon factory workers. Father stood three paces behind Dear Leader.

"It is a great day when Dear Leader poses for a photograph with you. Because my father was born in the South, I inherited Wavering *songbun*, but after Dear Leader posed for a photo with me and the other workers, my *songbun* increased to Core. Then I could finally marry your mother."

Father was an accountant at a vinylon factory. The factory managers enriched themselves by embezzling and using the funds to smuggle Russian electronics into Korea. Father enriched himself by taking bribes to cover the managers' thefts. Since he and the managers added a small portion of their smuggling profits into the factory's income, their factory seemed like the most productive vinylon factory in Korea. Thus Dear Leader came to congratulate the workers and their bosses, and everyone's *songbun* went up.

All of Ha Neul's relatives had done desperate things to improve their *songbun*. Now it was his turn.

Like all Korean families, they had Dear Leader's portrait hanging on the wall. Ha Neul felt Dear Leader's piercing eyes stare into his mind. Dear Leader could see his fear and disloyalty.

Ha Neul sweated and felt his stomach churn.

The lights went out for the evening.

*

ONE MONTH BEFORE LAUNCH DATE:

A grey-haired man with eyeglasses climbed out of Chollima 1's crew module and walked to Flight Director Jang.

"Comrade Communications Engineer Hong," Jang said, "can the Chollima play the song?"

Hong shrugged. "We may have a problem, Comrade Flight Director. The Chinese didn't complete the spaceship before they were, uh, removed. We've finished their work, but we still have trouble with the on-board broadcasting system. The radio uplink from the ground to the broadcasting system is erratic. Sometimes it works, sometimes it doesn't."

Jang grunted. "If necessary, can the cosmonaut manually activate the player and broadcast the song to Earth?"

Hong smiled proudly. "*That* part of the system works. *I* built the on-board playback mechanism."

"Well, at least we Koreans can build a tape recorder," Jang said. "We may have to depend on Cosmonaut Lee to broadcast the song. Let's go and see how the flight simulation is going."

*

The spacecraft simulator rocked gently back and forth. Inside, Ha Neul gazed at the images of Earth projected on the fake window.

Outside, Yoon Ah and Bon Hwa looked at the monitor showing Ha Neul's vital signs.

"You're breathing too quickly," Yoon Ah said over the radio. "Calm down."

"Temperature is okay, but heart rate and blood pressure are high," Bon Hwa said.

"Cosmonaut Lee, please relax," Yoon Ah urged. "Let Mission Control do all the work."

Ha Neul moaned over the radio.

They watched the simulator rise languidly. Bon Hwa shook his head.

"This simulator can't provide weightlessness. We need a reduced gravity aircraft," Bon Hwa said. "Well, at least it won't upset his stomach."

"I feel sick," Ha Neul said.

Jang and Hong arrived. The Flight Director looked at Ha Neul's vital signs and frowned. "Is he in any condition to carry out orders from the ground in case of emergency?" Jang asked.

"Let's try," Yoon Ah said, handing a microphone to Jang. "What do you have in mind?"

Jang said into the microphone, "Cosmonaut Lee, this is Flight Director Jang. Do you read me?"

Ha Neul moaned.

Jang shook his head. "Comrade Cosmonaut, there has been a malfunction in the uplink to the broadcast system. I authorize you to take manual control of the ship. Press the play button of the audio player."

No sound came from the simulator.

"Did he press the button?" Jang asked.

Hong looked at the monitor. "No, he did not."

"Cosmonaut Lee, do you acknowledge my order?" Jang said.

Again, no sound came from the simulator.

"His heart rate and blood pressure are sky high," Bon Hwa reported.

"Get him out of there," Yoon Ah ordered.

The technicians opened the simulator's door and pulled Ha Neul from his seat. He looked relieved to get out.

"How could anyone get nervous riding a children's toy?" Yoon Ah complained.

The simulator was a ride from Rungna People's Pleasure Park. It did not simulate the G-force, weightlessness, or movements of actual space flight. But it was the best simulator NADA could get. Dear Leader had killed the Chinese before they could build a simulator.

"The simulated images of Earth were very frightening," Ha Neul said.

"I know training is difficult, but on the day of the mission, you have to stay calm," Bon Hwa said. "Think of your family."

Ha Neul looked down at the floor. He would panic in space and bring shame and Hostile *songbun* to his family.

"Cosmonaut Lee, you could not even press a button, the simplest task possible!" Jang scolded. "Do not embarrass Dear Leader! The consequences of failure are unspeakable. Do you acknowledge?"

"Yes, Comrade Flight Director," Ha Neul stammered.

*

After dinner, Ha Neul and Bon Hwa watched videos of Russian, American, and Chinese space flights in the cosmonaut lounge. Dear Leader banned ordinary Koreans from watching foreign space flights; Koreans did not need to know that foreigners had technology more advanced than theirs. However, Yoon Ah used her Elite *songbun* to get the videos from the State Commission for Science and Technology.

"Look how easily these foreigners fly in space," Bon Hwa said. A Russian cosmonaut waved at his TV audience as his spaceship blasted off. "Imagine yourself like him."

Ha Neul closed his eyes. He saw himself riding the rocket, smiling at the camera, calmly reporting on his ship's systems to Mission Control.

"Can you see yourself flying into space like him?" Bon Hwa asked.

Ha Neul nodded silently.

"Good," said Bon Hwa. "You must learn to visualize without me. I will not be with you in the spaceship."

"But you will talk to me from Mission Control, won't you?"

Bon Hwa shook his head. "No, I won't be there either. There will be ten foreign journalists in the Media Office. Regulations require a military officer of sergeant's rank or above to monitor them. All such officers except me will be either guarding the launch centre or marching in Dear Leader's parade. I will be at the Media Office."

"Oh," said Ha Neul.

"I have to go home now, while the trams still get electricity. Continue practising visualization without me."

Bon Hwa went home, leaving Ha Neul alone to watch the videos. A half hour later, the blackout began, shutting off the lights and the video player.

His concentration crumbled. The lounge was like a tomb, all dark and silent. He thought only of plane crashes and dead pilots.

Ha Neul remembered Bon Hwa had saved his life by taking control of the plane as they returned from China. Since then, he could not calm down without Bon Hwa urging him.

Without Bon Hwa, he would fail in his mission and disgrace Dear Leader in front of the entire world. He would be dead without Bon Hwa.

*

LAUNCH DATE:

January 8, *Juche* 122: the entire nation celebrated Dear Leader's fiftieth birthday. In Pyongyang, fifty thousand people sang and paraded through Kim Il Sung Square. At Musudan-ri, a sole cosmonaut, Ha Neul, blasted into space on a different mission to honour Dear Leader.

The amusement park ride was nothing like real space flight. Ha Neul thought the G-force and violent shaking would tear his body apart. He urinated in his spacesuit.

The Chollima 1 spacecraft separated from the Unha-10 rocket. As the booster fell into the East Sea, Chollima 1 went into a low-Earth orbit.

The weightlessness turned his stomach. Ha Neul forced himself not to vomit.

He looked out the window. Chollima 1 flew one hundred and seventy kilometers above the Earth, about the same altitude that Gagarin had flown, seventy-two years earlier. Ha Neul thought of the distance between him and the ground. A new jolt of fear ran through his body.

*

At Mission Control, Yoon Ah stared at the cosmonaut's vital signs on a monitor. "He's hyperventilating. We better calm him down before Dear Leader watches the flight. Where is Dear Leader now?"

Jang looked at the TV. "He's still at the parade."

They watched a computer graphic of the flight on the large screen. Chollima 1's orbit stabilized.

"Given the time and budget, we're extremely lucky," Jang said. "The flight is as good as any by another country.”

Ha Neul moaned over the radio.

“But we can’t have our cosmonaut whimpering like a dog when Dear Leader watches the flight,” said Yoon Ah. “He needs to behave like a national hero.”

*

During the second orbit, Flight Director Jang’s cell phone beeped. He read the email and grabbed a microphone.

“Attention, all staff,” he said. “Dear Leader will watch the flight thirty minutes from now.”

The Mission Control crew murmured. Yoon Ah ran to Jang. “That’s an hour earlier than we expected.”

“Lunch with the Cabinet ended early,” Jang explained. “He’s running ahead of schedule.”

“We better test the broadcasting system *now*,” Yoon Ah said.

Jang went to Hong. “Let’s run a test. Play the song.”

Hong nodded and pressed a button.

Nothing happened.

“Hey, Hong, what’s going on?” Jang asked.

Hong looked worried. “The uplink failed. The ship’s broadcasting system isn’t receiving our signal.”

A drop of sweat flowed down Jang’s forehead for the first time. “If we can’t get the song playing, we’ll all be punished.” The Flight Director swayed.

Yoon Ah suggested, “Can we play the song from here, feed it into the Korean Central Television signal, and fake a broadcast from space?”

“The government has told the foreign countries to listen for the song,” Jang said. “They will report that no broadcast from space occurred. Our own people won't know the difference, but Dear Leader receives foreign news. He'll know what the foreign countries think of our failure."

"Then we have to depend on Cosmonaut Lee," Yoon Ah said.

Ha Neul moaned over the radio.

Jang said, "This is Mission Control to Chollima 1. Chollima 1, do you read me?"

Ha Neul moaned again.

Jang and Yoon Ah watched the video feed from the spaceship. Ha Neul looked stricken with panic.

"He never got cured," said Yoon Ah.

"That didn't matter as long as Mission Control did everything for him," Jang said, "but now, he's on his own."

Jang said, "Mission Control to Chollima 1. Chollima 1, do you read me?"

"Aaack—yes!" Ha Neul replied.

"Cosmonaut Lee, I need you to test the broadcasting system. Press the 'play' button. That is all you have to do."

They watched the video feed. Ha Neul did not press the play button. They could see the fear in his eyes.

"Are we going to crash?" Ha Neul asked.

Hong said, "Director Jang, tell Cosmonaut Lee that the on-board playback mechanism will work. It will not fail! I personally tested it twenty times. He can have confidence in it."

"I don't think it matters if he thinks your machine works or not," said Jang.

Yoon Ah looked at the monitor showing Korean

Central Television. Dear Leader's limousine drove towards Ryongsong Residence.

"Can we send the KCTV signal to the spaceship?" she asked.

"Hong, get to it," Jang ordered.

*

On the Chollima's video monitor, the scene suddenly changed from Mission Control to the Ryongsong Residence. Ha Neul watched in disbelief as Dear Leader got out of his limousine and walked through the grounds of his palace.

Why are they showing me Dear Leader's birthday news? Ha Neul wondered.

Instead of the news announcer's narration, Yoon Ah's voice came with the news video. "Cosmonaut Lee, this is Director Cho. Look at the TV news. Dear Leader has gone home. He will watch the space flight soon. Do your duty! Do not embarrass Dear Leader!"

Ha Neul sweated and panted as he watched Dear Leader stroll through the gardens of Ryongsong Residence. Dear Leader's smile inspired both love and terror.

"All of us depend on you. Your family depends on you," Yoon Ah urged.

I can do it without Bon Hwa, Ha Neul silently told himself. *I* must *do it without Bon Hwa. I need to prove to Bon Hwa that I can do it.*

Ha Neul closed his eyes and took a deep breath. He saw himself as a heroic cosmonaut. He imagined pressing the button, hearing the song play, bringing the ship back to Earth, and shaking hands with Dear Leader.

He smelled the fragrant flowers that the Youth Corps would give him at welcoming ceremony. He tasted the salty pork that would come with his increased rations. He felt his mother's warm embrace as they moved into a luxury apartment.

*

Jang's cell phone beeped. He looked at the email and frowned.

"Damn, we've run out of time," he muttered.

Jang stood at attention and said, "Comrade Cosmonaut Lee, Dear Leader orders you to play his theme song on the designated frequency. Perform your duty to the Fatherland."

No sound came from the spaceship.

Then Ha Neul broke the silence. "Flight Director Jang, I acknowledge the order and will perform my duty. Glory to Dear Leader and the Democratic People's Republic of Korea!"

Yoon Ah gasped and cried with joy.

*

Ha Neul pressed the play button.

The song "Kim Jong Un, We Follow Only You" played.

Ha Neul sighed in relief. He heard people applauding in Mission Control.

*

All over the Earth, foreigners heard Dear Leader's song from space. The Korean Central News Agency announced, "Today, the Korean people, led by their Dear Leader on his birthday, began their conquest of space. The radio signal of Dear Leader's theme song will travel into the cosmos forever, symbolizing the eternal spirit of the Korean people and the *Juche* Idea."

Ha Neul orbited the Earth four times. KCNA bragged, "Under Dear Leader's guidance, Cosmonaut Lee completed one orbit more than did John Glenn, the Yankee aggressor pilot who attacked Korea in the Fatherland Liberation War."

The crew module separated from the service module, descended back to Earth, deployed its parachutes, and landed on the Chaeryong Plain. According to KCNA, "The Democratic People's Republic of Korea has a terrain of mostly hills, mountains, and valleys. Its plains are few and small. Landing a spaceship on a plain was a triumph of Dear Leader's technology and science."

Ha Neul smiled for the TV cameras as the ground crew helped him out of the spacecraft.

*

Two days later, Dear Leader visited Musudan-ri Rocket Launch Centre. Dear Leader promoted Ha Neul to First Lieutenant and pinned the Hero Cosmonaut badge to his Air Force uniform. Again, Ha Neul smiled for the cameras.

The most important event of Dear Leader's visit came next. All the Mission Control crew gathered on the auditorium stage for a group photo with Dear Leader.

They wore their best clothes and red Dear Leader lapel pins.

Dear Leader stood to Ha Neul's left. To Ha Neul's right stood Bon Hwa and Hong. Ha Neul had insisted that they stand with him in the front row. Jang relented and let the two low *songbun* men stand beside the Hero Cosmonaut.

After the photographer snapped the photo, everyone cheered. They jumped up and down and waved their arms above their heads, as if they were at Dear Leader's birthday parade.

Dear Leader smiled and waved at them, overjoyed by their love for him. But they were also cheering for themselves. Their *songbun* had just increased.

*

Bon Hwa grinned. "Remember me if you get to hire staff. I want to work for a national hero. The guy who won the Olympic Gold Medal for archery is on the Olympic Committee now. His personal secretary gets two hundred grams of pork per day. Two hundred grams!"

"I'll get you a job, Flight Sergeant," Ha Neul said. "I'll call you when I settle into Pyongyang."

Ha Neul left to catch the train to Onsong. Although he had flown in space, he preferred to travel by train.

*

Ha Neul and his parents moved from Onsong to Pyongyang. Their apartment had its own bathroom *and* a flush toilet. Clean water flowed from the kitchen faucet. The elevators worked. Electricity ran until twenty-three hundred hours, when the day's TV broadcast ended. They each received three hundred grams of food per day. Pyongyang was paradise.

Mother hummed the children's song, "We Have Nothing to Envy in the World". She had finally regained the status that her ancestors lost. The family was Elite again.

Just like in Onsong, Dear Leader's portrait hung in the living room. But now, they also hung photos of Dear Leader in their bedrooms, in the kitchen, in the small hallway, and on the closet doors. Dear Leader looked at them everywhere.

They owed everything they had, from the food they ate to the clothes they wore, to Dear Leader. Putting his picture all over their apartment was the least they could do to thank him for his generosity.

One night, the TV announcer ended the day's broadcast by saying, "Think about serving Dear Leader in all your achievements. Good night and sleep well."

But when Ha Neul fell asleep, he did not think of Dear Leader. He dreamed about himself, Hero Cosmonaut of Korea.

About "Songbun"

North Korea really does have a caste system called *songbun*, which determines every factor of an individual's life, including career, income, housing, and even access to food.

North American science fiction has a trope of rebels fighting against dictatorships (*Star Wars*, of course, being perhaps the best known). I took a different approach in "Songbun"; its characters don't plot against the regime but exploit it for their own benefit, which is what many people in totalitarian regimes do.

Thanks to Susan Forest and Lucas Law for publishing the story that will forever get me banned from North Korea.

It Came to Eat Our Chicken Wings

Her friends thought her uniform looked silly: tight little orange shorts, white tank top with a picture of an owl, shiny beige pantyhose, and white running shoes. Her father wondered what type of restaurant would publish a swimsuit calendar of its waitresses. But despite the raised eyebrows of friends and family, Kyra Ling liked working at Hooters. At least she made more money serving beer and chicken wings than she had pushing a dim sum cart.

However, there were moments when the job seemed distinctly unglamorous, like this moment, when the two college frat boys were lolling their heads, nearly unconscious.

The guy in the Cocoa Beach University golf shirt shook his buddy's shoulder as she passed by. "Hey," he yelled to Kyra. "My friend thinks Asian girls are hot."

Kyra smiled. How could she get these two drunks out? "Thanks," she replied. "Do you guys want a coffee?"

His buddy drooled as he leered at her. "I'm looking for a geisha."

Kyra shrugged. "Go to Japan."

The student was unfazed. "So do you speak Asian?"

Kyra's lips curled into a bemused grin.

"*Non, mais je parle anglais, français, et un peu de chinois*," she replied.

The student didn't give up. "So can you teach it to me? It's one of those languages that's best taught by a..." he mumbled before he slumped over the table.

Kyra tapped him on the shoulder.

"I think you're done." She handed the cheque to his friend. "Here's the tab."

"Oh, sure," the frat boy said as he handed her a fifty dollar bill.

Kyra took the money and pushed the change into his shirt pocket. "We better get you into a cab. Don't drive, okay?"

"Sure thing," he muttered.

Kyra motioned to Maria, the manager. They walked the two frat boys out the door and into a cab. When they returned into the restaurant, the regular customers burst into applause. Kyra curtsied to the audience.

Maria laughed. "That was great. You should negotiate the Middle East peace treaty."

"Get out," Kyra teased. "Did you hear those two morons? 'I'm looking for a geisha.' I bet he doesn't know what a geisha really is. Is that all these guys think about when they see an Asian woman?"

"You, Kyra dear, can be a lot of things," Maria suggested as she gave a bag of chicken wings to her. "You and Nicole can munch on these. Brandy called in sick, and Nicole's at the car show alone, so you can stay there and work at the booth."

"Cool, my first promo." Kyra retouched her lipstick. "How do I look?"

"You look fabulous. Don't keep fussing. It's only a promo, not a calendar shoot," Maria reminded her. "Actually, it can be fun. Come on, get going, or you'll be late."

Kyra hopped into her red convertible, threw the bag of chicken wings into the back seat, and drove onto the highways around Cocoa Beach, Florida. With clear weather and no traffic jams, she should be at the convention centre in no time.

Then she saw a bright light in the sky. A shiny, silvery object, engulfed in red flames, was falling to the Earth.

"Oh my God, is that a crashing plane?" she wondered. The object plummeted steadily until it disappeared into the horizon. The sound of a crash boomed in the distance. Curious about the object, she sped ahead.

A mile later, she stopped her car, walked on to the side of the road, and looked at a nearby swamp, her eyes widening with awe. A cylinder, like a grain silo about thirty feet long, lay at the edge of the swamp. Its silver surface was charred black in spots, and it had a few dents and creases, but it seemed mostly undamaged. Steam rose from the water surrounding the cylinder, but no fire burned anymore.

She looked up and scanned the sky. It was blue and cloudless, quiet and peaceful. No storm or hurricane had brought this thing down.

Lowering her gaze back to Earth, she looked at the swamp again. She stood still for a long time, staring at the shiny, steaming cylinder.

A vehicle screeched to a halt behind her. She spun around and saw a NASA van beside her car. NASA workers, holding cameras and equipment, jumped out of the van, ran into the swamp, and waded towards the object.

"What is it?" she asked a man whose badge read: John Evans. Recovery Team Leader.

"I don't know," Evans admitted. "It doesn't look like one of ours or a Russian or a Chinese or any other country's."

"It doesn't have any markings," a recovery worker yelled from the swamp.

Evans gasped. "Darn, maybe it's somebody's secret weapon! Get out of there!"

"It's okay, it's okay," the recovery worker reported. "Nothing—no radiation, no biological or chemical contaminant—is registering on our equipment."

"It's not on fire now, but it was on fire on the way down," Kyra observed.

"That was probably the surface burning as it entered our atmosphere," said Evans. "Thank goodness it fell in the water. If it had fallen on trees or grass, the whole countryside could be on fire now."

He pulled out his notebook and glanced at Kyra's Hooters name badge. "Uh, Kyra? May I ask you some questions? Did you see the spacecraft come down?"

The spacecraft. The NASA guy had called it a spacecraft. But it wasn't from any country in the world. "Maybe it was from beyond this world," thought Kyra.

She told him about the fire in the sky, the spaceship's constant speed of descent, and the sound of the crash.

Then she remembered the chicken wings in the back seat of her car. "Oh dear, the car show," she muttered. "I am so late for the car show. Can I go now?"

"Sure, and thank you," said Evans.

Kyra smiled, ran back to her car, and drove off. A few minutes later, a recovery worker pointed out the open hatch to Evans. "Someone was flying this ship," Evans guessed as he swung the hatch door open and closed. He looked into the ship. "There's no one inside the ship. Where's the astronaut?" he asked. Nobody knew.

"Hey, look at this," cried Dr. Steve Potter, the biologist.

Evans walked back to the side of the road. Potter led him along a streak of blue liquid that stretched from the swamp to a stand of trees, to a pair of tire tracks in the mud. The tire tracks were where Kyra had parked her car.

"What could that be?" asked Evans.

"Mechanical fluid from the spacecraft?" Potter shrugged. "I dunno. I'll take a sample back and analyze it."

"Whatever it is, someone dripped it on a path from the swamp to the Hooters Girl's car," said Evans. "I hope she's not taking more than chicken wings to the car show."

*

"You're late," Nicole complained. She moved away from the racing car emblazoned with the orange and white Hooters logo on its hood. "What took you so long?"

"I saw a spaceship crash beside the highway," Kyra squealed. "It was so exciting. I think it was an alien ship."

"As if," Nicole replied. She pointed at a stack of posters of the contestants of the Miss Hooters of East Central Florida bikini pageant. "Come on, help me hand out posters to horny car show fans."

Nicole sat down and began autographing the posters, which showed her flipping her blonde hair while posing in a pink bikini. She signed each poster, "Breast wishes, Nicole XOXO," before handing it with a smile to the next guy in a lineup of car aficionados.

As Kyra passed another poster to Nicole, a teenager asked her, "Are you in the poster too?"

"No," said Kyra. "But I'm on the coupon for ten free chicken wings." She handed a coupon to him. "Do you want one?"

"Awesome," said the kid. "Uh, can you sign it?"

Kyra signed it "Hugs and hooters, Kyra" and gave it back to the teenager. As he walked off, she turned to Nicole. "Don't you love it when you can make the day of a fifteen-year-old kid because he's seen a Hooters Girl?"

Nicole laughed. "Sure, love it. Hey, I think those guys want to take a photo of us."

The car show promo continued: handing out posters, posing for photos, and selling the swimsuit calendar. A newspaper photographer took a photo of Kyra reclining on the hood of the Hooters racing car.

During a lull in the show, Kyra began eating the chicken wings. "So, Nicole, are you going to continue your modelling?"

"Oh, yes," said Nicole as she reached for a chicken wing. "I did a shoot for a travel magazine: Clothes for Hiking in Theme Parks."

"That's great!"

"And what about you? Still thinking of the State Department?"

"Yep. I figure when I get a degree in languages, I can get a job as an interpreter. Who knows, I might even get to work in an embassy in some place like Paris or London."

"Our little Kyra, in the diplomatic corps, talking to foreign VIPs," mused Nicole. "You can do it, girl."

*

Potter held the beaker of blue liquid up to the light. "Interesting stuff."

"What is it?" Evans asked.

"It's not mechanical fluid, that's for sure," said Potter. "It's biological; it has DNA."

"It has DNA? You mean it's from somebody's body?"

"Not somebody. Something. It has amino acids, but it's not human. I think it's something's blood."

"Blood? What animal on Earth has blue blood?"

Potter hummed. "Perhaps it's not from Earth."

*

Kyra and Nicole couldn't help but notice the babbling in the exhibit hall had suddenly grown louder.

"What's going on?" asked Kyra, staring at the crowd forming near the vintage Mustangs.

A creature stomped out from the crowd. Bellowing like an elephant, it waved its arms around. It walked upright on two legs and was the size of a man, but it wasn't human; it was a green reptile wearing a torn silver spacesuit. Its bulging eyes looked around.

"What's he trying to promote?" Nicole wondered.

"I don't think he's advertising anything. I think it's an alien, the outer space type," said Kyra. "But it seems harmless, like an overgrown iguana."

"Hey, look, I think it's bleeding blue blood," Nicole observed. "That spot on its upper arm."

"Godzilla! Godzilla!" a boy shouted. Squealing with delight, he ran to the alien, threw his arms around it, and hugged it. As he jumped up and down excitedly, he hit the alien's bleeding wound.

The alien growled and quickly pushed the boy away. Seconds later, flames burst from the alien's head, arms, and parts not covered by the torn spacesuit.

Screams of panic filled the air. As people stampeded past them, Kyra and Nicole watched the alien run from car to car.

"There's gas and oil in those cars," Nicole realized.

"He could blow up the place," Kyra said excitedly. "We have to stop it, but how?" She saw a fire extinguisher hanging on the wall. "Why don't we use the fire extinguisher?"

"Good idea, but look at it," Nicole said as they pulled the fire extinguisher from the wall. "It's running around. How do we make it stay still long enough to spray it?"

Kyra glanced at the alien. "I've got an idea. I'll get its attention, and when it's standing still, you sneak up behind it and spray it."

"It's a plan," Nicole agreed.

Kyra poured the chicken wings on a tray. Swaying her hips, she strutted up to the alien. "Hey, have you eaten yet?" she cooed the traditional Chinese greeting in

Cantonese.

The alien stood still, looked down at Kyra, and reached down for a chicken wing. Kyra flinched as she felt the heat from the flames, but she held out the tray and smiled.

Still on fire, the alien began devouring the chicken wings, bones and all. Kyra kept smiling; in the corner of her eye, she could see Nicole sneaking up with the fire extinguisher.

Nicole crept behind the alien. Without any warning, she blasted the foam all over it. The flames went out.

The alien roared, turned around, and threw foam on Nicole. Then it flung foam on Kyra.

Kyra brushed the foam off her hair. "You can have all the chicken wings you want, but you've gotta show some table manners!" she scolded.

The alien looked down at her and said, "Okay."

Kyra's eyes widened in surprise. "You speak English?"

*

Fifteen minutes later, NASA scientists and police officers stormed into the convention centre. They saw nobody, just an exhibit hall full of cars.

"We heard there was a monster," shouted a police officer. "Where is it? Is anybody here?"

"We're over here," came a reply from the Hooters booth.

They went to the Hooters booth and found the big iguana eating chicken wings as the two Hooters Girls watched.

The police officers drew their pistols and pointed

them at the alien. Kyra waved her hand at the guns dismissively. "Guys, you don't need the guns," she said. "We've negotiated an interstellar ceasefire here."

"A first-contact situation," Potter marvelled. "You're obviously feeding it. Does it need anything else from us?"

"Yes, he does," Kyra said. "Can you give this guy a lift back to his spaceship?"

*

The alien ship, a little dented and charred from its trip to Earth, blasted off from Kennedy Space Center. Kyra, Nicole, Evans and Potter watched the ship disappear into the sky.

"Our first contact with an alien species, and it came here to eat our chicken wings," Evans said, shaking his head. "Unbelievable."

"It's actually quite believable," said Kyra. "Our TV transmissions have been going into space for years. He saw our commercial and decided to drop in and try our chicken wings."

"And thus American consumerism paved the way for interstellar diplomacy," Nicole added.

"An amazing species," Potter remarked. "Even on its own world, it's the only species that can inflame itself to protect a wound from infection."

Kyra nodded. "Its fire wasn't intended to hurt us. It was intended to heal that nasty cut he got when his spaceship landed."

"You called it *he* early on," Evans remarked. "How did you know it was a male alien?"

Kyra and Nicole giggled. "He did what every male

tourist to Florida does at Hooters," Kyra explained. "He took photos of us."

*

Aboard his spaceship, Argon put the chicken wings into the cryogenic suspension chamber and wandered back to the control room. He looked at the photograph of himself between the two smiling Hooters Girls, evidence of contact with the inhabitants of the blue planet. Finally, all those years of learning their language from their television signals had paid off. At the next song festival, the Science Academy would sing his praises.

He would have to visit Planet Florida again, if only to try the cheese burrito.

About "It Came to Eat Our Chicken Wings"

RicePaper is a nationally acclaimed magazine of Asian Canadian arts and culture, published by the Asian Canadian Writers Workshop (ACWW). I had the honour of co-editing its Speculative Fiction issue in 2014. A dozen years earlier, ACWW asked me to write a science fiction story for its Technology issue. I wrote a story about a Chinese American Hooters Girl who meets an alien at a car show.

Hooters is a delightfully tacky yet unrefined restaurant chain, and I've visited at least twenty Hooters across the United States, Canada, and China. Carl Hiaasen's novel *Lucky You* (1997) has a Hooters Girl as one of its characters, chasing after a lost lottery ticket. *Lucky You* inspired me to write my own Hooters story. I later wrote another Hooters story, "Family Tradition" (2010).

The Faun and the Sylphide

Alan Cornwall, clad in a white T-shirt and black tights, finished his dance by jumping through the air. He was rehearsing the dance of the Rose in *Le Spectre de la Rose*.

Joan Silverton, artistic director of the Metro Toronto Ballet, clapped her hands together. "Okay, kids, that was wonderful. That's it for today."

As Alan walked back to the centre of the dance studio, Joan smiled and said, "Excellent *ballon*."

A slim young woman untied her blonde hair from its bun and let it fall over her shoulders. She walked over to Alan and put her arm around his waist. "I'm sure King Charles will be impressed."

Alan guffawed. "Oh, Denise, you think he actually wants to watch a ballet when he could be looking at an old building?"

"He certainly wants to watch a ballet," Joan said. "He supports a performing arts trust in Britain. He sees the local artists of every city he visits."

"Well, as if *that's* not any pressure," Alan remarked.

"Oh, come on, we've still got three weeks for rehearsal," Denise urged as she tugged his arm.

Joan nodded. "You've got nothing to worry about if you keep rehearsing. You're both developing well as dancers." She looked at Alan. "I picked you, a second soloist..." Then she looked at Denise. "...and you, a first soloist, when I could have picked two principal dancers. You've both got immense potential, and I want to give you a chance." She grinned, paused for a moment, and glanced at Alan. "You might even earn your promotion to first soloist in a few months."

Denise smiled and looked up at Alan. He gave her a thin, weak smile. Joan nodded and left the dance studio.

Denise ran her hand through Alan's brown hair. Then she tugged on the shoulder straps of her pink leotard. "Let me get out of these sweaty clothes, and I'll give you your best birthday present ever," she cooed.

*

Denise, holding a hot skillet, came out of the kitchen of Alan's apartment. At the dinner table, she flipped the salmon fillets off the skillet and onto Alan's plate.

"Just because I grew up at the National Ballet School doesn't mean I don't know how to cook," Denise said. "Mom made sure I learned all the homemaking stuff during the summer."

Alan tasted the salmon. "This is delicious, with the teriyaki sauce, the basil, the onions. You could be a chef at a restaurant."

Denise poured white wine into their glasses. "Now that's something to consider after I retire. Other dancers go into teaching. I could go into cooking."

"It would pay better," Alan joked.

"Unless I get promoted to principal dancer, and I will. And so will you," Denise predicted. She sipped her wine and leaned forward. "We can do it, I know we can."

Alan shrugged. "I don't know. There are people who've been in the *corps de ballet* longer than I've been. Why did I get promoted before them?"

"Alan, do you want to be a first soloist?" Denise asked.

"Yes, of course. I want the starring roles."

"Then don't stress yourself by worrying about it. You can do it." Denise reached out and took Alan's hand. "We'll do it together."

After they finished dinner, Denise handed a gift-wrapped box to him. "Happy birthday," she said.

"Thanks," said Alan.

He carefully unwrapped the box, opened it, and pulled out a small ceramic figure. It was a sylphide, a fairy creature seen in classical ballets. Like all sylphides, this one was thin, had long legs, tied her brown hair in a bun, and wore a long, full, white romantic tutu and little wings.

Alan smiled. "It's beautiful. It looks just like you when I first saw you," he said.

"You had just joined the company, and I was in the *corps* for *Les Sylphides*. You saw me at the dress rehearsal," Denise remembered.

"And I fell in love with you right away," Alan said. "I couldn't stop looking at you out of all the bunheads."

Alan kissed Denise and walked to a small table where a

dozen other ceramic figures stood. All were ballet and dance characters. Among them stood the Dying Swan in her short, white classical tutu; the clown puppet Petrouchka in his white shirt and red and green checked pants; and the Nutcracker prince in his red army uniform. He set the sylphide beside a horned, satyr-like figure with light brown skin and dark brown spots.

"I'll put him beside Nijinsky, *L'Après-midi d'un Faun*," he said, naming the famous ballet about an amorous faun who pursues a forest nymph. The great dancer Vaslav Nijinsky had danced the role of the faun before he went insane with schizophrenia.

He picked up the faun figurine. "Nijinsky also danced the Rose in *Le Spectre de la Rose*. I could never be as good as him."

"Oh, don't be so unsure of yourself," Denise said. "You're going to dance your best performance ever, the audience will love you, and Joan will promote you to first soloist and then to principal dancer. Just you dance and see."

She pulled him towards her and kissed him. "We'll do it together, hon. That's a promise."

*

Each day for the next week, Alan and Denise danced and sweated through three hours of morning classes followed by four hours of rehearsal of *Le Spectre de la Rose* in the afternoon.

In this one-act ballet, a girl brings a rose home from a ball, falls asleep in a chair, and dreams that the rose becomes a male spirit. In the first half of the ballet, the rose appears at the window, curls his arms overhead, jumps into the room, and dances a series of spectacular leaps and turns in the air. Then he lifts the girl out of her chair, and they dance a romantic *pas de deux* around the room. Finally, he gently returns her to the chair and leaps through the window. She awakens, still under the spell of the dream.

As ballet mistresses do, Joan suggested corrections to Alan during the rehearsals: changes to his timing, his gestures, the way he carried his body, and the way he held Denise as they danced around the room.

"Did you hear her?" Alan said as he and Denise left the rehearsal studio. "She corrected me on my *port de bras* after I jump into the room."

"It was really minor," Denise said.

Alan frowned. "I'm just not good enough. This is going to be a disaster."

"No, it won't," Denise said. "If you're not good enough, Joan wouldn't have picked you."

They stopped by a photograph hanging on the wall: a dancer dressed in the Rose costume. "I wish I could be as good as him," Alan said.

"Ah, Rafael Carmello. What a great dancer," Denise said wistfully. "What a tragedy too. How could he strangle Norma?"

"I don't know," Alan said. He turned away from the photograph. "I've got to go to Lisa for a costume fitting. See you later."

He kissed Denise and went downstairs to the costume department. Lisa Benton, the costume mistress, saw him and picked up a skin-tight pink costume covered with pink rose petals. It was the same design that Léon Bakst had designed for Vaslav Nijinsky in 1911.

"Try this on," Lisa said, handing the costume to Alan. He took the costume and went into a change room.

When Alan emerged, Lisa asked, "Does it fit well? Do you feel comfortable in it?"

"It's fine," Alan replied as he looked at himself in the mirror. "Is there a headpiece too?"

"Coming right up," Lisa said. She pushed a tight cap covered with rose petals over his head.

"It fits just fine," Alan said. He looked in the mirror again and remembered photographs of Vaslav Nijinsky and Rafael Carmello as the Rose.

If only he could be as great as those dancers…

He saw a similar costume hanging on the wall. "Why did you make another one?" he asked.

"Oh, that's the one that Rafael wore," Lisa said.

"I guess you don't want anyone to wear it after what he did to Norma," said Alan.

Lisa shook her head. "No, that's not the reason. I'm not superstitious. It's just that we haven't staged *Le Spectre de la Rose* since Rafael and Norma danced it."

She went to feel the costume. "It's also made from that experimental fabric, memory cloth."

"Memory cloth?" Alan asked, intrigued.

"It was invented by Dr. Jonathan Rand at University of Toronto," Lisa said. "Memory cloth absorbs the electrical signals that the brain sends to the muscles throughout the body. Dr. Rand thought a person's muscle memory and movement skills could be passed to the next person who wore the fabric. People could learn to dance, ski, swim, and do all sorts of things by wearing memory cloth that had been worn by an expert. At least that was the theory."

Alan felt the costume's smooth, silky fabric. "What happened to the experiment?" he asked.

"It was never completed. During the experiment, Rafael's paranoid schizophrenia grew worse, and he killed Norma. The memory cloth didn't cause Rafael's schizophrenia. In retrospect, he was showing signs of illness at least two years before the experiment. But the experiment ended anyway."

Alan returned into the change room, stripped off his costume, put on his T-shirt and tights again, and came back out. As he handed his costume back to Lisa, he eyed Rafael Carmello's costume again.

"May I borrow it? May I take it home?" he asked, still looking at Rafael's costume.

Lisa looked surprised. "You want to borrow Rafael's costume?"

"Rafael was one of our greatest dancers," Alan said. "Maybe the costume will inspire me."

"I suppose that would be okay. All right—I'll let you borrow it," Lisa agreed cautiously. She took the costume off the wall. "Bring it back in one piece."

*

Later that evening, after all the dancers had gone home, Alan returned to the dance studio. Now he wore Rafael's Rose costume.

He stood with his feet on *demi-pointe* and in fifth position, crossed so that the heel of the front foot touched the toe of the back foot. Then he curled his arms overhead and leapt across the room.

He flew through the air in a *grande jeté* and danced a stunning series of leaps and turns in the air.

He continued dancing, jumping, and turning around the room. He felt the vibrant spirit of the Rose take over his mind and body. In his muscles, he felt all the moves that Rafael Carmello had danced. Energy coursed through his body, and he felt his blood heat up with excitement.

Finally, he could dance like a star.

*

The next day, Alan wore the Rose costume at rehearsal.

"This isn't the dress rehearsal," said Joan. "Why are you wearing the costume?"

"It'll inspire me," Alan replied.

Denise giggled. "Oh, let's humour him."

Joan shrugged. Then she motioned to the pianist to start.

As the pianist played Carl Maria von Weber's waltz-like tune, Alan and Denise danced the ballet's *pas de deux*, where they galloped around the room in sequences of *chasses*, *arabesques*, and *sautés*.

When they stopped dancing, Denise blurted, "Wow, what's gotten into you?"

"The spirit of the Rose," Alan answered, grinning.

*

When the rehearsal ended a couple hours later, Joan clapped. "Kids, that was excellent," she remarked.

Denise laughed. "Wasn't Alan wonderful? I bet Nijinsky

couldn't have danced better than that."

"Nor could Rafael Carmello," Joan said. "I've not seen anything like that since Rafael and Norma danced."

"Thank you," Alan said, smiling as he bowed.

"You danced like Rafael," Joan said. "The way you jump, the way you turn, the way you hold your partner, the way you move your arms. It's as if you've copied his style exactly."

"That's great," said Denise.

"Uh, yes, I guess it is," Joan said, her voice uncertain. "You were developing your own distinct style, like every dancer does. I just didn't expect it to resemble Rafael's so closely."

"I watched videos of his performances," Alan lied.

*

Denise glanced at her watch. "We should go home," she shouted above the pounding music and the shrieks of the crowd.

Alan put down his beer bottle and grabbed Denise's hand. "Come on, one more dance," he urged, smiling. He pulled her out to the crowded floor of the nightclub.

Giggling, Denise danced with him amid hundreds of people. The strobe lights flashed like lightning in the darkness, and rock music blared from the speakers. All around them, people were shaking and laughing and shouting and drinking and kissing.

Denise kissed Alan and ran her hands through his hair. "I know it's Friday night, but we have a rehearsal in the morning. Shouldn't we go home?"

Alan looked puzzled. "What's wrong? Aren't you

having fun with me?"

"I am, I am," Denise said, "but tomorrow's rehearsal—"

"—can wait until tomorrow," said Alan.

"It's already tomorrow," Denise observed, looking at her watch again. The next song started, and they continued dancing.

*

They were rehearsing the scene where the Rose awakens the girl. Denise raised herself out of the chair and languidly fluttered her arms.

"You forgot to brush your hand near your mouth, as if you were waking up and covering a yawn," said Joan. "And move your arms more gracefully, more fluidly."

Denise nodded and fell back into the chair. "Can I try it again?"

"Of course," Joan replied. "Just concentrate."

Denise let out a small yawn and remembered last night. After yesterday's gruelling rehearsals, she wanted to sleep by midnight, but Alan kept her up dancing for hours. She didn't return to her apartment until three o'clock in the morning. She fell asleep without taking off her make-up.

But Alan had been so full of energy. His eyes were still glowing as he and Denise rode the taxi to Denise's apartment. Where had he gotten his energy?

Denise rose out of the chair again and stumbled. Giggling, she sat back down in the chair.

"I'm sorry, it's just that we stayed out too late last night," Denise confessed sheepishly.

"What's wrong with you?" Alan snapped.

Denise turned around in the chair and looked up. "Huh?"

Alan was wearing the Rose costume again. He crossed his arms and glared down at Denise.

"You're spoiling the rehearsal," Alan declared. His eyes looked angry.

"Alan, really," Denise said. "I'm sorry. Let's try that again."

Joan nodded and told the pianist, "Start at the awakening."

Denise raised herself out of the chair, brushed her left hand near her mouth, and joined Alan in a dance around the room.

As they danced, Alan said, "You don't care about me."

"What?" Denise whispered as she continued galloping across the floor with him. How could Alan speak during the intense physical workout?

Alan lifted Denise, and Denise's hands and legs lifted into a third *arabesque*, Cecchetti method.

When Alan lowered Denise back to the floor, he said, "You don't want me to be promoted to first soloist, do you?"

"What?" Denise blurted.

She stopped dancing and pushed herself away from Alan. Her partner frowned and glared at her.

"What was that?" Joan demanded.

Denise turned to Joan. "Nothing, nothing. We were just a bit—distracted."

Alan shook his head. "I'm not distracted," he snarled.

"Alan, what's gotten into you?" Denise asked.

"Kids, I know you're feeling some pressure, but you're both professionals. Stay focused," Joan urged. "Now again from the awakening."

Denise sat back in the chair and waited for the pianist to start. She watched Alan walk to his position behind the chair. As he walked, he stared at Denise. Never before had Denise seen so much anger in his eyes.

The pianist played the music again, and Alan and Denise danced the *pas de deux* again. They danced flawlessly for the next couple hours. But by the end of the rehearsal, they were not talking to each other.

*

Alan and Denise did not have lunch together, and they fled to their separate apartments. After eating a chicken sandwich, Alan lay down on his couch. He was still wearing the Rose costume.

How dare that girl sabotage his career, he thought. All that time Denise had been dancing and loving him, she was only raising his hopes. The higher she raised his hopes, the longer would be his fall downward. But he had finally noticed the evil of the devious little vixen. It was not too late. There was still time to expel her from the ballet company, time enough to find a partner less mean and more talented.

He looked over to the table that held his collection of ballet figurines. The faun seemed to be staring straight at him.

The faun's lips moved and snarled, "You don't deserve to be a first soloist."

Alan bolted upright. The little figure was pointing and snickering at him.

"You're a lousy dancer!" the faun said. "She hates you!

Quit now!"

The faun jumped from the table and flew at Alan's face. Alan cried out and swung his hands frantically. He batted the faun away. After the faun landed on the floor, it cackled and jumped up and down.

Alan watched the little figure run under the table. The faun dashed to the door. The door opened by itself, and the faun ran out of the apartment.

Taking a deep breath, Alan felt his heartbeat slow back to normal. How had that girl found a horned demon to destroy him?

*

"I'm going to call off this rehearsal if you two don't behave," Joan threatened. "What's wrong with you?"

Denise turned to look at Alan. He was still wearing Rafael Carmello's Rose costume. Denise turned away quickly when she caught Alan's hateful gaze.

Alan broke the silence. "I can't dance with her. She's not partnering well with me. There's no chemistry between us."

"What on Earth?" Joan said. "You were the perfect pair until yesterday. What happened?"

"I can't work with someone who's jealous of me," Alan said. "Just watch me. I'll be principal dancer, and you'll never be!"

Denise shook her head and held out her hand to Alan. "Is that what you think? Dear, I'm not jealous of you. I want you to be the best."

"Oh, stop insulting my intelligence," Alan said. He laughed bitterly. "And to think I slept with you."

"Alan, that's enough!" Joan scolded. "Apologize to Denise and focus or get out of the room now!"

"With pleasure," Alan said.

He turned to Denise and said, "I'll get that horned demon that you sent to me."

The two women stared at him as he stormed out of the studio.

Denise put her head on Joan's shoulder and hugged her silently for a moment. Then Denise burst into tears.

"I don't know what's gotten into him," Denise cried. "He's been mean and rude, and he won't see me anymore."

"There, there, just relax," Joan comforted her. "Do you think the pressure is getting to him?"

"I don't know, I don't know," Denise said. "He's always been driven to succeed, he's always wanted to be the best, but he's never been so awful before."

Joan pushed Denise off her shoulder and looked into her eyes. "Did anything different happen in the past week?"

Denise wiped the tears off her face. "No, nothing. Things went wrong suddenly, without warning."

She paused for a moment and said, "Things went wrong when he started wearing that costume."

*

Denise went downstairs to the costume department. Lisa was sewing "cookies" or padding into the breasts of a girl's costume.

"Alan's been wearing a Rose costume at rehearsals," Denise said.

Lisa looked up from her sewing. "So *that's* what he's been doing with it."

Denise nodded. "Yes. Did you give it to him?"

"I lent it to him. He said it would inspire him." Lisa looked shocked. "I didn't know what he would do with it, but I didn't expect him to actually wear it."

"He's been behaving oddly since he started wearing it," Denise said.

"That costume is special. It's made out of memory cloth, and Rafael was the last person to wear it."

"Rafael Carmello? He went mad and killed Norma Leonard."

"Has Alan done or said anything weird, anything not like him?"

"He said I sent a horned demon to him."

Lisa pulled a black book from her desk and opened it. "This is the diary of Rafael Carmello. He left it in his locker. Look at the pages."

Denise leafed through the diary. Each page was cluttered with scribbled words and drawings of geometric shapes, people, and animals of all sorts. One page was full of drawings of frowning, angry-looking dogs, fish with mouths full of sharp teeth, and men carrying swords. In the middle of the page, surrounded by the drawings, was a rambling poem about swimming through a lake.

"Every inch is covered with words and images, all the pictures are asymmetrical. A lot of the people in the pictures are in authoritarian poses," Lisa pointed out. "Schizophrenic people often draw and write in this cluttered, asymmetrical style.

"Now look at this page," Lisa said, pointing at a

drawing.

Denise gasped at the drawing. It was a faun, like the figurine Alan had. Obscenities filled a speech balloon above the faun's head.

Under the faun was the caption "The horned demon that Norma sent to destroy me."

*

Denise knocked on the door a dozen times before Alan opened it. He was still wearing the Rose costume. Without waiting for Alan to invite her, Denise barged into the apartment.

"Alan, take off that costume," Denise demanded.

Alan chuckled. "Oh, are we going to have sex?"

"Come on, please take off the costume," Denise pleaded. "It's making you do strange things."

"If you think that, you must really hate me!" Alan yelled. "This costume has inspired me. Before I wore it, I was nothing. But now, I can dance like a star. I know how the great Carmello danced, I know his every move!"

"Alan, that's the problem," Denise insisted. "The costume captured Rafael's brain waves and memory, and you absorbed them. But the costume captured his insanity too, and now you're going mad just like Rafael. Please take off the costume."

Alan sneered at her. "I will not. Unlike you, I will become a principal dancer."

"You won't become a principal dancer if you wind up in a mental institution like Rafael did," Denise warned.

Alan suddenly leapt towards Denise and grabbed her throat. "You bitch!" he snarled.

"Rafael strangled Norma," Denise gasped.

Alan released Denise's neck, and she ran from the apartment. Alan stared silently at the open door.

Then he saw the faun walk through the doorway. The little horned demon leapt into the air and floated to Alan.

"You fool, you let her get away," the faun said. "She's turning Joan Silverton against you, and other dancers will get promoted to principal dancer and leave you well behind. Denise is sleeping with each of the male dancers, so why would she need *you*? She's betraying you just like Norma Leonard betrayed Rafael Carmello."

The faun floated around Alan's head and continued. "It'll be easy for Denise to destroy you because you're untalented. After Denise has ruined you, you'll be a male stripper dancing naked in a gay bar.

"But you can stop her," the faun urged. "You know what to do."

Alan smiled, marched into the kitchen, and picked up the steel skillet. As he walked back into the living room, he muttered, "I'll bash her head in, I'll bash her head in."

He looked at the skillet. It reminded him of a dinner.

"I'm surprised the bitch didn't poison me," he said, remembering his birthday.

He remembered something else from his birthday.

He looked at his table of figurines and spotted the sylphide. He picked up the sylphide and examined it. How much it looked like Denise when he first saw her, he noticed again. She had looked like a graceful, beautiful fairy in her tutu and wings, and he couldn't stop looking at her long legs and svelte body and pretty face. It was love at first sight.

They had danced and loved each other for five years.

Why did she want to destroy him now?

"Hey, what are you waiting for?" the faun yelled, jolting Alan out of his daydream. "You've got a mission to do."

"No," Alan said as he put the sylphide back down on the table. "No, I can't do it."

"You loser," the faun said as he floated in front of Alan.

Alan swung the skillet at the faun, and in a flash of light, the faun disappeared.

After dropping the skillet to the floor, Alan took off the costume.

*

When Alan arrived for rehearsals in the morning, he was wearing a white T-shirt and black tights again, and he held the Rose costume in his hands.

Denise approached him slowly, cautiously. "Alan, you're not going to wear the costume?"

Alan shook his head. "No more. I'll only wear the new one that Lisa made for me." He looked at Rafael Carmello's old costume. "Nobody will ever wear this one again."

He kissed Denise and said, "I'm sorry. I wasn't myself for the last few days. But now I'm back, and I'm ready to dance as myself again."

Denise threw her arms around him. "Welcome back, dear."

They rehearsed the entire ballet perfectly.

*

After the royal command performance, the dancers of the Metro Toronto Ballet lined up to meet King Charles III and Princess Consort Camilla.

"You danced wonderfully. Congratulations," said the King.

"Thank you, sir," Alan said before bowing.

After the royal couple had moved to the choreographers, Denise whispered to Alan, "See, you did it all on your own. You never needed Rafael Carmello's memory. Just be yourself, hon, and you can do anything."

"Thank you for making me trust myself again," Alan said.

Lisa went to Alan and pulled the rose petal headdress off his head.

"Why are you taking it now?" Alan asked. "Can't you wait until I get changed?"

"I noticed some minor damage," Lisa said. "I'll fix it before it gets worse."

*

The security guard opened the steel door at the Ontario Hospital for the Criminally Insane. Lisa walked into the lobby to meet a man with a gaunt face and grey hair.

"Did you bring the cap?" the man asked.

Lisa handed the rose petal headdress to the man. "Here it is, Dr. Rand. I hope this works."

"We've got nothing to lose," Dr. Rand said as they walked into a corridor of spotless white doors, each with a little window. An occasional moan or laugh broke the silence as they passed the cells.

They stopped at a cell, and an orderly unlocked the

door. Lisa and Dr. Rand entered and looked at a man sitting on a bed.

The man stared wildly at them. His face was pale from years without sunshine, and his black hair was long and dishevelled. Leather straps bound his wrists and ankles, but he did not struggle against his bonds.

Dr. Rand pulled the rose petal headdress over the man's head and stood back.

"Thanks for making the cap out of memory cloth," Dr. Rand said. "If memory cloth can transfer insanity to a person, maybe it can transfer sanity too."

"It's worth a try. Rafael was a splendid person and talented dancer," Lisa remembered. "It'll be wonderful to bring him back."

Lisa and Dr. Rand stayed in the cell, staring at Rafael Carmello.

Slowly, Rafael's wild stare softened.

About "The Faun and the Sylphide"

This is an indirect sequel to my novella "All Dancers Go to Heaven". Dr. Rand appears in both stories. Thanks to Mark Leslie Lefebvre for publishing this story.

Seventy-Two Virgins

Say to those who reject the Faith: "Soon, you will be vanquished and gathered together in Hell, an evil bed to lie on!"

The Koran, Surah 3 (Al-'Imran), verse 12

*

In them [two gardens in Paradise] will be maidens, chaste, bashful, whom no man or Jinnee has touched before; then which of Our Lord's favours will you deny? Virgins like rubies and coral.

The Koran, Surah 55 (Most Gracious), verses 56-58

*

When Qabeel arrived at his father's apartment building, he saw Farouk and Faisal leaving a small house across the street. The two young men had moved into the house after Faisal's uncle had died. For some reason, the uncle had left the house not to his children but to Faisal. To add to the intrigue, Farouk and Faisal had initially said that they were cousins, and later, that they were friends, but local gossips suspected that they were more than friends.

Farouk and Faisal were buying suitcases from one of the vendors who pushed his cart along the streets. Why did they need luggage? Certainly they could not be on a martyrdom mission.

After Farouk and Faisal paid the vendor, Qabeel crossed the street and looked at the luggage. "Are you travelling?"

Faisal nodded. "We are going to Canada. My uncle left me some money. We can go on vacation overseas."

"It is better than spending our free time here," Farouk said. "Nothing but bombs and bullets."

"So you flee, leaving others to do the fighting," Qabeel said, sneering. "I hear that marriage between man and man is legal in Canada now. Leave, go to Canada, get married. Then go to San Francisco for your honeymoon. But do not come back. If the Americans and Crusaders are good for anything, it is that they will house perverts like you."

"We are merely going on vacation," Farouk said.

Faisal motioned for Farouk to stay silent, but Farouk continued. "You are a disturbed individual."

"Not as disturbed as you," Qabeel said. "You two will soon go to the fires of hell, an evil bed to lie on! God wills it!"

*

Qabeel accepted the coffee from Al Majuj, leader of the Al

Ghazu Jihad Brigade. He sipped the bitter drink and looked at the decorations on the wall: a large gilt-framed photo of the Dome of the Rock; a Palestinian flag; a portrait of Saddam Hussein in military uniform; a caricature of an Israeli soldier as a rampaging monster; and a dartboard made from a photo of Yasser Arafat.

Al Majuj said, "Cursed be the traitors of the Palestinian Authority who conspire with the Zionists and the Americans to build a casino on our sacred soil! May they all go to hell, an evil bed to lie on!"

Qabeel set the coffee on the table. "Uh, great leader, is the merchandise designed yet?"

"Ah, yes, my friend, yes!" Al Majuj opened a bag and poured a smattering of objects onto the table. "You will be famous, my friend!"

Qabeel's eyes lit up when he saw the merchandise: key chains, postcards, stickers, and buttons printed with his face and the word Martyr. He was most impressed by a poster showing him, grinning and holding a rifle, superimposed over the Dome of the Rock. This was how he wanted to be remembered, as a brave fighter laughing at death as he fought for his people.

"There is also a video of your farewell speech," Al Majuj said. "All proceeds from its sale will go to your family, of course."

Qabeel nodded. "My father will appreciate the proceeds. He has been unable to work since the Zionists ruined his leg in the *intifada*. Who needs a carpenter who cannot get around a construction site?"

"Cursed be the Zionists," Al Majuj said.

"What about the Saudis?" Qabeel said. "Did you ask them again? Will they give anything for my family?"

Al Majuj shook his head. "I asked the Saudi Interior Ministry, but it will not make an exception to its policy. It is unfortunate that you do not have a wife. Yes, the Saudis pay twenty thousand rials to the widow of each martyr, but they will pay only the widow."

A widow, Qabeel thought. If only I could leave a widow. All who would honour me would revere her too. Rich benefactors like Al Majuj and bin Laden—if anyone could find him—would shower her with gifts and money to compensate for her loss.

Areej had missed her chance. She would soon regret her rejection of him. She could have been the wife of a hero, widow of a martyr. But instead, she chose to be a harlot of the Zionists, the Americans, and their traitorous allies in the Palestinian Authority.

"But cheer up," Al Majuj said, "for you will be our first bomber martyr." He picked up a collector's card. "Look, my friend, here is your rookie card. Actually, all suicide martyr cards are rookie cards, but that only makes them more special."

Qabeel took the card and smiled. He was number one in the Al Ghazu Martyrs series. Unlike other organizations' martyr cards, Qabeel's was in full colour, showing him raising his fist before a Palestinian flag.

He reached into his shirt pocket and pulled out another martyr card showing Mohammed Attah. It was a spectacular card, in colour on brilliant white cardboard, with the words "Magnificent 19 Al-Qaeda Aerial Combat Martyrs of New York and Washington" embossed in gold foil. Comparing his card to Mohammed Attah's, Qabeel suddenly felt sad.

"Great leader, why cannot I have a card like this with

gold foil, maybe a hologram?"

Al Majuj smiled sympathetically. "Ah, my friend, do not be disappointed. Attah's card is part of a special edition made by friends of Al-Qaeda. They had the money to print coated, gold-embossed cards. As for us, we must make do with a dwindling trust fund from Saddam Hussein. Mind you, the publishers of the Magnificent 19 set cannot get money from Al-Qaeda anymore."

"Still, I would like to be remembered by a more attractive card," Qabeel said.

Al Majuj patted him on the back. "But your martyrdom mission against the casino will guarantee that our people will celebrate you as a hero. Then our youth will seek out and treasure your card, despite its lack of gold foil or a hologram."

"Yes, the martyrdom mission will give meaning to my life," Qabeel said. "All those people who sneered at me, what will they be? All those people who laughed at me, what will they be? All those people who called me a loser, what will they be? My uncle, who fired me from his company, what will he be? They are like swine, who simply eat and sleep and do nothing with their lives."

"Exactly! Better to fight and die like a lion than to cower and live like a pig," Al Majuj said. "For them will be the fires of hell, an evil bed to lie on. But for you awaits the gardens of paradise, place of flowing rivers, fruit trees, and seventy-two virgins to serve you."

Will they look like Areej? Qabeel hoped so.

*

Qabeel left Al Majuj's office. A young woman ran up

beside him on the street.

"Qabeel, do not do anything stupid," she said.

"Areej," Qabeel said, "what is that dreadful costume you are wearing?"

Areej glared at him, straightened her red pantsuit and pointed at the button that proclaimed in Arabic and English, "CASINO TRAINEE: Ask me about the Slot Club Bonus Points."

"I am training to be a hostess," Areej said. "It will bring much needed employment and revenues to our town."

"You lie with the traitors," Qabeel said. "You are an affront to your own people."

Areej's brown eyes burned with anger as she put her hands on her hips. "And what about you? How are you helping our people by joining a terrorist group?"

"Al Ghazu is not a terrorist group. It is a freedom fighter brigade."

"Hah, I have heard that before," Areej said, smiling sardonically. "You are correct, how can it be a terrorist group? How can anyone be terrorized by a group whose own people drowned while training dolphins to attach bombs to Israeli boats?"

Qabeel forced himself to stay calm. "Perhaps we should have gotten dolphin trainers who knew how to swim. How were we to know that the dolphins would head for the deep end of the pool? But you must admit that Al Majuj's concept was brilliant. Only the execution was flawed."

"You are a loser," Areej said, "a bum who wastes his day loitering in the streets, spending what is left of his father's money.

"Look around you." She pointed at the dilapidated

apartments, the rotting pavement, and the forlorn people shuffling through the street. "Look at the unemployment and poverty.

"But your family, among all others in Ramallah, does not live in this trap. Your father found a good school for you, one that offered you a scholarship, but it expelled you for truancy. Your uncle gave you a good job, but he fired you for laziness. How can your own uncle fire you from the only successful computer company in the area? All you ever wanted is money and girls, and you got neither. Now you are consorting with Al Majuj's gang of morons. Do not mess up your life any further!"

Qabeel pulled Areej into an alley and shook his finger at her. "Do not insult the great leader and Al Ghazu! I am finally doing something right with my life, and I will not mess it up!"

"Al Majuj's people mess everything up!"

"You who refused me, you who would lie with the Zionists and Americans, you who would help corrupt Saudi princes and Jews gamble, you will go to hell, an evil bed to lie on! God wills it!"

Areej laughed. "I rejected you after dating you for three months, and you ask God to send me to hell. Go ahead. At least I am helping our so-called country. I admit that a casino is not the most stable basis for an economy, but we must start somewhere. How are you helping? You loser, when will you realize that it is you who will go to hell?"

"When the time comes, God willing, I will not go to hell," Qabeel said. "I will enter paradise and be served by seventy-two virgins."

Areej laughed scornfully.

"All more beautiful than you," Qabeel added.

"Like hell you will find a girl more beautiful than me." Areej ran her hand through her wavy, black hair. Then she took a deep breath, and the anger faded from her eyes.

"Listen, Qabeel, our families come from the same village. My father fought alongside yours in the *intifada*. I do not want harm to come to you. Do not do anything stupid with Al Majuj's group."

She looked at her watch and gasped. "Oh, today is the day to switch to Daylight Savings Time! I forgot to turn my watch ahead one hour. It is 17:30 already. I am late for my training!"

"Bah, Zionist time! It is only 16:30 Palestinian time," Qabeel said.

"Live in whatever time zone you wish, but the casino is in the Zionist time zone, and I get paid according to the clock there," Areej called as she ran off. "Remember, Qabeel, do not do anything stupid."

As he watched Areej run down the street, Qabeel stared at her svelte body and gentle curves, beauty that the pantsuit could not hide. Seventy-two virgins awaited him in paradise. They would all look like Areej, and they would squeal in pain and ecstasy as he forced them into positions he had briefly glimpsed when a friend had found a discarded American magazine called *Hustler*...

I will be a hero, I will be a hero, I will be a hero, Qabeel chanted to himself as he walked away, admiring a key chain showing his face.

*

Jalut, the explosives expert, handed the time bomb to Qabeel. Among the wires and plastic explosive, a digital clock counted off the time.

"The clock is set to explode at 18:00," Jalut said.

"18:00," Qabeel repeated.

Al Majuj nodded and handed a set of car keys to Qabeel. "Take the blue car parked outside. Run the car through the front door of the casino, and the blast will wipe it off the face of the Earth, God willing."

Qabeel held the bomb. It felt so light, so easy to carry. How could something so little carry a blast so big? That mass destruction could come in such a small package impressed him.

Jalut took the bomb from Qabeel and put it into a black briefcase. "Place it in the trunk so that no one can see it," Jalut said.

"May you have a successful mission," Al Majuj said, "and may the gates of paradise open to you."

Qabeel nodded, picked up the briefcase, and walked toward the door. Before he left, he turned and said, "Glory to God, and glory to Al Ghazu Jihad Brigade!"

Al Majuj and Jalut raised their fists to salute Qabeel, and Qabeel left the office, smiling.

"Ah, there goes another fine young fighter," Al Majuj said, "our first martyr. I feel so proud of him." He looked at his watch. "It is only 16:00. I still have time to catch the end of the Lebanon–Syria football match on TV."

*

Qabeel parked the car in front of his family's apartment. He looked at his watch: 16:45. Well over an hour—plenty of time to leave a suicide note for his father and Areej.

Farouk and Faisal were hauling their suitcases onto the street. Qabeel could not resist the urge to insult them one last time.

He got out of the car and yelled, "Faisal, did you remember to pack a white dress to wear at your wedding?"

Farouk shouted back, "You are a disturbed individual!"

Qabeel laughed. "At least when I die, I will go to paradise, a place of sparkling rivers and nubile virgins. But God has a different fate for you. For you will be the fires of hell, an evil bed to lie on. And when you lie with the demons, it is you who will take the female position."

Farouk grunted with the luggage. "Be silent, swine. Our airplane does not leave for several hours, and we have plenty of time to beat the goat cheese out of you." Clenching his fists, he stalked toward Qabeel's car.

"Farouk, please do not," Faisal said.

Farouk looked rather scrawny to Qabeel. "You think you can fight me and win?"

Farouk swung his fist at Qabeel. Qabeel ducked, dodging the blow.

"You are a useless, lazy swine who cannot even make falafels for a living!" Farouk said.

Faisal shouted, "Farouk, please stop!"

"Take this, pervert!" Qabeel punched Farouk on the nose.

Stunned, Farouk reeled backwards. Faisal wailed.

"Ah, this is what is important in life, to hear the cries and lamentations of his woman," Qabeel said, paraphrasing an American movie he had seen years ago.

Farouk stood up sluggishly and raised his fists. Then

Qabeel remembered his mission. He looked at his watch. 16:59. Did he have time to beat up the pervert?

Yes, plenty of time.

Rushing forward, he raised his fist again and smashed it into Farouk's eye.

The last thing he heard was the bomb exploding.

*

The angel had white, feathery wings like a dove's, and he wore a white robe, a gold belt, and a white turban. He sported a long beard the same black colour as his eyes.

Behind the angel lay acres of green grass and shrubs; flowing rivers of sparkling white water; large, shady palm and pomegranate trees; a brilliant blue sky; and sunlight, bright yet cool instead of blistering.

Qabeel looked at the angel and the scenery beyond. As he smelled the fragrance of roses, jasmine, and spices, he realized that he was not in Ramallah anymore.

"Praise be to God, I am in paradise!"

"That is what they all say when they arrive here," the angel said. He smiled and bowed. "Welcome, Qabeel, most honoured martyr. We have been expecting you."

"How many Americans and Zionists were killed?" Qabeel asked with excitement.

The angel shrugged, making both his shoulders and wings move. "I do not know. Perhaps they went to the other place."

"Of course, of course."

"You must be eager to see the rest of the grounds," the angel said. "Will you follow me, please?"

The angel led Qabeel to a bed lined with rich red and

gold brocade. Beside the bed stood a pomegranate tree surrounded by its own spring.

Qabeel knelt, put his hands into the spring, and lifted some water to his mouth. He had never tasted water as cool, clean, and refreshing as this. He certainly was no longer in Ramallah.

"Make yourself comfortable on the bed," the angel said. "I will fetch the *houris* for you."

Qabeel said, "Praise be to God, I will finally have my seventy-two virgins!"

The angel clapped his hands, and dozens of young men appeared from nowhere and paraded in front of the bed.

They were incredibly handsome, with oil glistening on their strong, muscular bodies and hairless chests. They wore only loincloths that barely covered their male parts. As they passed Qabeel, the men gazed at him and smirked and flexed their muscles, showing off their bodies.

The fragrance of flowers and spices gave way to the musky stink of male sweat. Qabeel squirmed, unnerved by the sight of half-naked men displaying themselves to him.

"Are these my servants?" Qabeel asked.

"No, these are the houris," the angel said. "Your seventy-two virgins."

But they did not look like Areej! Indeed, some of them looked like suicide bombers who had martyred themselves before Qabeel had. Others looked like local ruffians who had died in brawls.

Two men stepped forward from the crowd. Qabeel gasped. Farouk and Faisal.

Qabeel shrank back into the bed and looked furtively

at them. "How can these be the virgins of paradise?"

"It is true. I am a virgin, thanks to you," Farouk said, scowling. "No man or woman had ever used me before your bomb killed me."

"Not even Faisal?"

Faisal shook his head sadly. "We never got to Canada."

A chill shot through Qabeel. "What are you doing here?"

"I should not have falsified my uncle's will," Faisal confessed. "The house was not intended for me."

"Or for me," Farouk said.

The angel smiled and put his hand on Faisal's shoulder. "Make our latest arrival comfortable, beautiful houri."

Faisal knelt on the bed and began to rub Qabeel's shoulders. Qabeel stiffened in fear as the dead man's hands caressed him.

"Your muscles are very tense," Faisal said. "Just relax, Qabeel. Soon, none of us will be virgins. But we will be gentle with you. You will be sore only for the first eighty days."

The virgins laughed, their voices filled with bitterness and sarcasm rather than humour and joy. Qabeel looked up and saw Farouk frowning at him.

Qabeel tried to get off the bed, but Faisal pushed him down on his back and began unbuttoning Qabeel's shirt.

"Just relax," Faisal said as he ran his hands over Qabeel's chest.

Qabeel bolted up again, but the virgins crowded around, held him down, and stripped him naked. He yelled as the young men forced him onto his knees and elbows.

Farouk climbed onto the bed and crouched behind Qabeel. With a long, mournful sigh, Farouk said, "How awful that I should lose my virginity to a disturbed individual like Qabeel!"

Farouk tore off his loincloth and flung it on Qabeel's head.

"No, no, no!" Qabeel shrieked as he struggled against the virgins.

The angel bowed. "Excuse me, but I must check on Mohammed Attah and his friends. I left them in the same room with Meir Kahane."

"Merciful God, is this how paradise should be?"

The angel said, "Paradise? Who said you are in paradise?"

Qabeel screamed when Farouk's rough hands caressed his buttocks. "Merciful God, save me from this evil bed to lie on!"

The angel shrugged. "The Americans have a saying: you made your bed, now lie on it."

About "Seventy-Two Virgins"

Thanks to horror writer Lee Allan Howard for publishing "Seventy-Two Virgins" in *Thou Shalt Not...*, an anthology of horror stories based on the Ten Commandments. Before the submission deadline, he mentioned online that almost all stories received were about the Sixth Commandment (Thou shalt not murder), with some about the Seventh Commandment (Thou shalt not commit adultery), and very few about the other commandments. He needed to spread the stories among all Ten Commandments.

I figured that if I wrote something about one of the less popular commandments, my story would have a higher chance of getting into the anthology. I chose the Third Commandment: thou shall not take God's name in vain, that is, do not misuse His name.

Choosing the Third Commandment worked, and Lee accepted the story despite it having no Jewish or Christian characters.

There actually was a Palestinian casino. The Palestinian Authority and Casinos Austria International Limited opened Oasis Casino in Jericho in 1998. It employed more than one thousand people and attracted thousands of Israelis every day. It was the first legal casino anywhere near or in Israel, and Israelis didn't mind entering Yasser Arafat's territory to gamble. However, some local people thought it was a scheme to enrich corrupt Palestinian leaders.

Oasis Casino shut down during the Second Intifada in 2000, only two years after it opened.

Cloned to Kill

The teenaged girl slammed the young vandal into the church door. "Let me take him down!" she yelled as she held the boy against the door.

"No, let him go!" said Father John Markham.

The girl turned her head, and her long blonde hair swept the air. She scowled at Father Markham. "But he defaced the church."

The priest looked at the graffiti scribbled in black marker ink on the door: GO, LEAFS!

Due to its downtown location, St. Joan of Arc's Church suffered more vandalism than other Toronto parishes did. Markham smelled alcohol on the boy's breath. No doubt the boy had drunk too much beer and been egged on by his friends, the noisy bunch fleeing down the street. Only a combination of alcohol and stupidity could have made the kid write about hockey in June.

"Only God can help the Leafs," Markham muttered.

The boy laughed.

Markham stepped up to the boy. "The Toronto Maple Leafs haven't won the Stanley Cup in over one hundred years. Do you really think defacing a house of God is going to help them?"

The boy lashed out with his fist, and Markham dodged the blow. The girl grabbed the boy's head and banged it against the door. He screamed and sobbed.

"That's enough. Let him go," Markham said.

"But Father, he attacked the church!"

"Stand down, Lorraine!"

Lorraine released the boy. As he walked away, he glared at Markham.

"I'll get you charged with assault!" the boy threatened.

Markham grunted. "Get out or I'll have you arrested for under-aged drinking and vandalism. Go!"

The boy ran away. Markham sighed. In less than half an hour, the Rodriguezes would arrive for the baptism of their son. The custodian would have to clean off the graffiti right away.

Lorraine stared at the ground. She looked lost in her thoughts.

"Lorraine, are you okay?" Markham asked.

"I am, Father, I am," she replied. "I heard that voice again."

"What did it tell you to do?"

"To defend the church against its enemies."

"Did it tell you to attack that boy?"

"Yes."

"Did it tell you to kill him?"

"No. It said that non-lethal force would be sufficient."

"Good. Let's keep it that way."

The petite girl wore a white sundress and a gold cross of Lorraine around her neck. She looked like any other pretty girl out on a summer afternoon. Yet in the month since she came to the church, she had gotten into three fights with the local troublemakers. Her combat skills astounded Father Markham.

A black limousine arrived in front of the church. The chauffeur opened the car door for a man with stylishly trimmed brown hair. The man's blue suit looked expensive and exquisitely tailored. He talked to his chauffeur, who stayed by the driver's door.

A guest arriving early for the baptism, Markham wondered? He didn't know that the Rodriguezes had friends or family who were so wealthy.

When the man turned around, Markham saw his face and recognized it from the television news.

"Oh, it's him," he muttered.

Two other men came out of the car and stood guard around it. They were big, muscular men who looked around, scanning the neighbourhood. Markham guessed they were the man's bodyguards, probably former mercenaries. It was fashionable for the extremely wealthy to hire ex-mercenaries.

Here comes more trouble, Markham thought. He looked at Lorraine and said, "Go back into the church."

Lorraine looked at the man, frowned, and silently went inside. Markham closed the church doors and stood in front of them, preventing the man from entering.

The man smiled as he shook hands with the priest. The hostility in his eyes belied any sincerity in his handshake or smile.

"You must be Father Markham," the visitor said.

"Yes, you guessed from the black suit and the shirt with the funny collar, didn't you?" Markham said. "Are you Mr. Dennis Rowicki?"

The man frowned. "That's Doctor Rowicki, vice-president of product development, Clymene Biogenesis."

"Oh, sorry, doctor. I didn't know you are a physician."

Dr. Rowicki smiled again. "Apology accepted. Actually, I'm not a physician. The University of Western Ontario gave me an honorary doctorate in recognition of my financial support of the university. I got my Master of Business Administration there. I'm an M.B.A., but you can call me Doctor."

"Of course," Markham said. "Then we have something in common. I have a Ph.D. too."

"Oh?"

"It's in psychology. I got mine by studying and researching. I'm a doctor, but you can call me Father."

Rowicki stopped smiling. "I called earlier," he said. "I've come to take my company's property."

"I don't have anything that belongs to your company," Markham said.

Rowicki pulled out his pocket computer. A photo of Lorraine appeared on its monitor. "This is the clone Warfem version one, created by Clymene Biogenesis. Several people have observed her here. Do you deny that she is on the grounds of this church?"

Markham took the pocket computer from Rowicki and looked at the photo. Lorraine's blonde hair was pulled behind her head, and her eyes had no emotion.

"Have you seen the Warfem clone?" Rowicki asked.

"Her name is Lorraine," Markham said.

Rowicki sighed. "That's just a pet name that one of our nurses gave her. That nurse had such silly ideas. We dismissed her after the clone escaped. This particular clone has no personal name yet."

"I won't deny that she's here," Markham said as he gave the pocket computer back to Rowicki. "I disagree that she's your property, though."

"A clone is not a human being under Canadian law. It belongs to my company."

"The Church considers clones to be human. She belongs to nobody except herself. She came here seeking sanctuary, and she'll have it," Markham said.

"The Church can't offer sanctuary to something that isn't human."

"Yet Pope Christopher approved the baptism of clones last week."

"He did? Why?" Rowicki said.

"The Church considers them human, so they're entitled to the same sacraments given to natural-born persons," Markham explained.

"The baptism of clones shows the hypocrisy of the Catholic Church," said Rowicki. "For years, the Church opposed the cloning of humans. For years, you said only God has the right to create human beings through natural procreation. Yet you eagerly baptize the clones created by the process you condemn."

"Clones are not responsible for the sins of their creators," Markham said. "They are children of God, like us."

"It still doesn't make them human under the law," Rowicki argued.

"Maybe not by secular laws, but in God's eyes, they can be purified and initiated into the Christian family. Baptism is a sacrament we reserve for humans," Markham said.

"The Warfem version one was created in a cloning hatchery; how can that be human?" Rowicki said. "She's a manufactured product. She has some manufacturing defects that you've undoubtedly noticed. She hears voices in her head."

"I know about that. I think that's a side effect of the neuro-programming you gave her."

"Perhaps. The voices tell her to attack people."

"I know that too. That's what you get when you create a clone to attack people," said Markham.

"She's prone to violence."

"Oh, I've noticed that too."

"She's a military prototype, created and trained to be the ultimate soldier," Rowicki explained. "But a good soldier shouldn't be hearing voices that aren't there."

"I agree. I was a military chaplain, so I know about the mental health of soldiers," Markham said.

"Then you'll agree that she's in a bad state," said Rowicki. "Your psychology degree is impressive, but you can't help her without medical facilities and doctors, nurses, and therapists. She'll be better off receiving psychiatric treatment at Clymene Biogenesis, from people who care about her."

"You mean from people who will dissect her and find out what went wrong?" Markham said. "You want to fix the factory defects so you can sell a defence contract to the government."

Rowicki glared at the priest. "I want to avoid trouble, but if you don't cooperate, I'll tell the police that you've stolen my property."

"Save yourself the time. I've already called them," Markham said. "The police chief is a friend of mine from the wars. He won't intrude on the sanctuary of a church, especially after that fracas with the clone rights protesters at St. Patrick's Basilica in Montreal."

"Just let me talk to her," Rowicki demanded. "If she's as human as you insist, you'll let her talk to me so she can make her own decision about where to go."

Markham shook his head. "No. Get off my church's property now or I'll charge you with trespassing."

"You can't say that to me!" Rowicki protested. "I'm the richest man in Canada. I want to be nice and get things done without going to court, but I can get a judge to order you to hand over the clone."

"You can get the court order, but no police officer or bailiff will carry it out after that incident in Montreal," Markham said. "Your money can't buy good public relations for the cops."

"We'll see about that," Rowicki said.

As Rowicki and his bodyguards drove away, Father Markham sighed in relief, but he also wondered when Rowicki would return.

*

Father Markham approached John and Ava Rodriguez and their baby boy Daniel. Daniel wore a white garment decorated with intricate lace. Markham had seen that christening gown before, when he had baptized Daniel's brother Andrew two years earlier.

The boy, quiet in his mother's arms, stared up at Father Markham. Markham dipped his hands in the sacred oil, touched Daniel's forehead, and made the Sign of the Cross.

"Daniel Paul, the Christian community welcomes you with great joy. I now trace the Cross on your forehead and invite your parents and godparents to do the same," he said.

Markham invited them to the baptismal font. As Ava held Daniel, Father Markham dipped his hands into the holy water and poured it over Daniel's head.

"I baptize thee in the name of the Father, and of the Son, and of the Holy Spirit," Markham said. "This child is now reborn in baptism. He is now a child of God, so indeed he is."

As in all baptisms, the Rodriguezes and their family and friends posed for photographs. After the ceremony, they left the church, passing the statue of St. Joan of Arc on their way out.

Lorraine had been standing by the statue and watching the baptism. A woman wearing a blue jacket and skirt stood with her. Father Markham approached them.

"That was a beautiful ceremony," the woman said.

Markham said, "Thank you, Sister Clara." He turned to Lorraine. "What did you think about it?"

"Is it part of the human experience?" Lorraine asked.

"For some humans, it is," Markham said.

Sister Clara said, "I'm going to call the Big Chicken Coop. What do you want?"

"The usual," Father Markham said.

"The roast quarter chicken dinner," said Lorraine.

"Gravy with your French fries again?" Clara asked.

"Gravy," said Father Markham.

"I will have baked potato with sour cream instead of the French fries," Lorraine said.

"Money," Clara demanded.

"Oh, yes," Markham said as he gave his money card to Clara. "It's still got fifty dollars."

"That should be enough," the nun said as she took the card. "I'll call the Big Chicken Coop and go pick up the order. I'll be back soon."

She turned to Lorraine. "Place the plates and knives and forks on the table, like I showed you, will you?"

Lorraine nodded. Clara left for her car, leaving Lorraine alone with Father Markham.

"Is it true that only humans can be baptized?" Lorraine asked. "Sister Clara told me that you do not baptize animals or equipment."

Father Markham had noticed that when Lorraine was fighting, she spoke in an angry, emotional tone. But when she was calm, she spoke in an emotionless monotone. She never seemed happy, and she never smiled. This had to be due to a life without family, friends, and schoolmates, a life of only neuro-programming and combat training, Markham thought.

"That's true, only human beings can be baptized," Markham replied.

"Was the baby human before he was baptized?"

"Of course, he was."

"Then why does he need to be baptized if he was already human?" Lorraine asked.

"While it's true that only humans can be baptized, baptism does not make someone human," Markham explained. "Baptism is for people who are already human. It's a ceremony of purification and entry into the Christian community."

"Purification? Was that baby impure?"

"In a limited sense. He was born with original sin. The baptism is a remission of original sin."

"Original sin. I read about it in *L'Osservatore Romano* in your library. Sister Clara talked about it with me. It is a general condition of sinfulness into which all humans are born. However, I am not sure how it exists and works," Lorraine said. "Unlike you, I was not born from humans. I was cloned from a donor's cell. Do I have original sin?"

"I think you do, and for once, I think that's wonderful," Markham said.

"Wonderful? How can being sinful be wonderful?"

"Because it means you're human."

"Only inside this church. I am non-human outside it," Lorraine said. She paused for a moment and asked, "Father, if I am truly human, will you baptize me?"

She was unsmiling and unemotional as usual when she asked about baptism. She did not fully appreciate people's feelings for life's milestones. Not yet.

"I'll baptize you if you are willing to learn and join the Christian community. The choice is yours."

"Perhaps I can do that. I will read more articles in *L'Osservatore Romano*."

"You might have to read more than *L'Osservatore Romano*," Markham said. "Don't worry, I won't make you recite the names of the sacred monkeys in the Vatican."

"If the monkeys in the Vatican are sacred, have they been baptized?" asked Lorraine.

Markham wondered if Lorraine had developed a sense of humour.

*

The rectory was in a house separated from the church but still within the church grounds. In the rectory, Father Markham, Sister Clara, and Lorraine again dined on take-out food from the Big Chicken Coop.

"What do you say when I pass the bread to you?" Markham asked.

Lorraine took the basket of bread. "Thank you?"

"That's right. You're learning."

Lorraine bit into the bun.

Father Markham felt happy about Lorraine's progress. Her neuro-programming and combat training had included no social graces, but she was learning them faster than he had expected.

"So how was your day?" Clara asked.

"Why do you need to know?" Lorraine said in her flat, emotionless tone.

"It's just something people do when they eat together. They make 'small talk,' harmless conservation about things that happened," explained Clara.

"Oh, okay," Lorraine said. "I heard the voice in my head again."

"Do you recognize the voice? Do you know whose it is yet?"

"No, I do not. All I know is that it is a man's voice."

Father Markham took a sip of wine. "Does it remind you of a voice you heard during neuro-programming?"

"I do not remember."

"Could it be an instructor at the mercenary training camp?"

"No, it is not one of them. They are within my recent memory. I would remember them."

After the dinner, Father Markham brought a decanter

of port to the table. Drinking port after dinner was a tradition of Canadian military officers' messes.

"May I have some port too?" Lorraine asked.

Father Markham shook his head. "You're too young. Do you want coffee or tea?"

Lorraine also shook her head and stood up. "No, I will go back into the church and look at the statue."

"Don't leave the church grounds," Father Markham said. "The Clymene Biogenesis people might try to capture you."

"I can protect myself if they try to capture me," Lorraine said.

"I know you can," said Markham. "It's your enemies I'm worried about."

"All right," said Lorraine as she left the room.

As Sister Clara poured some port into her glass, she said, "She seems to like that statue of St. Joan of Arc. I think she identifies with St. Joan after reading about her in *The Lives of the Saints*."

"Like St. Joan, she hears voices in her head," Father Markham observed.

"At least she doesn't think it's God's voice. We get enough people hearing Him," said Clara.

"I suspect the voice is someone she remembers from her neuro-programming. I've heard of other neuro-programmed and force-grown clones experiencing voices or visions. Some of them become mentally ill due to the way they grow up. After Lorraine was created, her creators force-grew her to a sixteen-year-old size in five months, and she learned eight years of primary schooling in six months of neuro-programming."

He sipped his port. "What she doesn't have is all the

people and experiences that develop a teenager's mind: family, friends, schoolmates, or any memories of childhood or adolescence. She has none except the cloning hatchery and the mercenary training camp.

"In addition, clones are brainwashed into slavish devotion to a specific role, usually dangerous or low-paid jobs, like uranium miner, landmine sweeper, garbage picker, or prostitute."

"But Lorraine's different. She's the first of her kind, an elite combat soldier," Clara said.

"Yes, a soldier who can get killed without any pensions or payments to a surviving family," Father Markham said. "She's the perfect expendable human. Sorry, non-human."

He shook his head. "Have we come to this: creating people just so they can kill? Or just so they can die?"

"You were a military chaplain," Clara said. "Is creating a clone any worse than recruiting and conscripting people into the military, where they may also be forced to kill or die?"

"No, that's different," Markham said. "Society considers natural-born people to be human, and they keep all the rights of a human being and citizenship when they join the military. They have the free will that God gave them. Even a conscript can disobey orders that are illegal. I told my soldiers that it was their duty to refuse any orders that violate the laws of armed conflict."

He put down his glass. "We treat clones differently. They have no human rights, and they don't have any rights of citizenship. And we neuro-program, brainwash, and train them so they won't have any free will, just an urge to obey us."

"Not Lorraine," Clara said. "She escaped from the mercenary training camp because she wanted a different life."

"She resisted her programming and training," said Markham. "Something must have gone wrong in the factory."

"Perhaps," said Clara. "She got some rather intense training, though. I'm amazed that she hasn't attacked us."

Father Markham grinned. "She came here on Victoria Day, when I was wearing my medals for the parade. I must have imprinted on her mind as a military officer, and therefore, a commander.

"But she hears voices that aren't there, so I don't know how long I can control her."

*

After Sister Clara went home, Father Markham went into the church to find Lorraine. She was still staring at the statue of St. Joan of Arc.

St. Joan wore a white armour breastplate, a blue peasant's skirt, and boots. She held a sword in her right hand, and in her left hand, a shield of the traditional coat of arms of France, blue with three gold fleurs-de-lis. Unlike many medieval depictions of her, in which she has short hair, this statue showed her with long blonde hair, flowing as if swept by the wind.

"She heard voices too, did she not?" Lorraine asked.

Markham nodded. "Yes, she did."

"And she defeated a whole army, did she not?"

"Yes, she did. She defeated the English at the siege of

Orléans."

"The voices told her to fight the English invaders, kill them, and drive them out of France, did they not?"

"Yes—I think they did," Markham replied uneasily.

"Based on the evidence, people who hear voices are programmed to fight," Lorraine said. "I should not have left the training camp. I should return and fulfill my purpose."

"No, you're free to do what you wish with your life. Don't let your creators tell you what to do," urged Father Markham.

"But St. Joan heard voices telling her what to do. How is she different?"

"St. Joan heard voices by the grace of God. You hear voices because of your neuro-programming, which definitely isn't graced by God."

"I have received no training for any other purpose in life," Lorraine said. "I was created and trained just for fighting. But I wanted to escape from the training camp. I did not want to be a soldier, at least not only a soldier. My trainers said that any other desires were mental problems."

Markham put his hands on Lorraine's shoulders. "They're wrong. What else do you want to do?"

"I saw many things on the web and television that I would like to try. I want to dance, cook, play baseball, fix cars, paint pictures, and grow flowers," she answered. "However, I cannot predict which duties I will like. I suspect that I will have to try many of them before I know what I like."

"That's the way humans learn and grow," Markham said. "You can try anything you want to do, then choose what you like. God created humans to be free."

"You think I am human. Not everyone agrees," Lorraine said. Her face turned grim.

"They're wrong. You're human," Markham assured her.

The church doors swung open, making a loud noise. They turned towards it and looked down the aisle.

"What on Earth?"

Dennis Rowicki walked into the church.

"Mass isn't until noon tomorrow," Markham said.

"I'm not here for that," Rowicki said. "I'm here for her."

Lorraine's eyes widened. "That is the voice in my head."

"He's the voice?" said Father Markham.

"I'm the one who created you," said Rowicki, holding out his hand to Lorraine. "Come back where you belong. I command you."

A trance-like stare came into Lorraine's eyes. Silently, she walked to Rowicki.

"Lorraine, wait," said Markham as he touched Lorraine's shoulder. She kept walking as if he did not exist.

Markham ran in front of her and grabbed her shoulders. "You don't have to go with him. You're a free person," he insisted.

Lorraine gently pushed his hands away and continued walking to Rowicki.

"I'm the control voice, the one you're programmed to obey," Rowicki reminded Lorraine.

"And when she was at the training camp, when she was away from you, she broke free," said Markham.

Rowicki nodded. "The model has some defects. That's why we need her back."

"No!" said Markham as he grabbed Lorraine. "She must be free!"

"Warfem version one, neutralize the enemy, use non-lethal force," ordered Rowicki, pointing at Markham.

Lorraine slugged Markham in the jaw. As he staggered back, Lorraine punched him in the ribs. Caught unaware, Father Markham gasped and fell to the floor.

"Lorraine, it's me, Father Markham!" he yelled.

He rolled over as Lorraine's foot stomped down, just missing his chest. Markham rolled again, sprang up, and dodged Lorraine's fist as she swung for his head.

Although chaplains were not required to take combat training, Markham had taken it so he could understand his soldiers better. As he felt his pulse quicken, he remembered the hand-to-hand fighting.

Lorraine thrust her fist at his nose, but he threw up his arm to deflect her. Then he kicked one of her thighs before she could kick him. The girl groaned and stumbled back.

"Warfem version one, continue and neutralize the enemy!" Rowicki shouted.

Attack the officer, Markham silently told himself.

He rushed at Rowicki and tackled him. As Rowicki fell on the floor, Markham landed atop him. The two men hit the ground face to face with each other.

Markham punched Rowicki's left eye, blackening it immediately. Next, he hit Rowicki's nose. Blood gushed down Rowicki's face. Markham scrambled up and kneeled beside Rowicki. He pressed his knee against Rowicki's throat.

Rowicki made choking noises. Since he was lying on his back, his nosebleed was flowing down his throat.

Lorraine, her eyes full of anger, approached them.

"Tell her to stand down or I'll crush your throat—if you don't drown in your own blood first," Markham said.

"Warfem version one, stand down," Rowicki choked out.

Lorraine stopped and stared at the two men. Markham stood up and pulled Rowicki to his feet. Blood flowed down Rowicki's white shirt.

"You must've broken a commandment, you hypocrite!" Rowicki said before coughing up blood.

"It was self-defence. You ordered her to attack me, remember?" said Markham. "Get out of here and don't ever come back!"

He pushed Rowicki through the doorway, and the man tripped and fell outside the church. Markham quickly closed and locked the doors.

Looking confused, Lorraine stared at Father Markham. "What happened?" she muttered. "There's blood on your collar, and you have bruises."

"The blood is Dr. Rowicki's," Markham said. "Don't worry about me."

Lorraine gently touched a bruise on Markham's cheek and quickly pulled her hand away. "Oh no, did I do that to you?"

Markham nodded. "You did, but don't let that bother you."

"Did I try to kill you? No, please, it can't be true!" Lorraine said. A tear ran down her cheek.

Father Markham had never seen Lorraine cry before.

Lorraine looked grief-stricken. "I tried to kill a priest!

That's a terrible sin, isn't it? Is that all I can do? Sin? I'm so full of sin. I'm less than human because of my sin."

They heard a loud bang. Something heavy had smashed into the door. The banging noise repeated.

"He's trying to break down the door," Markham said.

He pulled out his pocket computer and dialled the emergency telephone number, 9-1-1. A message appeared on the monitor: "NO SIGNAL AVAILABLE".

"Damn, he's jamming my signal."

The banging on the door echoed through the church.

Lorraine grabbed Father Markham. Her face had changed from grief to panic.

"I'm afraid," she said. "I'm afraid of my powers. I destroy things. I can kill people. If I hear his voice again, what will I do?"

"Fight it. Resist him," Markham said.

"But I'm a clone. I'm programmed like a machine!" said Lorraine.

"You can resist your programming. God gave you free will," Markham argued.

"I wasn't created by God! I was created in a lab."

Markham pulled Lorraine down the aisle to the baptismal font. He dipped his hands into the water and traced the Sign of the Cross on the girl's forehead. Then he scooped up some water with his hands and poured it over her head.

"I baptize you, Lorraine, in the name of the Father, of the Son, and of the Holy Spirit," he said.

Lorraine stared in bewilderment at him.

"Now your sins are gone. Feel free again," said Father Markham.

"I don't feel any different," said Lorraine.

"Now you are one of us, a member of the community of Christ, a human child of God."

Father Markham grabbed Lorraine's hand and led her back to the statue of St. Joan of Arc.

"God gave you free will. Now you just have to find it within yourself. You have the strength to do it. Ask St. Joan and God to help you find that strength," Markham urged her.

Lorraine dropped to her knees and looked up at the statue. She whispered so softly that Father Markham could not hear the words clearly, but he knew she was praying.

The banging noise continued. Markham saw cracks spreading across the wooden doors. Rowicki must be using a heavy battering ram.

The doors burst open. The chauffeur and bodyguards carried a steel battering ram into the church. Rowicki, his face and clothes stained with blood, walked behind them.

"Warfem version one, come to me," he ordered.

Lorraine stood up, turned to him, and said, "No, I'm staying here."

Rowicki looked stunned. "Warfem version one, come to me," he repeated.

"No."

"I'm your control voice! I order you to come to me!"

"No, I'm not going with you!" Lorraine protested. "You can't control me anymore."

Rowicki went to Lorraine. "Listen to me, listen to me," he demanded. "I'm your control voice! Recognize my voice. You are programmed to obey me."

Lorraine punched Rowicki in the stomach. As he

staggered back, howling in pain, Lorraine jumped and kicked his face. His two front teeth flew through the air. Rowicki crumpled onto the floor.

The chauffeur and bodyguards stepped forward. Lorraine held out her hand and snarled at them.

Crouching over Rowicki, she grabbed his head and pulled it to look up at her face. She put her hands around his neck and squeezed.

"Tell your men to leave or I'll snap your neck," she said.

Rowicki coughed and said, "Get out of here, get out of here, get out of here."

The men turned and ran out of the church, leaving the battering ram behind. Lorraine let go of Rowicki's neck and searched his pockets.

She pulled out his pocket computer and tossed it to Father Markham. "He didn't jam his own pocket computer. Call the police," she ordered.

Markham stared at Lorraine for a moment before calling the police.

*

"...and that's how I fought with a young girl and assaulted a man and threatened to kill him," Father Markham said.

"Wow, that was a busy day," said Archbishop Tolbert.

They sat in Markham's office, drinking coffee in the church's sacristy, the office behind the altar. The archbishop sipped more of his coffee.

"I understand why you had to fight your young ward. Nobody can fault you for defending yourself," said

Tolbert. "What about Rowicki? Would you have killed him had he not ordered Lorraine to stop attacking you?"

"I honestly don't know what I would've done," Markham said. "I had to think and act quickly, moment by moment."

"Part of being human is having choices but not knowing which one to choose," said Tolbert. "That's what makes us different from animals and machines."

"I guess it does."

"When you confessed about fighting in the church, I was very curious about what happened. You told me some of it, but I thought there had to be more details. I knew you would tell me when the time was right. You've been absolved already, but thanks for giving me the whole story."

"Thank you for seeing me," said Markham. "Six months have passed since the fight, and I'm relieved to finally talk about my feelings with you."

"Given the circumstances that befell you, I don't think God blames you for the violence in the church. Perhaps you are guilty of anger, but maybe it was necessary to preserve yourself," said Tolbert.

"Thank you, Your Grace," said Markham.

"How is the girl coming along?" Tolbert asked.

"She's living with Sister Clara and doing very well in school," said Markham. "She has several friends, has no disciplinary or behaviour problems, and scores B-plus or A on all her subjects."

Tolbert picked up a framed photograph of Lorraine wearing a white judo costume. "I see she has taken up martial arts as an extracurricular sport."

Markham nodded. "It's a safe outlet for her past

training."

"It was a good idea to enrol her in high school. Now she'll have the life she never had," said Tolbert. "Does she still hear voices in her head?"

"No, not anymore."

"That's great. Some of our saints have a reputation for hearing voices, but it's not always a healthy thing."

"Especially if the voice is from an imprisoned clone creator," Markham added.

*

A little later, Markham walked out to the cold December air. He saw Sister Clara and Lorraine returning from a hockey game.

Lorraine carried a blue pennant showing a white maple leaf, the logo of the Toronto Maple Leafs.

"Who won the game?" Markham asked.

"Only God can help the Leafs," said Sister Clara.

Lorraine groaned and said, "Montreal won. Six to zero!" She shrugged and added, "What can you do?"

Markham stifled a laugh. "That's what you get for being a hockey fan in this city. Our baseball team's doing better. But you aren't a baseball fan, are you?"

"I find hockey more interesting," Lorraine said. "I know it's embarrassing to be a hockey fan in Toronto, but that's my choice. I guess that's part of growing up human here."

About "Cloned to Kill"

I first wrote on Roman Catholic themes in the Aurora Award-winning story "Transubstantiation". Karina and Robert Fabian were looking for stories for their second Roman Catholic-themed science fiction anthology, and so I wrote "Cloned to Kill".

Lorraine is another one of my female main characters. She's damaged by trauma, but ultimately, she overcomes her demons and defeats a dangerous man.

Father John Markham is loosely based on a real priest, a former U.S. Army chaplain, whom I had met while on vacation in Las Vegas. The ex-chaplain had served during the Vietnam War and was rather unorthodox. He had written a book about how to be Catholic if you didn't want to be too conservative or strict; he hoped the Pope would condemn it so its sales would increase.

Father John Markham isn't as eccentric as the priest I met in Las Vegas, but he is certainly different from your regular parish priest.

Thanks to Karina and Robert Fabian for publishing "Cloned to Kill", especially since "Roman Catholic-themed science fiction" is a hard sell.

Family Tradition

"...and Chelsea is the new Miss Hooters of Cocoa Beach!" said Maria, the restaurant manager. Amidst the cheers and hoots of the audience, Chelsea Van Helsing received the aluminum tiara from last year's winner, Sara. Seconds later, Sara and Maria threw the "Miss Hooters of Cocoa Beach" sash over her shoulder and handed her a bouquet of red roses. As she clutched the tiara to keep it from wobbling, Chelsea posed and smiled for the photographers.

Chelsea hugged and kissed the runner-up and the other contestants. "This is way cool!" she cried. "I won a bikini pageant! This is way cool!"

Hooters, the restaurant chain with waitresses who wore white tank tops and tight orange shorts, had a series of beauty pageants for its waitresses. Now she was Miss Hooters of Cocoa Beach. To what heights would she strut next?

Maria grabbed the microphone again. "Chelsea will represent Cocoa Beach at the Miss Hooters International Pageant in Las Vegas. In addition, she'll receive a hundred-dollar gift certificate from the Econo-Mall."

The gift certificate wasn't the university scholarship that the Miss America Pageant gave its winner, but Chelsea didn't complain. She needed all the money she could get for college.

On her way out of the crowded restaurant, Chelsea stopped to autograph a poster of the contestants, which showed her in the red bikini. Too tired to change into her civilian clothes, she grabbed her duffle bag, threw on an overcoat, hopped into her white convertible, and drove back to her apartment.

As she unlocked her door, a balding man wearing the black suit of an Eastern Orthodox priest approached her. He was Father Boris Buca, a new visiting professor at the Department of Theology, Cocoa Beach University.

"So how did the contest go?" he asked.

Chelsea showed him the tiara. "Oh, just fabulous! I won!"

"Congratulations," Father Buca said. "I hope that my blessing helped. Never before had anyone asked me to bless a beauty pageant contestant."

Chelsea nodded. "For that, you get ten free chicken wings. I'll get a coupon for you. Good night, Father."

She entered her apartment, went to the bedroom, and threw off her overcoat, leaving herself clad only in her bikini.

"I say, young lady, must you display yourself in public wearing immodest apparel such as that?" a voice said in the Dutch accent of Chelsea's ancestors.

She spun around and saw an old man dressed in a black morning coat and pants, white shirt with upturned collar, and a plaid bow tie. His straggly, unkempt hair and goatee were as white as snow, and his hostile eyes stared at her through thin wire glasses. In his Victorian clothes, he would have looked like an actor from a play, except that he was semi-transparent. Chelsea could see right through him.

Chelsea moaned. "Great-great-granddad, don't you ever knock? Like on the door?"

The ghost of Abraham Van Helsing scowled. "I keep telling you that I have no solid form to knock on doors."

Chelsea put on her overcoat. "So you just appear in a girl's bedroom unannounced—like your old buddy, Dracula?"

Abraham sighed, and Chelsea smirked. She knew the old ghost hated being compared to his old enemy.

"Chelsea, I am distressed to see you squandering your life serving beer to ruffians of the lower classes and displaying yourself in a manner that would embarrass even the most shameless trollop," he said. "You should take a more respectable trade, like our family tradition."

"I'm having too much fun serving beer to horny frat boys, posing for swimsuit calendars, and hanging out with my friends. Why should I go skulking around in cemeteries at night?"

"That is what our family does," Abraham said. "I pledged myself to rid the world of the evil of vampirism."

"There are no vampires in Cocoa Beach," Chelsea said.

"Before I died, there were rumours that Dracula was somehow revived after I beheaded him," Abraham said. "Now I suspect that he may have come here to Cocoa Beach, America."

"Why do you think he's here?" Chelsea demanded. "Did a ship come in with its entire crew dead? Is a plague of rats infesting the city? Are mental cases eating flies and spiders?"

"There are increasing numbers of Romanian immigrants arriving to these shores," Abraham said. "He and his acolytes could be among them."

"That's why you think Dracula is here? Oh, so like, they passed the Homeland Security anti-terrorist test, but they didn't pass the Abraham Van Helsing anti-vampire test?"

"Chelsea, do not take my warnings lightly. Dracula is King of the Undead. Being undead is the worst state of evil. You must destroy Dracula to stop the evil."

"Oh, he's undead, so he's evil," Chelsea mused. "What about you, then? You're just as dead as he is."

Abraham shook his head. "No, no. Dracula is undead. I am dead. There is a difference."

"Oh, as if!" Chelsea cried.

"It is our family tradition to kill the undead," Abraham urged. "Please, be like your father and help me lay a trap for vampires at the cemetery."

"I'll tell you what a trap is. Our family tradition is a trap," Chelsea said. "Well, forget that!"

"It is your destiny!"

"Get out of here! Go haunt someone who cares!"

Abraham Van Helsing's ghost disappeared with a "poof" noise, which he made when he was extremely annoyed. Tired and exasperated, Chelsea fell onto her bed.

*

"Hi, my name's Chelsea, and I'll be your Hooters Girl,"

Chelsea cooed as she leaned over the table to talk to the customer. By leaning over, she gave the customer a good look at her deep cleavage. She didn't mind, though; he was only looking, not groping, and flashing her cleavage at him would guarantee her a big tip.

But instead of staring at her cleavage, the customer looked into her eyes.

Chelsea stared into his deep green eyes. They seemed intense and hypnotic, as if they could pierce a girl's soul and discover her deepest desires and fantasies. She drifted into a daydream...

Chelsea snapped back to attention. "Oh, sorry, I got a little distracted." She wiped the drool off her lips. "Uh, as I said, my name is Chelsea."

"It is a pleasure to meet a beautiful lady such as you, Chelsea," the customer said. His voice sounded soft and seductive. "My name is Ivan Teppish."

"Great to meet you too, Ivan. Are you visiting from out of town?"

"I have recently moved here to start a business. I am from Romania," he said.

"Oh, so cool," Chelsea said. "You've got a cute accent. You sound just like Count Chocula."

Ivan's smile faded.

Chelsea flipped her black hair. "So can I get you something to drink? A beer? Or a wine?"

"I never drink wine. Please give me, uh, what do you call it, a Bud Light?"

*

Ivan ordered a steak sandwich cooked extra rare, pink

with blood oozing. After bringing the steak to him, Chelsea rang up the tab for another customer. As she stood by the cash register, she stared at Ivan eating his blood-soaked steak.

In a restaurant full of guys in golf shirts, jeans, and baseball caps, Ivan wore a white shirt, a deep red tie, and an elegant black suit that Chelsea recognized as an Armani. This man dressed to impress.

He was also incredibly gorgeous, with his handsome face and thick black hair. And he filled out that designer suit well, Chelsea noticed. She fantasized about the finely-sculpted, athletic, toned body under the designer suit: the muscular biceps, the strong chest, the flat stomach, the firm butt...

The other waitresses ogled Ivan too. As they passed his table, the girls swayed their hips and twirled their hair around their fingers.

"Oh, your customer is soooo adorable," Kate squealed as she approached the cash register. "He is stud material."

"I can see all the other girls going all droolly and hair-twirly around him. The power of male pheromones," Chelsea said. "But hah, he's at my table tonight."

She sauntered over to Ivan's table, sat down, smiled, and asked, "So, how's the steak?"

Ivan smiled back at her. "It is excellent, very juicy and tender, as young, beautiful, fresh meat should be."

"Another satisfied customer. Great! Did you say that you're here to start a business? What kind of business is it?"

"I own a multi-million dollar enterprise in Romania. I am establishing a branch of my business here."

He handed a business card to Chelsea. She looked at the card:

Carfax Jewelers
Diamonds and Gold Jewelry

"Wow, you deal in diamonds and jewellery," Chelsea said.

Ivan looked seductively into her eyes again. "I like to acquire things of beauty."

Chelsea nodded and looked into his eyes. Those eyes could hypnotize her into doing anything with him, she realized.

She regained her senses and shifted her gaze to a brooch pinned to the lapel of his suit. It looked like a gold reptile curled into a circle with diamonds for its eyes.

"What's that?" she asked.

"Ah, that is a dragon. My ancestors were Romanian nobility. They were members of the Order of the Dragon, a noble society pledged to free our lands from invaders."

"Way cool. It's so pretty," Chelsea said.

"It is gold with inlaid diamonds," Ivan told her.

Kate came by. "Did I hear someone say gold and diamonds?"

"Look at that cool brooch he has," Chelsea pointed out.

"Oh, I want to take a closer look at it," said Kate.

As Kate bent over, a large silver cross dangled from a chain around her neck. As the cross swung, light glinted from it.

Ivan hissed and put his hands in front of his face.

"Ivan, what's wrong?" Chelsea asked.

"Uh, nothing, nothing at all." Ivan settled back into his chair. "Uh, I got startled, that's all."

"Oh, sorry for bothering you," Kate said before going to the kitchen.

As she watched Kate leave, Chelsea felt a hand touch hers. She turned to Ivan.

"From the time I first saw you on the poster of the Miss Hooters Pageant, I knew that I must have you," Ivan said. "I want you. And you want me."

"Are you asking me for a date?" she said.

Ivan gripped her hand tighter. "Yes, you will join me. I can feel your blood boiling with desire."

His smooth, manly voice was hypnotic. It could put a girl into a trance, Chelsea thought.

But then her mind jolted, as if she awoke.

Chelsea pulled her hand away and giggled. "We Hooters Girls get hit on all the time. I've never gone out with a customer. Why should you be any different?"

"You American girls always play hard to get," Ivan said.

He fished into his pocket and pulled out a gold chain. He dangled it in front of Chelsea, and she saw the diamonds suspended from it.

He glanced at the other men in the restaurant. "These boys will give you flowers and chocolates as if they were diamonds, but I can give you diamonds as if they were flowers and chocolates."

Chelsea hadn't seen diamonds like these before. "Ooooooh. Diamonds are a girl's best friend."

"You have such a beautiful neck," Ivan said. "This chain would add to its beauty. I would be honoured to put it around your neck as a simple memento of our first date. Come with me tonight."

"Not tonight. I'll be too tired after my shift," Chelsea said, "but I have the day shift on Friday. It ends at seven. Drop by then, and we'll do the date thing."

"It would be an honour and a pleasure," Ivan said. He rose from his chair, bowed to Chelsea, and kissed her hand.

*

On Friday, Ivan returned to the restaurant just as Chelsea's shift ended, and they went dancing at a local nightclub. After midnight, they arrived at Chelsea's apartment.

"This has been a wonderful evening," Chelsea said as she put the key into her door.

"The pleasure is all mine," Ivan said. "You are a desirable woman, all that a man can ever want."

He lifted the gold chain from his pocket and placed it around Chelsea's neck.

"A beautiful chain for a beautiful woman," he whispered. He moved behind her and placed the chain around her neck.

He lifted her hair and nibbled on her ear lobe. He stroked her shoulders and arms.

Chelsea purred with pleasure. "Oooooooooh, you move quickly on a first date."

"I fly with the speed of a raven, and I can take you to heights you have never before imagined," Ivan said.

He licked her neck. Chelsea closed her eyes and moaned as she felt his hot breath upon her tingling skin. As Ivan's arms encircled her just below her breasts, Chelsea felt the heat of his body, as if their clothes had melted away.

She gyrated and ground her butt against his groin in a lascivious dance. She felt sensual and lustful.

His lips and tongue caressed her neck. Then she felt his teeth upon her skin.

"Good evening," a voice said.

"Father Buca!" Chelsea cried out as she broke herself from Ivan's grip. "Uh, you've been out late tonight."

Ivan hissed and backed himself against the wall. He glared at the priest.

"Uh, Ivan, this is Father Buca from the university," Chelsea said.

"Pleased to meet you," Ivan said, still pressing his back against the wall.

"Glad to meet you too," Father Buca said. "Well, I'm really tired. Good night."

After Father Buca entered his apartment, Chelsea quickly kissed Ivan on the cheek.

"Thank you for a wonderful first date," she said. "I'm kinda tired too, but we must do this again. Just look for me in the restaurant."

"Uh, uh…"

Chelsea opened the door, rushed into her apartment, and shut the door, all in a few seconds. She giggled as she bolted the lock.

Her great-great-grandfather's ghost appeared.

"Young lady, where have you been?" Abraham demanded.

"I've been on a date," Chelsea said. "You know, girl meets boy, boy spends ton of money on girl, boy hopes girl will put out, and girl denies sex to boy but promises it for next time. And then the cycle starts over again."

Abraham grunted. "I viewed your suitor before you shut the door in his face. He looks like Dracula."

"Oh, knock it off," Chelsea said. "He's just a millionaire diamond dealer from Romania."

Abraham gasped. "Romania! I knew it."

"You know nothing. He's some horny guy who thinks I'm hot."

"He's King of the Undead!"

"Oh, he's not undead. He's definitely alive. I know because I felt his hardness when I ground my butt against his groin when we were dirty dancing."

Abraham looked aghast, and Chelsea grinned.

"Oh, come off it, stop obsessing over a dead vampire and just go to heaven," Chelsea said.

The ghost frowned at her. "I cannot rest in peace until I am satisfied that Dracula, King of the Vampires, is destroyed."

"He's been a dead undead person for over a hundred years. Go to your afterlife and get out of my life."

"What an ungrateful brood I have sired! None of you have taken up the family tradition," Abraham said. "Do you realize that only my constant vigilance against Dracula has guaranteed the survival of our family?"

"The survival of our family?" Chelsea laughed and pointed at a photo of her parents. "What family? You broke up Mom and Dad's marriage."

"I had to ensure that Dracula and his acolytes were not stalking them," Abraham said.

"They got tired of you dropping in on them," Chelsea said. "And you also broke up Granddad and Grandma."

Abraham's face remained stern. "Unfortunately, your grandparents did not appreciate my protection of our family."

"We have no family. There's only a lot of divorced singles," Chelsea said. "You've destroyed the family."

The air turned ice cold, and a strong draft blew through the apartment. But Chelsea did not fear these ghostly threats.

"And I, the last direct descendant of yours, can't even keep a boyfriend because you keep scaring them away," Chelsea said. "Our family's going extinct on its own."

"Such disrespect!" Abraham scolded.

"I'm not going to become another divorced, depressed, drunk, single, sexually dysfunctional Van Helsing," Chelsea said. "I'll go to a normal college, I'll get a normal college degree, I'll get a normal job, I'll get a normal boyfriend, and I'll live a normal life."

Abraham sneered and wagged his finger. "Young lady, you are taking a great risk with your life—"

"Get out now!" Chelsea said.

With a poof sound, Abraham's ghost disappeared, and Chelsea stormed into her bedroom.

*

The next morning, Chelsea knocked on Father Buca's door. When the priest opened the door, she smiled and gave him a coupon.

"Here's a coupon for ten free chicken wings," she said.

"Ah, thank you," Father Buca said.

"And by the way, I know you're not Catholic, but do you eat fish on Fridays?" Chelsea asked. "I can get you a big fish sandwich on the house. I have just one more request..."

*

Father Buca walked into Chelsea's apartment and looked around. Clutching a large silver cross, he said, "I'll try my best at this, but this is my first time. We Orthodox don't do this often. Catholics have a lot more experience with exorcisms."

"Uh, they do?" Chelsea said, wondering if Father Buca was the best choice for the ritual.

"But don't worry, I know how to do this—I think. I did some research on Eastern Orthodox prayers of exorcism. Those should do the trick. Well, I hope they work."

"Okay, let's get started," Chelsea said.

Father Buca held out a bottle of holy water and sprinkled it around the apartment. "Father O'Hara from Introduction to Catholicism 101 says this stuff really works."

"Paging Abraham Van Helsing, paging Abraham Van Helsing," Chelsea said. "Mr. Van Helsing, please report to the apartment."

The ghost of Abraham Van Helsing appeared in front of Father Buca.

Father Buca screamed and dropped the holy water bottle. "You weren't kidding, there really is a ghost here!"

Abraham looked confused. "What is a priest doing here? Are you holding a religious ritual without consulting me?"

Father Buca held the cross out to the ghost. With his other hand, he pulled a piece of paper from his pocket and chanted in Greek.

"What is this man saying?" Abraham said. "It's all Greek to me."

"He doesn't understand Greek," Chelsea said.

"Oh, dear," Father Buca muttered. He turned over the paper. "Okay, I downloaded the English translation too."

"What is going on here?" Abraham asked.

"Hail, God of Abraham. Hail, God of Isaac. Hail, God of Jacob. Jesus the righteous Holy Spirit Son of the Father," Father Buca said.

The temperature in the room plummeted, and a cold draft blew across the room. Abraham stared at Father Buca and Chelsea.

"Again I ask you, young lady, what is going on?" Abraham asked.

"It's an ancient Christian liturgy of exorcism, fourth century, originally in Greek and Coptic," Chelsea said.

"An exorcism!" Abraham's eyes lit up like fire. "How dare you subject me to a sacrament for driving out evil demons!"

"Come out, demon, whoever you may be. Stay away from Chelsea Van Helsing's home," Father Buca said.

The air turned freezing cold, and the draft grew stronger and swirled around the apartment and knocked over a vase. The coldness whipped Chelsea's face and hair.

"Oh my God, it's cold in here," Father Buca said. "Oh, where was I? Ah, here it is: Quickly! Now! Come out, demon!"

Abraham scowled. "I have devoted my whole life and afterlife to exterminating creatures of evil. I have destroyed scores of the undead, the vilest of Satan's spawn. I have killed Dracula. And now you treat me as a Hell-born demon."

Already a semi-transparent ghost, Abraham became

wispier as Father Buca chanted.

The air above Abraham turned blood red and spun around. Like smoke being sucked into an exhaust fan, the ghost stretched and drifted up to the whirlwind.

"It is that boyfriend of yours, the Romanian. He turned you against me!" Abraham yelled. "You are making a mistake! You are not in love! You are under his hypnotic spell! By the time you swear your eternal love for him, and he swears that he will never hurt you, make a note of this: both of you are lying!"

The whirlwind spun faster. Abraham groaned. Then the whirlwind sucked him in and disappeared. The air shot back up to normal temperature, and the draft stopped blowing.

Father Buca sat down. His hand trembled as he put the cross down on a table.

"Well, at least nobody vomited green bile on me, and nobody's head turned around a hundred and eighty degrees," he said. "My goodness, you have such unusual requests."

"Thank you so much," Chelsea said. "Your next big fish sandwich at Hooters is on the house."

"Thank you," Father Buca said. He looked at his watch. "Ah, I better leave soon. It's my turn to celebrate the noon Mass at St. Constantine's."

"Is that St. Constantine's Romanian Orthodox Church downtown?" Chelsea asked. "Does it have a gift shop?"

*

That evening, when the night shift ended at the restaurant, Chelsea phoned the number on the Carfax

Jewelers business card.

"Hello?" Ivan answered.

"Hi, Ivan. This is Chelsea."

"Ah, the most beautiful and glamorous woman I have met in my travels."

Chelsea chuckled. "Yep, that's me, though I don't feel so glamorous by the end of the night shift. I hope I didn't wake you up."

"No, not at all," Ivan said. "I was working. I often work late."

He's still awake at two in the morning, Chelsea thought. He'll certainly agree to go to an after-hours dance club that stays open until dawn.

"I'll be free tomorrow night," she cooed. "In case you didn't notice, I really love dancing. I could dance the whole night away. Want to take me dancing again?"

"I would love to, my dear."

"Way cool. By the way, did I tell you that I took jewellery design a year ago? A night class at community college, that's all. Could you bring some more diamond and gold stuff? I want to see some of your designs."

*

True to her word, Chelsea kept Ivan dancing the whole night. Eventually, she wanted a drink and dragged him away from the crowded dance floor and to a table.

"Wow, most guys can't keep up with me," she said. "You've been dancing for hours. You've got such stamina."

"I do not tire easily," Ivan said. "I can maintain a girl's pleasure for a very long time."

"Oooh, I bet you can."

Chelsea raised the banana daiquiri to her lips. There was a banana stuck in the drink. She plucked out the banana and sucked it while looking at Ivan.

Ivan stared into Chelsea's eyes. "You want me, you want me, you want me," he repeated.

With a banana in her mouth, Chelsea stared back at Ivan and felt herself become drowsy. Her jaw dropped, and the banana fell to the floor.

"Oops, what a klutz I am," Chelsea said.

She stood up, turned her back to Ivan, and bent over at the waist to pick up the banana. She knew that her black miniskirt was so short that it would ride up and expose her red thong panties and her butt, but she didn't care if Ivan caught a glimpse under her skirt.

She sat back down, crossed her legs, put the banana on the table, and picked up her glass. "Uh, where were we?"

Ivan took a deep breath, stared into her eyes again, and said, "You want me, you want me, you want me..."

Chelsea looked into Ivan's eyes. Then she tipped her glass and spilled her drink over herself.

"Oh, my top! It's all wet and sticky," she said as she grabbed a napkin. She patted the napkin against her low-cut gold halter top. "Oh, I got wet and sticky in there too," she said as she wiped her cleavage. "And I'm wet and sticky there too," she said as she wiped her bare midriff.

"I heard about American girls being hard to get, but this is ridiculous," Ivan said.

"Okay, I'm finished wiping myself," Chelsea said. "Hey, were you watching me wipe my breasts and belly?"

"Yes, how could I not look at you?" Ivan said with a

smirk.

Chelsea straightened her back and thrust her breasts forward. "And did you see anything you like?"

Ivan leaned over and kissed and licked her neck. Chelsea closed her eyes and purred. She gyrated slowly and sensuously as Ivan ran his hands over her back, her arms, her belly, and her breasts.

She felt the hardness of his teeth upon the soft skin of her neck.

With a giggle, she pushed herself away and flipped her hair. She motioned at the scores of people packed onto the dance floor, sitting at tables, and clustered around the bar.

"This place is way too crowded to be a make-out spot," she said. "Why don't we go back to my place?"

"Okay, let's go," Ivan said as he rose from his chair.

"And you can show me your jewellery samples too," Chelsea reminded him as she grabbed her handbag.

*

When they entered the apartment, Ivan groped her and nuzzled her neck. She pulled herself away and laughed. A frustrated, desperate frown appeared on Ivan's face.

"Oh, you horny hound, not in here," she said. "Let's do it in the bedroom."

Ivan's lips curled into a smile. As he parted his lips, Chelsea saw how brilliantly white and long his teeth were.

Chelsea grabbed his hand and pulled him towards the bedroom. She giggled, spun around to his back, squeezed his butt, and pushed him into the room. She rushed into the room and slammed the door shut.

Ivan gasped and threw his hands in front of his eyes.

Silver and wooden crosses and crucifixes covered the bedroom walls. Strings of garlic hung from the window curtains. Jars of water sat on her dresser and desk.

"I wanted to redecorate my apartment, so I bought some crosses at a church's gift shop," Chelsea said. "Aren't they pretty?"

Ivan hissed and spun around to face Chelsea. She pulled a water pistol out of her handbag and squirted jets of water into his eyes.

He screamed as his eyes turned red. Wisps of white smoke rose from his eyes. He threw his hands over his face.

"Holy water from the church," Chelsea said. "It's free."

Ivan staggered towards her, and she ran to her dresser and its jars of water. She picked up a jar and flung water on Ivan's hands. His skin turned black as charcoal, and smoke rose from his hands.

Howling with pain, he threw his hands into the air. Chelsea splashed water on Ivan's face.

As Ivan shrieked, his cheeks turned black like his hands. Cracks and boils appeared all over his face, and white smoke and red blood oozed from the wounds. Chelsea smelled the stench of burning skin.

She pressed her back against the door, blocking the exit from the room.

Ivan dropped his jaw, raised his upper lip, and exposed his long, canine fangs. He snarled like a wolf as smoke kept rising from his face.

"Cheap hussy," Ivan said. "I could have given you sensual pleasures beyond your imagination. I could have given you eternal life free of mortal pain. I could have made you Queen of the Undead."

Chelsea shrugged. "Queen of the Undead sounds awesome, but I'll settle for being Miss Hooters of Cocoa Beach."

Ivan lunged at her. Chelsea darted away from the door. Ivan slammed face first into the door, which was covered with crosses and strings of garlic.

He howled as the garlic and crosses burned his face and hands. As Ivan clutched his cheeks, Chelsea rammed a chair into his chest, and he fell onto his back.

Chelsea grabbed a mallet and a wooden stake. She rushed to Ivan and held the stake over the left side of his chest.

"Toys from the family," she said.

Chelsea slammed the mallet down on the stake. As the stake plunged into Ivan's heart, he screamed, and a geyser of blood gushed from his chest.

Chelsea panted as she fell to the floor. "Whew, that was close!" she said as she wiped the vampire's blood and her own sweat off her forehead.

She crawled back beside the vampire, who was groaning and twitching on the floor. Still panting, Chelsea plucked the golden dragon brooch off his Armani jacket.

"You should never have come back, Dracula," Chelsea said. "Everyone except my great-great-granddad thought you were dead. When you showed up, I had to kill you."

She reached into his pockets and grabbed the diamond pendants, bracelets, and rings.

"This won't pay for all the emotional trouble you've

made for my family, but it'll help pay for college," she said. "I'll get a normal life. Nobody in my family could live a normal life while you and my great-great-grandfather loitered in the land of the living."

"Your great-great-grandfather?" Dracula murmured.

"Oh, too bad the bikini pageant poster doesn't show my last name. It's Van Helsing," said Chelsea.

Dracula groaned and gripped the stake. He convulsed as he tried to pull it out.

Chelsea went to the window and grabbed the window curtains. "You know what I like about that after-hours dance club? You can dance all night till dawn."

She pulled open the curtains and let the sunlight pour into the room. Dracula wailed as light bathed him. His skin and flesh began crumbling into grey ashes, exposing his bones. Minutes later, only a pile of grey ashes and a black Armani suit remained of the King of the Vampires.

Chelsea smiled. "The Van Helsings may be dysfunctional, but at least we have a family tradition."

About "Family Tradition"

Another story about a plucky Hooters Girl! However, Unlike Kyra Ling in "It Came to Eat Our Chicken Wings", Chelsea Van Helsing has emotional demons. However, she ultimately triumphs against the two most toxic men in her life. Again, the beautiful girl is also a strong woman. I wanted an attractive woman character who can also be a smart, determined heroine.

The opening scene is based on the annual bikini contest held by the Hooters in downtown Toronto. The tiaras really were cheap aluminum, and one year, the restaurant manager forgot to remove the clear plastic wrap from the tiara before crowning the winner. Of course, the prizes were far below the level of the Miss America scholarship fund.

When I was young, I collected Marvel Comics' *Tomb of Dracula* comic books, which had Rachel van Helsing, great-granddaughter of Abraham Van Helsing, Dracula's nemesis (Note that the Marvel Comics character uses a lower-case v in "van", whereas the Bram Stoker character uses a capital V, which my character uses). Rachel van Helsing inspired me to create Chelsea Van Helsing.

Many thanks to Barbara Custer, editor of *Night to Dawn*, for publishing my first vampire story.

Kleinheimat

June 10, 1967, West Jerusalem, Israel:

Emil Hirsch watched his television in disbelief. On the news, Shlomo Goren, Chief Rabbi of the Israeli Defence Forces, blew a *shofar* at the Western Wall in Jerusalem. Behind him, some Israeli soldiers watched in silent bewilderment.

"One hundred thousand Israelis have defeated two hundred and forty thousand Arabs," the TV reporter announced. *"David has slain Goliath."*

In only six days, Israel had defeated Egypt, Syria, Jordan, and Iraq and captured the Gaza Strip, the Sinai Peninsula, the Golan Heights, and the West Bank.

The TV showed Lieutenant General Yitzhak Rabin, Chief of the General Staff. He said, *"Nobody planned it in advance. Nobody prepared it, and nobody prepared for it. It was as if Providence had directed the whole thing."*

"Providence did not give us this victory," Emil said in German to his wife Clara. "Someone has changed history."

"Do you think one of the time travellers did it?" Clara

asked.

"I don't doubt it. Twenty-nine years ago, Aviva Loew told us that Israel would lose this war. Someone must have gone back in time and changed something."

"Could it be your old friend Mehmet Tasci?"

"Perhaps. Or maybe it was Aviva."

Emil went to a desk and took out a black and white photograph of a dark-haired girl in her twenties. She wore an Israeli Army uniform with a badge depicting a robot. No such badge existed yet.

Clara picked up the photo and smiled. "Ah, our little lieutenant."

"Are you talking about me?" said a voice in Hebrew from behind them.

Emil and Clara turned around to see their granddaughter Rachel enter the living room. She was a slim, pretty girl who left her blonde hair untied so that it flowed out from under her beret and down past her shoulders, and was attired in her Air Force uniform of beige shirt, pants, and beret.

At age twenty-five, Rachel had been promoted to second lieutenant just in time for the war. Emil was glad that his granddaughter had survived the last six days. A disproportionate number of officers had died.

Rachel picked up the photograph of the girl. "Grandpa, why are you looking at this again?"

"She could be here," said Emil.

*

November 11, 1920, Kleinheimat, Bavaria, Germany:
It was the second anniversary of the end of the Great

War. For war veterans like Emil Hirsch, it was a bittersweet day. He felt pride in his military service, but Germany's defeat still saddened him.

Emil stood behind the ribbon that was suspended in front of the Veterans Hall. The ribbon had three stripes of black, white, and red, like the flag of the German Empire.

In contrast to the ribbon, the black-red-gold tricolour of the Republic fluttered above the doorway. Like many people, Emil did not like the new flag. He preferred the Imperial colours.

The people of Kleinheimat had gathered in front of the Veterans Hall. Despite the grey sky and chilly air, many had come. Emil waved at Clara and three-year-old Helena, who were at the front of the crowd. His wife and daughter smiled and waved back at him.

Emil wore the Iron Cross First Class and the Ottoman War Medal on his black frock coat. Other war veterans, wearing either their civilian suits or old uniforms, stood beside him.

A man approached Emil and saluted. He wore glasses, a Bavarian Army cap, and a blue business suit. On his jacket was the Military Merit Cross, Third Class with Swords, Bavaria's main decoration for bravery and military merit for enlisted soldiers.

Emil returned the salute and shook the man's hand. "It's a pleasure to see you again, Otto. Or should I say, Doctor Schmidt?"

Otto laughed. "No, don't call me 'doctor' until I get my Ph.D."

"As you wish, Corporal Schmidt. Fall in line."

"Yes, sir, Lieutenant Hirsch!"

A minute later, Conrad von Seyfried arrived, looking impressive in his Army uniform. Of all the soldiers from Kleinheimat, Seyfried had advanced the highest, to the rank of Captain. After the defeat, he stayed in the Republic's army.

"Attention! Officer coming!" Emil shouted as Seyfried approached the veterans. They snapped to attention and saluted.

"Thank you, gentlemen," said Seyfried. "As you were."

After chatting with each of the veterans, Captain Seyfried stood beside Emil as they waited for the ceremony to begin.

"This is a very nice reunion," said Seyfried. "Thank you for organizing it. I haven't seen some of these guys since they were demobilized."

Emil nodded. "I'm glad that we could get together again. How are things in the army?"

"It's a lot easier after we beat the Reds," Seyfried said, "but now there's a new group with brown uniforms."

Looking at his watch, Otto said, "The mayor is late. What disrespect and lack of discipline at a military ceremony."

The band suddenly started playing the song "The Watch on the Rhine". The musicians were students from St. Joseph's Roman Catholic School. Their headmaster, a priest named Bernhardt, conducted the band.

"Finally, the mayor is coming," said Otto.

A car screeched to a halt in front of the Veterans Hall. The chauffeur rushed out and opened the door for the passenger. A man in a black frock coat and top hat came out. He was Karl Wettig, the mayor of Kleinheimat.

Karl Wettig was in his twenties, the same age as the

veterans. However, he did not serve in the war. Instead, he received a deferral of military service from the High Command, where a general owed a favour to his father, a wealthy lawyer. He spent the war at Ludwig Maximilian University in Munich, where he earned a degree in political science. After the war, he returned to Kleinheimat, ran for mayor, and won just a week ago.

Wettig nudged some veterans out of the way and took the centre position behind the ribbon. When the band finished playing, the mayor spoke to the crowd.

"Thank you, my fellow townspeople, for coming to the opening of the Veterans Hall," he said. "This grand building will be more than just a meeting place for our veterans. It will be also be a shrine to our glorious sons who fell while defending the Fatherland. Let us honour our war dead. Please face the war memorial and stand for a minute of silence."

"Veterans, about face!" Emil ordered.

The veterans turned in unison to face the building. They stared at a bronze plaque mounted into the limestone wall. The plaque's first line read:

OUR GLORIOUS WAR DEAD, BROTHERS UNITED BY
THEIR LOVE OF THE FATHERLAND

This was followed by a list of the dead. Each name had a small cross beside it except for two: Werner Goldstein and Helmut Luxembourg. Their names had Stars of David beside them.

At the top of the plaque was a large *cross pattée*, the Iron Cross. Regardless of whether the soldier had a Christian cross or a Jewish star beside his name, all were underneath the Iron Cross, the symbol of the German military.

When the silence ended, Father Bernhardt approached the war memorial and prayed, "Dear God, our Father in heaven, please protect the souls of our fallen sons... bless this war memorial as a sacred shrine to our glorious dead, in the name of the Father, Son, and Holy Ghost, amen."

He made the Sign of the Cross, and the band played the national anthem. Everyone sang the song, *"Deutschland, Deutschland über alles, über alles in der welt..."*

Next, a pretty girl in a dirndl gave a pair of scissors to Mayor Wettig. He cut the ribbon, and the crowd cheered.

"Veterans, fall out!" Emil ordered.

The veterans broke out of formation, applauded, and entered the building with the mayor. The people followed them.

Clara, holding Helena by the hand, rushed through the crowd to join her husband. "Oh, Emil, that was a beautiful ceremony. Our soldiers deserve so much. They didn't get enough gratitude after the war."

The Veterans Hall had numerous rooms, including those dedicated to the Army and the Navy. It was profusely decorated with paintings, badges, swords, medals, flags, guns, and other artifacts of the German military.

Emil and his family went to the main dining room, where a large portrait of Kaiser Wilhelm the Second hung. For the opening day reception, the guests went from table to table, gathering snacks and drinks.

"*Herr* Hirsch, this is a lovely building. We could not

have asked for a better architect," said Mayor Wettig as he grabbed a glass of schnapps from the bartender.

"Thank you, sir," Emil replied. "It was an honour to build this monument to my comrades."

Wettig took a sip of schnapps. "Thank you for returning to Kleinheimat to practice architecture. We need people like you. Kleinheimat is a large town that was growing into a small city before the war. As the economy recovers, we'll need new buildings."

"I'm glad to be back," said Emil. "I have the opportunity to open my own firm here. In Nuremberg, I would have stayed a small fish in a big pond."

"I'm glad you came back," said Wettig. "Like I said, we need people like you."

The mayor went to talk to a businessman. Clara gave a pastry to Helena, who ate it quickly. At a food station, Emil picked up a pair of tongs but hesitated to take some small sausages.

Captain Seyfried came to Emil's side and said, "Go for the sausages, Lieutenant. They're beef, not pork."

"Thank you," said Emil as he put some sausages on his plate. "I'm not especially religious, but I do follow the kosher rules."

"Like many of us, you love tradition," Seyfried observed, "but weren't those dietary rules a pain in the army?"

"They were, so I didn't follow them all the time," Emil admitted. "Getting kosher-like food was possible in Gallipoli. The Turks are Moslems, and their food rules are similar to Jewish ones. But in France, I ate whatever I could get. There were no kosher butcher shops in the trenches."

"Just getting food of any sort was difficult near the end," Seyfried recalled. "I almost ate the rats."

Otto, holding a sandwich, approached them. "Don't remind me of army food," he said.

"Corporal Schmidt, what are you doing now?" Seyfried asked.

"Resuming what I was doing before the war interrupted me," Otto replied. "I've returned to Berlin to finish my master's degree in physics, and then I'll go for a doctorate. I want to teach at a university."

Emil, Otto, and Captain Seyfried reminisced about the war. They had served together in Gallipoli, and later, were transferred to France, where they stayed until the surrender.

Seyfried looked out of the dining room. "Let's look at the rest of the building, shall we?"

In the hallway, they saw a painting of a knight on horseback. The knight's shield bore the coat of arms of the Seyfried family. The Captain's family had been local nobility, barons, since the First Crusade. They had donated a small fortune for the construction of the Veterans Hall.

"Look, Gallipoli!" said Otto, pointing at a photograph of German and Ottoman soldiers. "We won there."

*

The Hirsches went home after the reception. Emil tidied his study, gathering up the plans and drawings of the Veterans Hall. Then he swung aside a portrait of the Kaiser on the wall. Behind the portrait was a small vault with a combination lock. He locked the papers in the vault. Then he moved the Kaiser's portrait back into place.

The Veterans Hall was the most important building he would ever design. It was a sacred shrine to the men who had paid in blood for their country's honour. Its plans deserved the protection of the Kaiser.

*

December 18, 1932:

Each year, Kleinheimat's veterans gathered for Christmas at the Veterans Hall. They wore their best clothes and followed the customs of a formal mess dinner. After Father Bernhardt said grace, they toasted Kaiser Wilhelm the Second and President Field Marshal Paul von Hindenburg, whose portraits hung side by side in the main dining room.

Doctor Otto Schmidt sat at Emil and Clara's table. Although he lived in Berlin and taught physics at Humboldt University there, he returned to Kleinheimat once each year for the Christmas dinner.

Otto, with his neatly-cut brown hair, crisp white shirt, custom-tailored blue suit, and military medals, still looked like a soldier on parade. However, when Emil asked him what he was doing at the university, he shed his military formality and rambled about his work with a famous colleague.

"...and Professor Einstein says that space-time can be locally curved," Otto said. "Theoretically, that's possible. I wonder if we could ever do it practically."

"And what would that achieve?" asked Emil.

"Time travel," said Otto.

"You mean going a thousand years into the past or the future, like in the adventure stories?"

"Yes, like a story by the British author H.G. Wells."

"Oh, *The Time Machine*! I've read it," said Clara. She straightened the white orchid pinned to her blue party dress. "Is that the one about people splitting into two races, and one eats the other?"

Otto nodded. "Yes, that's the story. It's a scientific romance."

"A romance, yes, but it has a moral lesson," said Mehmet Tasci, a Turkish veteran at their table. He wore a black tuxedo, red fez, and Ottoman war medals. "People can split into predators and prey all too easily. We must always be on the lookout for signs of such trouble."

Clara turned to Tasci. "I hear you have a scientific education."

Tasci nodded. "Yes, also in physics."

"Germany has so many physicists. We are such a scientific nation," Clara remarked. "But you're not teaching or working as a physicist. May I ask why you came here and opened a jewellery shop?"

"After the war, the Turkish government did not need my services anymore, so I learned my brother's trade and came to this country."

Tasci said nothing more and quietly ate his apple strudel while listening to the others.

*

After dinner, the guests retired to the various rooms in the Veterans Hall. Clara went to look at a Red Cross booth in the Navy Room, while Otto and Emil decided to go to the bar for a drink. They paused to look into the Stahlhelm Room, where the teenagers were holding their own party. Fifteen-year-old Helena was laughing and dancing around the Christmas tree with a boy of her age.

"My little girl is growing up," Emil remarked.

"That's Lieutenant Schultz's son, isn't he? Is he your future son-in-law?" Otto joked.

Emil guffawed and shrugged. "Who knows? Helena's got a mind of her own, and I can't control her. Why couldn't she be spending more time with Corporal Tannenbaum's boy? At least he's Jewish."

Helena saw her father and his friend by the door, so she went to meet them. She was wearing a green dirndl, and her blonde hair was tied in a ponytail.

"Well, you look lovely tonight," Otto said.

Helena curtsied and said, "Thank you, Doctor Schmidt."

"What's that?" Otto asked, pointing at a gilt medal hanging from a black, red, and gold ribbon around her neck.

"Oh, that's the award I won at the regional swimming competition," Helena replied, beaming. She looked back at Lieutenant Schultz's son. "Fritz wanted to see it."

"We German men are obsessed with medals and badges," Otto joked. "Congratulations. How did you place? In which event did you win it?"

"I placed first in the hundred meter backstroke," said Helena.

"She wants to compete in the Olympics," Emil added.

Helena giggled. "Watch me go to Berlin in 1936."

Otto smiled. "I'll be there, cheering for you, I promise."

As a new song started, Helena ran off to dance with Fritz Schultz again. Emil and Otto continued to the bar, where they drank and chatted near a painting of the Battle of Tannenberg.

Mehmet Tasci came to the bar to say good night to Otto and Emil.

"It's good to see a fellow professor of Humboldt University," Tasci said to Otto. "It's a pity we don't speak more on campus."

Otto nodded. "Let's keep in touch, shall we?"

"Yes, we should."

Tasci said good night to several other people, and then he left the Veterans Hall.

"I was surprised to see Doctor Tasci here," said Otto. "When did he come to Kleinheimat?"

"Just a few months ago," said Emil.

"He used to teach in my department, but he resigned suddenly and left without saying where he was going. We hardly spoke at Humboldt. Has he told you why he left the university?"

"No, he hasn't. He doesn't talk about his past. Now he's a jeweller. Do you know why?"

"I don't know. He's a mysterious fellow. At the university, he was conducting research in theoretical physics. But I heard rumours that he worked on a secret weapon for the Ottomans during the Great War."

"Secret weapon? Like an airplane or a tank?"

"Nobody knows. Ataturk exiled him after the war," said Otto. "That's the rumour."

"Oh, look, the mayor is free," Emil observed. "I haven't had any luck trying to talk to him tonight. Excuse me."

"Of course, go ahead," said Otto.

Emil walked towards Karl Wettig. Before dinner, Wettig had turned his back to talk to someone else whenever Emil had approached him. If Emil had not known any better, he would have suspected that Wettig was avoiding him.

Now the mayor was alone, drinking beer while studying a display of artillery badges.

"Ah, *Herr* Mayor, how nice to see you again," Emil said.

Wettig turned to face Emil. The mayor looked startled. He held his near empty beer glass over his jacket's left lapel.

"Hello, *Herr* Hirsch," Wettig blurted.

Emil held out his hand, but Wettig did not shake it. He kept holding his beer glass in his right hand.

Undeterred, Emil said, "Congratulations on your twelve years as Mayor."

"Thank you, *Herr* Hirsch. Is that all you wanted to say to me?"

"There is one more thing. Please excuse me for asking. When may I get a permit for *Herr* Michel's office building? I want to start construction soon."

"Ah, I know the application. I'm afraid that I've been so busy that I haven't looked at it. I'll review and approve it tomorrow. How does that sound?"

"That would be wonderful," said Emil. "Thank you. We don't want to keep *Herr* Michel waiting."

"No, of course, not."

A waitress came and said, "Oh, *Herr* Mayor, your glass is empty. Let me take it from you."

"No, Freida, I'm fine, you need not bother," Wettig muttered.

"It's my job, sir," Freida insisted. "We're running out of

glasses upstairs, so the maitre d' ordered me to retrieve all unused ones for cleaning."

Freida snatched the beer glass from Wettig's hand. Then Emil saw what the mayor had been hiding with his hand and the glass.

On Wettig's lapel was a circular pin showing a black swastika.

*

November 11, 1935:

It was the seventeenth anniversary of the end of the Great War. All the veterans in Kleinheimat would receive a new medal today. Emil should have been happy, but instead, he was annoyed. Nonetheless, he put on his black frock coat and medals and left his house.

On his way to the synagogue, he stopped in front of the Veterans Hall and looked at the flag above the doorway. The Republic's black–red–gold was gone, replaced by a flag of the old colours. But it was not the beloved Imperial tricolour. Instead, it was the National Socialist flag, a black swastika within a white disk on a red field.

The sign posted on the door upset Emil more than the flag did:

NO JEWS ALLOWED INSIDE!
BY DECREE OF KARL WETTIG, MAYOR OF
KLEINHEIMAT

The swastika flag and the ban on Jews were not the only changes Mayor Wettig had made at the Veterans

Hall. When the National Socialists came to power two years ago, Wettig removed the portrait of the Kaiser and replaced it with Adolf Hitler's.

When Hindenburg died on August 2, 1934, the mayor removed the Field Marshal's portrait. Now Hitler's image alone dominated the main dining room.

Otto Schmidt came out of the Veterans Hall. Like Emil, he was wearing his medals of the Great War. But unlike Emil, he had the new decoration.

"Ah, Emil, what a lucky coincidence to see you now," said Otto. "I've just received my medal from Colonel von Seyfried. Come on, let's go."

"Isn't there a reception? Don't you want to stay for it?" Emil asked.

"It's crawling with Brownshirts, all staring at me," said Otto. "I feel insecure in there despite being a Roman Catholic."

"You're also a Social Democrat," Emil added.

"Which I bet will be the next group banned from the Veterans Hall. Come on, let's go."

"What about the Colonel?"

"He's got to stay for the reception, but he'll join us in an hour."

After years living and teaching in Berlin, Otto had returned to Kleinheimat. In 1933, the National Socialists took over Humboldt University and expelled him. No state-funded school or university would have him, but Father Bernhardt hired him to teach science at St. Joseph's Roman Catholic School, which was privately-funded.

They walked to Kleinheimat's only synagogue. As they entered, Emil put on his yarmulke and said, "We must cover our heads." Otto nodded and put on his old Bavarian Army cap.

They went to the basement, where the Jewish war veterans were gathering. Due to the commandment forbidding graven images, the synagogue did not have any pictures of people or animals, except the Lion of Judah, on its main floor. However, in the basement, away from the Torah, the veterans put the portraits of Wilhelm the Second and Paul von Hindenburg on a table.

Hoffman, a tailor who had served as an artilleryman, gave a glass of red wine to Otto. "Good afternoon, Doctor Schmidt. You didn't have to come here, but I'm happy that you did. I'm sorry that you're the only Christian at this reception."

"Oh, don't apologize," said Otto. "We're all comrades here, united by the blood and limbs we lost fighting for the Fatherland. I would rather be here than at the other reception, with the Brownshirts."

"What a bunch of golden pheasants," said Berl, a medical doctor who worked in the Michel Building.

"Golden pheasant" and "Brownshirt" were nicknames of the Storm Division's or SA's members due to their brown uniform. The SA preferred to call its men by a more flattering term, "Stormtroopers."

Otto sipped the wine and remarked, "Oh my God, that's sweet. Are all Jewish wines like that?"

Hoffman laughed. "No, only when Berl buys the wine."

"Hey, you were not so picky about your liquor when we were at Flanders," Doctor Berl said. "It's good, drink it up!"

"We will," said Hoffman. "Now please excuse me. I better go upstairs and watch for the Colonel."

"And keep the golden pheasants out," Berl added.

A short time later, Colonel Conrad von Seyfried came to the synagogue. Resplendent in his Army uniform, Seyfried looked like an Aryan hero from a National Socialist poster. However, he was secretly visiting a synagogue.

"You didn't have to come here," Emil said. "You're taking a risk."

"Any old comrade is worth the risk," Seyfried replied. "Hindenburg would have approved."

"Where is your adjutant?" Emil asked as he gave a drink to Seyfried.

"I said I had to run a personal errand for my family, so I gave him thirty marks and told him to go to Schneider's Tavern, buy himself dinner, and pick me up at the Veterans Hall in two hours."

Schneider's Tavern was at the outskirts of town, so the adjutant would not see Seyfried come and go from the synagogue.

"Congratulations on your promotion to Colonel," Berl told Seyfried.

"Thank you," Seyfried said.

"I'm happy that you suggested this ceremony."

"If the Gentile veterans of Kleinheimat have a ceremony, the Jewish veterans should have one too. It's only fair. Were we not all comrades in the same trenches?"

The veterans nodded in agreement.

"Let's get started," said Seyfried.

"Reich Association of Jewish Frontline Soldiers, attention!" Emil ordered. "Fall in!"

The veterans organized themselves into a row. Otto,

the only non-Jew aside from Seyfried, went to the Colonel's side.

Seyfried put his briefcase on the table and took out some small envelopes and boxes. Each envelope had a name on it.

"Gentlemen, when I call out your name, please come forward and receive your medal and certificate," Seyfried announced. He looked at the first envelope in the stack. "Lieutenant Emil Hirsch."

Emil proudly stepped forward and stood at attention in front of Seyfried. Otto opened one of the small boxes, and Seyfried took out a cross-shaped bronze medal and pinned it to Emil's frock coat. Then Otto handed an envelope to Seyfried, who gave it to Emil. Finally, Seyfried saluted Emil, who returned the salute.

The military ritual repeated for each man until all had the Cross of Honor for Combatants, created by President Paul von Hindenburg just two weeks before his death. It was a belated reward for soldiers who had fought in the Great War.

The veterans sang "*Das Deutschlandlied*": "*Deutschland, Deutschland über alles, über alles in der welt...*"

As they sang, they looked wistfully at the portraits of Wilhelm the Second and Paul von Hindenburg. Their Kaiser was in exile in Holland. Their general had died. Both men, heroes of the old Germany, were gone forever. Conspicuously missing from the table was a portrait of the current leader of Germany, the *Führer* and Chancellor, Adolf Hitler.

Emil opened his envelope and pulled out a certificate. It read:

*In the name of the Führer and Chancellor,
by the decree of July 13, 1934 to remember the World War of
1914 to 1918, the Cross of Honor for Combatants, created by
President Field Marshal von Hindenburg, is awarded to
Emil Hirsch*

The certificate and medal gave some hope to Emil. By awarding this medal to Jewish veterans, the *Führer* showed his appreciation for their defence of the Fatherland. Despite his disdain for Jews, would the *Führer* have a place for the Jewish veterans and their families in the new Germany?

*

After the ceremony, the veterans chatted about their status in the new Germany. For the Jews, 1935 had been a humiliating year, the worst since the National Socialists had come to power. The Brownshirts had bullied Jews throughout the country. In May, the government forbade Jews from joining the military, and then in September the *Law for Protection of German Blood and German Honor* outlawed marriage between Jews and non-Jews. Next, *The Reich Citizenship Law* stripped the Jews of their citizenship.

"Colonel, you're a senior officer," Berl said. "What have you heard in the army? I hear a lot of officers don't like the National Socialists."

"It's true," Seyfried replied. "Many officers are nobility. The National Socialists don't like the nobility, and we don't like them. But what can we do? They're the elected government, and it's our duty to serve them."

"I hope the National Socialists are only temporary," Emil said. "All regimes since the end of the Empire have been short-lived. The Bavarian Soviet Republic lasted only a month."

"The only stable regime was the Empire," said Seyfried. "That's who should run the country: the Kaiser, the army, and the nobility."

"Hear, hear!" said the veterans.

"To the Kaiser!" Hoffman cried, raising his glass of wine.

As Emil drank the toast, he felt reassured. Compared to other places, Kleinheimat was still safe for Jews. The majority of the townsfolk didn't care for National Socialism. They were mostly farmers and small businessmen, people who concentrated on work rather than politics.

Like every town, Kleinheimat had its Brownshirts and Jew-haters, but they weren't as influential as their colleagues in larger cities like Nuremberg or Munich. The *Ortsgruppenleiter*, head of the National Socialist local chapter, was weak. He was a slacker named Joachim Rumeder, who spent more time drinking and sleeping than harassing Jews.

But Mayor Karl Wettig was whipping up anti-Jewish feelings on his own. He issued hate-filled decrees independently of the national government. Some people gossiped that Wettig wanted to replace Rumeder as the *Ortsgruppenleiter* and climb up the National Socialist ranks, possibly to *Gauleiter*.

*

Emil's firm had several architects, including his most devoted employee, Gunther Schloss. Years ago, when Gunther was seventeen years old, Emil hired him as an apprentice draftsman. The boy's enthusiasm and hard work impressed Emil so much that he paid for Gunther's education as an architect. Gunther repaid his boss by leading important projects, like the design and construction of the Michel Building.

A week before Christmas, Gunther Schloss handed in his resignation.

"Gunther, this is a surprise," said Emil. "Why are you leaving?"

"Please understand that I have no personal complaints against you. I like working here," Gunther replied. "It's just that, uh, I can't help but notice that our firm doesn't get as much business as it used to."

"Because nobody wants to hire a Jewish architect," Emil said bitterly.

Gunther frowned and nodded. "I have to think of my own financial security. I think I should look for employment with other firms."

"How can I argue with you under the circumstances?"

"*Herr* Hirsch, I'm grateful for the opportunities that you gave me. It's strictly an economic decision, nothing personal against you. I do not support National Socialism."

*

April 6, 1936:
Emil left Hoffman's tailor shop with the gefilte fish hidden inside a brown paper bag. Passover would begin

tonight, and Clara's family had a tradition of eating gefilte fish at their Seder. Hence, Emil adopted the custom after their wedding.

He was lucky to get the fish. No grocer sold kosher food anymore. However, Hoffman's American relatives had sent him some cans, which he generously shared with Emil.

Perhaps things will get better this year, Emil hoped. Under international pressure, the National Socialists were relaxing their restrictions on Jews prior to the Summer Olympics. They had removed "Jews Not Wanted" signs from Berlin's main tourist attractions and had appointed a Jewish war veteran, Captain Wolfgang Fürstner, as commandant of the Olympic Village. They even allowed a few Jews, like the fencer Helene Mayer, to compete for Germany.

Business had even picked up a little. Father Bernhardt had hired him to redesign parts of St. Joseph's School, repair its chapel, and renovate the local church. "God, not Hitler, tells me who can do the best job at the best price," the priest had said.

As Emil passed the Veterans Hall, he saw a man slamming a mallet into the war memorial plaque.

Emil's heart beat faster. What was going on?

As Emil approached the man, he recognized him as a construction worker.

"Klaus!" Emil said. "What are you doing?"

Klaus turned and looked embarrassed. "*Herr* Hirsch, I'm just repairing the war memorial."

Emil looked at the bronze plaque. Creases and dents surrounded the names Werner Goldstein and Helmut Luxembourg.

"You're defacing the war memorial to get rid of their names, aren't you?" he said, aghast.

"I'm sorry, *Herr* Hirsch. The mayor ordered me to remove Goldstein's and Luxembourg's names from the war memorial."

Klaus paused for a moment and continued. "I wish the names were engraved. Then I would only have to fill in the letters with stucco. But the letters are raised, and it's very difficult to flatten them. The bronze is hard. I'm not sure I can do it without damaging the other names, sir."

Emil couldn't believe Klaus was talking to him as if they were discussing common problems at a construction site.

"This is outrageous!" Emil yelled.

"What's going on here?" asked a voice from behind. Emil turned around to see Father Bernhardt.

"Father, they're defacing the war memorial!" said Emil.

Bernhardt looked at Klaus. "What? Is that true?"

Klaus nodded silently.

Bernhardt frowned. "I blessed the war memorial. Now you're desecrating it. Why?"

"There are two Jewish names on it."

"They're children of God and martyrs of Germany too. Who told you to do this?"

"The mayor."

Karl Wettig came out of the Veterans Hall. "Is there a problem?"

The priest turned to the mayor. "Did you order the Jewish names removed from the war memorial?"

Wettig snorted. "Yes, I did. Minister Goebbels wants Jewish names off all war monuments."

"But those men are heroes," Emil protested. "They fought for the Fatherland."

"No, they didn't! You Jews stabbed us in the back."

"What do you mean? Twelve thousand Jewish soldiers died for Germany."

"They didn't die for Germany. They martyred themselves to fool us into thinking that Jews were loyal. It was a great deception."

Wettig pointed at Emil. "Meanwhile, *you* were plotting against us. All Jews in the army were traitors, profiteers, or cowards. Germany was stabbed in the back by its Jews."

"I never heard of such nonsense," Emil said.

"Tonight is Passover, isn't it? I know all about it, Jew." Wettig grinned. "Passover is a remembrance of the time when Jews lived in Egypt. Tonight you will celebrate the killing of innocent Egyptians and their children. It's a Jewish tradition to stab Aryans in the back."

"That's not true!" Emil argued. "Passover is a celebration of our liberation from slavery. It is not a wish for violence against anyone."

Anger blazed in Wettig's eyes. "Then why do you recite the list of plagues that befell Egypt, as if they were great victories? We know the truth about you, so stop lying, Jew. You celebrate the death of Egyptians just like you celebrate the defeat of Germany. A race that brags about killing innocent people is a race that stabs its countrymen in the back. That's how Germany lost the Great War."

Father Bernhardt grabbed Emil's arm and urged, "I think we better leave."

As the priest led him away, Emil heard Klaus moan,

"Mayor Wettig, I don't think I can avoid denting the other names. Can you think of another way we can do this?"

*

When Emil arrived home, he found Clara and Helena looking at a letter. They looked dejected, and for some reason, Clara wore her swimming medal.

"What's wrong?" Emil asked.

Helena gave the letter to Emil. It came from the Reich Sports Office.

To Miss Helena Hirsch,

The Reich Sports Office, seeking to ensure that our Olympic athletes represent the best of the German people, considers you unfit for international competition. We regret to inform you that you have been disqualified from trials to select the swim team.

"Oh, dear, I'm so sorry," Emil said. Helena's greatest dream was to swim in the Olympics. Driven by the desire for a gold medal in Berlin, she had trained hard to win local and regional competitions, each a step towards qualifying for the Olympics.

"I competed for the glory of Germany, but Germany doesn't want me," said Helena. "Palestine is the only hope for Jews."

Emil shook his head. "No. Jews have suffered insults before, but we always bounce back. That's because we're Germans, we've been here for centuries, and we're part of this country. This is just a temporary setback."

"The National Socialists are not a passing fad. The

Zionists say we'll never be safe until we have our own country. The Tannenbaums have gone to Palestine. We should go too."

Like most members of the Reich Association of Jewish Frontline Soldiers, Emil opposed Zionism. He had raised Helena to be a proud German: Jewish in religion but also German in culture. She had grown up German, wearing dirndls during town festivals and organizing the teenagers' Christmas party at the Veterans Hall.

But in the last year, as anti-Jewish bullying grew, Corporal Tannenbaum's son had been telling Helena about Palestine and kibbutzim.

"Palestine?" Emil said. "You want to live in the middle of a desert, surrounded by Arabs, ruled by the British?"

"Is that any worse than living surrounded by Brownshirts, ruled by Hitler?"

"I'm sure that the National Socialists are only a temporary regime. They will certainly not last the one thousand years that Hitler predicts. The German people will come to their senses and remove them from power. Just wait and they'll be gone."

"And I'll be gone too, next year in Jerusalem."

Clara interrupted them. "Come on, my dears, let's not argue now. It's the first night of Passover. We're supposed to be celebrating, remember? Let's have our Seder. I'm getting hungry, and we have to recite the whole Haggadah before we get to the real food."

She grabbed the bag of gefilte fish and led them to the dinner table, where she had laid out the Passover Seder plate, with the bitter herbs, the paste of fruits and nuts, the celery, the lamb shank bone, and the hard-boiled egg. These were the ritual foods, each symbolizing a part of the story of Exodus. The actual meal was still roasting in the kitchen. Smells of roast beef brisket and sauerkraut wafted into the dining room.

They sat down for the ritual meal. Like Jews had done for centuries around the world, the Hirsches listed the ten plagues that God sent to punish Egypt: blood, frogs, lice, wild animals, pestilence, boils, hail, locusts, darkness, and the deaths of the first-born.

But before listing the plagues, Emil read a passage from the Haggadah, the ancient script of Passover:

"These plagues came to the Egyptians due to their evil, but we do not rejoice over their decline and defeat. Judaism teaches that all people, even the enemies who wish to destroy us, are children of God. We cannot be glad when anyone needlessly suffers, so we mourn the loss of the Egyptians and are sad over their destruction."

*

The Olympic Summer Games began on August 1, 1936. On August 16, the last day of the Games, Helena left Kleinheimat against Emil's wishes. She went to Hamburg and boarded a ship bound for Palestine.

Helene Mayer won a silver medal in fencing for Germany but immigrated to the United States after the Games.

A month before the Games, the National Socialists demoted Wolfgang Fürstner to vice-commandant of the Olympic Village and told him that he would be dismissed from the Army. Three days after the Games ended, Captain Fürstner, career Army officer, veteran of the Great War, and recipient of the Iron Cross First Class, committed suicide with a pistol.

Jews were leaving Germany, one way or another.

*

April 26, 1937:

Some Jews stayed on. Emil refused to leave Germany. He had served in the Bavarian Army and received the Iron Cross First Class. He had designed and built a hall for German war veterans. He had a portrait of the Kaiser hanging in his study. He spoke German fluently and Yiddish not at all. He knew only enough Hebrew to recite a few Torah verses for his bar mitzvah. Nobody could be more German than Emil.

His daughter, however, was shedding her German heritage. Helena had turned Zionist and left her home without his permission. Such disobedience would have angered most fathers. But Emil felt only sadness, not anger.

Helena's news from Palestine pleased him. In letters home, she told him about her job teaching swimming and physical education at an elementary school, the apartment she shared with a French girl, the friends she made, and her strolls through the beautiful Old City in Jerusalem. She had even found the Tannenbaums and reported that the Corporal and his son were working for the Jewish Agency for Palestine. However, Helena still had not set foot in a kibbutz. Maybe she did not like collective farming.

Emil grudgingly admitted to himself that Helena had more freedom and opportunity to build a good life in Palestine than in Germany. He was glad that Helena was a happy model citizen somewhere in the world.

As Helena's twentieth birthday approached, Emil thought about sending a gift to her. What would she like? What could he send her?

One day, Helena sent him a postcard showing the Zionist flag, which had a blue Star of David in the centre. The flag gave him an idea: he would give his daughter a gold Star of David. She had never worn the religious star before, but she could wear it now as a Zionist symbol.

But what jeweller in Germany still sold Stars of David? The government had deported Kleinheimat's only Jewish jeweller to his birthplace in Poland a month ago. Perhaps Mehmet Tasci had Star of David jewellery. Tasci, being Turkish, had no Aryan heritage to insult by selling Jewish symbols. As long as the sale stayed secret, Tasci might sell jewellery that nobody else wanted.

As Emil walked through the streets, he realized that he still knew nothing about Tasci's past. Emil used to talk to Tasci at events in the Veterans Hall until Jews were banned there. After that, Emil saw Tasci a few times to buy jeweller's copies of his war medals. But Emil had not learned what Tasci had done during the Great War or why Turkey had exiled him.

Tasci's shop was at the edge of the downtown. The street's other buildings had fallen into disrepair, with wooden boards across their broken windows. During the Great Depression, most of the street's businesses had closed. Except for Tasci's customers, few people ventured to this street.

Two years ago, Emil asked Tasci why he didn't move to a better area to attract more customers. Tasci had replied merely, "I like the privacy." Tasci showed various jewellery items in his window, but he also had the curtains drawn behind the display so that nobody could look into the shop.

Emil entered the shop and saw Tasci sitting behind the counter. The news was playing on the radio.

"The Luftwaffe has bombed the city of Guernica in Spain. Our aerial bombardment has crushed the Communists."

Tasci turned off the radio and said, "They're practising for a larger war." He looked up at Emil and smiled. "*Herr* Hirsch, welcome back. It's been a while since I've seen you."

"Yes, it has, too long," said Emil.

"What can I do for you today?"

"I've come to buy a birthday gift for my daughter."

"Feel free to look around. I have a vast selection of items in various shapes and sizes, in different metals, for young and old. I have something for everyone."

Emil looked at the counter and display cases. There were necklaces, pendants, rings, brooches, hairpins, and bracelets in various shapes, including crosses, but nothing like a Star of David.

"Do you have anything shaped like a Star of David?" Emil asked.

Tasci looked intrigued. "What a coincidence that you should ask. But then, perhaps it's not a coincidence at all."

The jeweller stood up and said, "Follow me."

He led Emil to a back room. There was a table with tools, gold and silver coins, and other items that Emil did not recognize. Tasci put on a pair of gloves and picked up an irregular plaster object.

"I use the lost-wax method to make castings," Tasci

explained. "This is the mould for a pendant that I'm making."

Tasci opened the cooled mould, and Emil could not believe what he saw inside it: two gold Star of David pendants.

"These aren't old stock that you have in storage. You're making new Stars of David," Emil said. "Why?"

"It's a personal project," Tasci said. "Did you say you want one?"

"Yes."

"Wait outside. I'll attach it to a gold chain to make a necklace. I'll need only a few minutes."

Emil returned to the salesroom. As promised, Tasci came out shortly and put the necklace in a gift box.

"I hope your daughter likes it," Tasci said as he accepted some reichsmarks from Emil.

"I'm certain she will," said Emil.

Tasci was silent, as if deep in thought. Then he finally spoke. "I hope you don't feel offended by what I'm about to say. I'm surprised that she would want to wear a Star of David in these times."

"She's in Palestine now. She can wear it freely over there."

"Ah, Palestine. Does she have a British passport now? Is she coming back? Is that when you'll give the necklace to her?"

"No, she's not coming back. I'll send it to her."

"Don't send it to her. Go to Palestine and give it to her personally."

"Clara and I have special Jewish passports," Emil said ruefully. "If we leave the country, we can't come back."

"Exactly," said Tasci. "Get out of Germany and stay

out."

"You too?" Emil said. "First the National Socialists, then the Zionists, then Tannenbaum, then my daughter, and now you. Everyone wants me to leave Germany."

"Today, you bought a gold Star of David for your daughter to wear, but in the future, the government will force you to buy another Star of David for her, one made of yellow cloth, and you won't want her to wear that one," Tasci predicted.

Emil was puzzled. "What are you talking about?"

"The National Socialists will force the Jews to wear a yellow star as an easy way to identify and capture them."

"I've heard of no such law. True, there are anti-Jewish laws, but there is none forcing us to wear a yellow star."

"That law is coming, believe me."

"And even if that's true, what can I do about it?"

"Get out of the country," Tasci said. He pointed to a chair and gestured for Emil to sit down.

"Listen to me, Lieutenant Hirsch. I haven't told anyone, but I will tell you, from one war veteran to another. The National Socialists are planning to murder all Jews in Europe. They will kill over six million Jews."

"Six million?" Emil said in disbelief. "That's unreal. No massacre in history was that large."

Tasci looked serious. "I'm not talking about history. I'm talking about the future."

"Have you talked to Adolf Hitler?" Emil asked.

"No," Tasci admitted.

"Have you seen any plans to kill all the Jews of Europe?"

"No."

"Then how do you know what's in the future?" Emil

demanded.

"Because I've gone to the future," Tasci declared. "I travel through time."

Emil leaned back in his chair and stared at Tasci. If this was a joke, it was in poor taste. But if Tasci was serious, he was insane.

"You can travel through time?" Emil asked skeptically.

"And I can travel through space too," Tasci said.

Emil decided to humour the mad jeweller.

"This is very interesting. How do you travel in time and space?" he asked, pretending to believe Tasci.

"I worked on secret research for the Ottoman Army. We were competing against the Germans." Tasci grinned. "You could have beaten us, but you undervalued and underfunded your scientists, especially the Jewish ones like Doctor Einstein."

"You invented a *time machine*?"

"Technically, it's a space-time portal creation system. It creates a portal in space-time at a programmed time and location. A person walks into the portal and appears at another time and place. To retrieve the person back to when and where he started, the system opens another portal and sends him back to his point of origin."

"So if you know that there will be a mass murder of Jews in the future, why don't you do something to prevent it?" Emil asked.

Tasci cast his eyes down, as if in shame. "I've tried to change the future by changing the past. By playing Allah, I wound up killing more people than I saved."

"What do you mean?"

"In 1969, an American meteorologist named Edward Lorenz will describe a theory called 'the butterfly effect,' which says that a small change in a complex system can create unpredictable large effects elsewhere. But in 1917, we had not completely thought out the effects of time travel, and we were rushing to prevent a war."

"The Great War?"

"No, originally, there was no Great War until I changed history," Tasci said with a sigh. "The unaltered timeline—if one can call any timeline unaltered—had the Archduke Franz Ferdinand of Austria visiting Turkey in 1914. The Archduke, you'll remember, wanted to give greater autonomy to the Austro-Hungarian Empire's ethnic groups, naively thinking they would appreciate his support. During his visit to Turkey, he told Turkish newspapers about his views. He unwittingly inspired the Ottoman Empire's own ethnic groups to demand greater autonomy. When the Ottoman Government violently ended their protests, a rebellion broke out across the empire. Two thousand people died before the rebellion ended.

"The Ottoman Army developed time travel in 1917, just as the rebellion ended. I volunteered to go back in time and space four years, to Vienna in 1913. Posing as an Ottoman diplomat, I visited Emperor Franz Josef and told him that Greek terrorists were in Istanbul and that it was unsafe for the Archduke to visit Turkey. The Emperor agreed, and instead of going to Istanbul, Archduke Franz Ferdinand went to open a new museum in Sarajevo.

"You know what happened next. Serbian assassins killed the Archduke, the Great War started, millions of people died, and both the German and Ottoman empires collapsed."

Emil was speechless. Tasci's story was so far-fetched, so unreal, that it must be a joke. But Tasci sounded sincere. Maybe the jeweller truly believed his story because he suffered from a mental illness. But if this were so, how had he hidden his insanity for so long?

Emil asked, "*Herr* Tasci, tell me more about the upcoming murder of the Jews."

"It will occur all over Europe," Tasci warned. "Those who are not killed immediately will be forced into slave labour and starved to death. The details will be too horrible to describe."

"I don't believe it," Emil argued. "This is Germany in the twentieth century. This is a civilized country and a civilized time."

"Believe me, it will happen. The National Socialists are not civilized."

"You've stayed silent about this for years. Why are you telling me now?"

"Because you're still here, and you're not thinking of leaving. You're running out of time," he said without intentional irony.

"If all you tell me is true, then you must do something to prevent the killing of the Jews," Emil urged. "It's your moral duty."

"I would consider it, if only I could be certain of the outcome," Tasci said. "But the butterfly effect is against me. Look at the mess I made of Europe. If I kill Hitler before he took power, would I create a larger problem? Would I wind up causing the deaths of millions more than would have died otherwise? I don't know."

Emil had heard enough. He wanted proof of time travel.

"Where's your space-time portal creation system?" he asked.

"It's in a room in the back," replied Tasci.

"The room we were in a moment ago?"

"No, another room in the back."

"May I see the time machine?"

"No. It has been unstable. Being near it is potentially dangerous."

Emil concluded that Tasci was insane.

"Thank you for your advice," Emil said as he stood up. "It's getting late, so I should go home to my wife now."

"Will you go to Palestine and give the necklace to your daughter?" Tasci asked.

"Yes, I'll do that," Emil lied.

"Good," Tasci said, smiling. "I'll visit you in Jerusalem someday."

"Yes, next year in Jerusalem!" Emil agreed as he left the shop.

*

April 26, 1937:

A day after visiting Tasci, Emil talked to Otto about the jeweller. The former physics professor listened quietly until Emil finished.

"Do you think Tasci is insane?" Emil asked.

"I don't know," said Otto. "I do know that he was researching the theories of time and space."

"How can someone travel through time and space?" Emil asked.

"We travel through space frequently. You travel through space just by walking across the room. We're also travelling through time; we're one hour further into the future than we were sixty minutes ago. There's nothing inherently difficult about travelling through time and space. The great challenge is to go between points of time and space at rates and directions different from what other people are experiencing. For example, everyone goes forward in time at the same rate, but it's practically impossible to go forward faster than everyone else or to go backwards in time."

Otto picked up a piece of paper and wrote an "A" at one end and a "B" at the other end.

"Let's imagine time and space as being this sheet of paper," he continued. "One could walk from point A to point B in a given length of time over this plane. But if we could bend space-time..."

Otto bent the paper so that the letters touched each other.

"...then we could go from point A to point B faster than anyone else. And we make A and B occupy the same point in time-space, we can go back and forth between their two times."

"If you say so," Emil said, shrugging. "This is just a theory using a piece of paper as an analogy. Aside from letting time pass naturally, it's not practically possible to travel through time, is it?"

"I don't think so, but who knows what Tasci did? Turkey must have exiled him for a reason," said Otto. "By the way, what a coincidence; before you came here, I was going to visit him."

"Oh? Why?"

"I'm going to buy an Ottoman War Medal. He told me to come and pick it up today."

Many German officers did not wear their military-issue medals, which were often poorly made. Instead, they bought and wore attractive copies made by jewellers.

"May I come with you?" Emil asked. "Now that he's talking, he might say more."

"Certainly, come along," Otto said as he got his coat and hat. "We don't have much time before he closes."

As they walked out the house, Otto looked at the lapel pin on Emil's coat. "Which organization is that?"

"*Reichsbund Jüdischer Frontsoldaten*," Emil replied proudly. The pin was a white shield with the black initials "RJF".

"Oh, good. I had to ask because 'RJF' also stands for *Reichsjugendführung*," said Otto, referring to the national leadership staff of the Hitler Youth. "Be careful. They might not like you wearing a badge with their initials."

"The Reich Association of Jewish Frontline Soldiers was founded first, long before the Hitler Youth," Emil said. "We have an older claim to the initials."

The sky was dark when they arrived at Tasci's shop. The "CLOSED" sign was on the door.

Otto looked at his watch. "He still has another twenty minutes before closing time."

"There's light in there," Emil observed, pointing at a crack in the curtain. "He might still be in there."

Otto turned the doorknob. "It's unlocked."

They entered the shop and stared in shock at the sight.

A silver metal figure stood in front of the counter, and a girl lay unconscious on the floor.

The metal figure reminded Emil of a robot he had seen in the Fritz Lang film *Metropolis*. It was over two meters tall, shaped like a human with a head, torso, legs, arms, and hands. But unlike the *Metropolis* robot, this one did not resemble a woman. Instead, it had a male shape. And whereas the *Metropolis* robot had a face with eyes, nose, and mouth, this robot had only a black, rectangular lens where the eyes would be. The inhuman face stared at Emil and Otto.

Emil marvelled at how seamless the robot was, without a single rivet, as if it were made from a single sheet of metal moulded to human form.

A blue Star of David was painted on its chest. Who had built this monster? Certainly not the National Socialists.

The girl wore an olive green blouse, matching short skirt and beret, and black boots. Her clothes looked like an army uniform, but not like any that Emil had seen before. From which country was she?

A shoulder bag lay near her. It too was olive green, with the words "MELOG PROJECT" on it. Emil didn't know what "MELOG" was, but he suspected "PROJECT" meant *projekt* in English.

"What is it?" Otto asked, looking at the robot.

"I was going to ask you the same question," said Emil. "You're the scientist. Have you ever seen anything like this?"

"Never."

"Do you think it's dangerous?"

"I don't know."

The girl moaned softly and moved her arms and legs.

"She's alive," said Otto. They approached her cautiously, glancing at the robot.

She sat up, grimaced, took off her beret, and rubbed her head as if she had hit it on the floor.

She was in her twenties, looked pretty, and had a slim body. Her brown hair was tied into a ponytail. Her blouse had shoulder straps with unknown rank insignia, and she wore a silver badge showing a robot and words in Hebrew.

The Hebrew words surprised Emil. No German military unit had Hebrew words on its badges. Was she from one of the Jewish sports clubs? Maybe she was, but they didn't have uniforms like hers.

The girl said something in a foreign language.

"What did you say?" Otto asked.

Emil was astounded. "It sounds like Hebrew, but I don't know that language well."

He knelt beside the girl and asked in German, "Miss, are you feeling well?"

"German," she murmured. "Do you speak German?"

"Yes."

"I can speak German too. I took it as an elective in university." Her accent was foreign, possibly American. She looked around anxiously. "Where am I?"

"In Tasci's jewellery shop."

"Doctor Tasci! Where is he?"

"I don't know," Emil replied.

Otto pointed at the robot. "Miss, do you know what that thing is?"

"It's—it's just a machine," she replied.

"Is it safe to approach?"

"Yes, for now."

Otto walked past the robot, saying, "I'll check if Tasci is in the back."

The girl asked, "What year is this?"

"It's 1937. What else would it be?" Emil thought it a

strange question.

"And where am I? The city and country, I mean."

"Kleinheimat, Bavaria, Germany." How could she not know where she was?

The girl scowled. "Damn it, Nazi Germany! I have to go!"

She grabbed the shoulder bag and stood up quickly. Emil got up and followed her, but she stumbled, turned, and fell into Emil's arms.

"Miss, what's wrong?" Emil asked.

The girl groaned. "I feel so dizzy."

She grabbed Emil's coat and stared at his lapel pin. "RJF. Is that *Reichsbund Jüdischer Frontsoldaten* or *Reichsjugendführung*?" she asked warily.

"Reich Association of Jewish Frontline Soldiers," Emil replied. Since the girl wore a badge with Hebrew words, he did not fear telling her the truth.

The girl smiled weakly. "I'm Jewish too. Will you hide me? Only until I feel well enough to travel."

"Uh, yes," Emil said. Although he knew nothing about the girl, Jews had to help each other in these times.

The robot, however, looked menacing.

"Thank you," the girl said.

"What's your name?" Emil asked.

"Aviva," the girl replied. "And you?"

"Emil."

Aviva felt her neck, as if looking for something. "Oh, damn, where's that necklace? I must have been carrying it in my hand. Where the Hell is it?"

She glanced at the floor. "Do you see a necklace with a gold Star of David?"

Emil spotted the gold star. It was like the one that he

had bought for Helena. He remembered that Tasci had made two stars from the same mould.

After seating Aviva in a chair, he picked up the necklace and examined it. Unlike Helena's birthday present, it had a black button on its back.

"No! Don't touch it!" Aviva shouted. Then, in a softer voice, she said, "Please, give it back to me."

Emil gave the necklace to Aviva, who put it around her neck.

Otto returned and said, "I can't find him."

"He didn't come with me," Aviva said.

"She's not feeling well," Emil said. "Let's take to her to my house, and we'll call Doctor Berl."

Emil and Otto helped Aviva out of the chair and walked her to the door. They paused and looked back at the robot.

"What about that thing?" Emil asked.

Aviva spoke to the robot in Hebrew. It walked towards them. Emil thought the automaton would make loud, mechanical sounds and stomp on the floor, but it moved silently.

"Is it coming with us?" said Otto. "Won't people see it?"

Aviva spoke in Hebrew again. The robot turned transparent.

She grinned. "Now they won't."

The robot looked like glass. Emil could see through it, but he could tell something was there.

Emil, Otto, and Aviva went into the dark streets, with the metal ghost following them.

*

Aviva was the same size as Helena, so Clara helped her take off her uniform and change into one of Helena's nightgowns. Then they put her in Helena's bed and called Doctor Berl. The doctor rushed from his home and examined the girl.

"Well, fortunately, you're showing no symptoms of serious injury," Berl said. "You have a mild concussion at worst, but we need more time to tell for sure. Don't exert yourself for a day and get some rest."

"Yes, doctor," Aviva said.

Berl smiled. "I didn't know *Herr* Hirsch had such a lovely niece."

"She's visiting us for the spring," Emil lied, trying to explain Aviva's sudden appearance in town.

Berl looked back at Aviva. "Are you from Czechoslovakia or Hungary or Poland? Your accent is different from ours."

"Uh, I'm from Munich," she said. Emil was sure that too was a lie.

"Munich?" Berl said. "The mayor there has banned Jewish doctors from treating non-Jewish patients. I hope that doesn't happen here in Kleinheimat. I've lost too many patients already."

Otto shook his head. "That's appalling. Doctor Berl, I've been your patient for years, and I'm not going to leave you for another doctor."

Berl smiled weakly. "Thank you, Doctor Schmidt. I wish all non-Jewish patients were like you."

After saying good night, Berl left the house. The robot silently climbed up the stairs from the basement. No longer transparent, it looked like a silver giant again.

"My God, that thing is creepy," Clara remarked. "What

is it?"

"Only our guest knows," said Emil. "She controls it."

The robot walked across the living room and stood at the front door.

"What's it doing?" Clara wondered.

"Aviva told it to guard the house after Berl leaves," Emil said.

He turned to Otto. "When you were in the back of Tasci's shop, did you see a time machine?"

"I have no idea what one would look like, but I didn't see anything odd. Just jeweller's supplies and tools," said Otto.

"Then I wonder how she and the robot got here without anyone noticing. Let's ask her."

They went back upstairs to Helena's bedroom, but Aviva had fallen asleep.

"We'll have to wait until the morning," said Emil.

"I want to talk to her too," Otto said. "May I join you for breakfast tomorrow?"

Clara shrugged. "Why not? The mystery girl and her robot are coming too. At least you'll be a normal guest."

*

At breakfast, Aviva devoured the bread rolls and beef sausages.

"I'm glad to see that you've got an appetite," Clara observed.

"Thank you for this wonderful food," said Aviva. "I'm sorry for eating like a pig. I haven't had a good meal for a while. You're too kind."

Emil put down the newspaper *Kleinheimat Zeitung*.

The front page had a photograph of Joachim Rumeder in his *Ortsgruppenleiter* uniform. He was an obese man, even larger than Hermann Göring.

The article read:

"For purposes of population control and monitoring, the Party prefers that Jews be concentrated in large cities, not spread among small towns... Julius Streicher, the Gauleiter *of Franconia, has ordered Rumeder to encourage Jews to leave the town. Rumeder has called all local SA Stormtroopers to attend a planning meeting at Schneider's Tavern..."*

Of course, Rumeder would call a meeting at a tavern. The lazy fool knew only how to drink and sleep. He got his Party position through family connections. The fat slob couldn't organize the local Brownshirts to do anything.

The next article was more disturbing:

"While visiting Munich, Mayor Karl Wettig hosted a reception in honour of Party officials who had received the Blood Order. Many important people attended this glittering event. Gauleiter Streicher thanked Wettig for his hospitality..."

Unlike Rumeder, Wettig knew how to work to get what he wanted. The mayor was entertaining Julius Streicher, a powerful National Socialist and rabid anti-Semite. Wettig had banned Jews from the Veterans Hall and had hammered their names off the war memorial. What would he do next to obtain favours from the Party?

Emil stood up and looked into the living room.

"The robot's still standing there," he observed.

"As I had ordered it to do," said Aviva. She pointed at the photo of Rumeder. "You need protection from guys like him."

Emil sat down, poured himself some coffee, and asked, "Aviva, what's your last name?"

"Do you really need to know?"

"Of course. I want to know who my guests are."

"Loew."

"That's a German Jewish name, isn't it?"

Aviva nodded.

Otto, who had been quiet so far, spoke up. "Miss Loew, what do you know of Mehmet Tasci?"

"I don't know who he is."

"Yet you recognized his name yesterday."

Aviva said nothing.

Emil asked, "Are you in the army?"

Aviva said nothing.

"I don't recognize your uniform. It looks military. It's got a patch and a badge with Hebrew words." Emil paused for a moment. "Are you in the Jewish Legion of the British Army?"

Aviva said nothing but took another bread roll.

Emil grunted, grabbed the breadbasket, and put it on the kitchen counter. Aviva looked worried.

"You can have more bread after you talk to us," Emil declared.

"I can't tell you much about myself," said Aviva, "but I can say this. You've been very nice to me, calling a doctor and giving me food and shelter, hiding me from the Nazis. I don't want anything to happen to you, so take my advice."

"What are you advising?" asked Clara.

"Leave the country now," Aviva urged.

"Everyone's telling me to leave," Emil said. "Why?"

"If you don't go, Hitler will kill you."

Emil remembered the same warning from Tasci. "How do you know?"

"I just know!"

"Are you a time traveller, like Doctor Tasci?" Otto asked.

Aviva hesitated before answering, "Yes."

"Another one," Emil muttered. "Everyone is a time traveller. Has the whole world gone mad?"

"She might be telling the truth," Otto said. "Look at her robot. That's not modern technology. That's *future* technology."

"I agree it's advanced, but that doesn't prove it's from the future." Emil faced Aviva and asked, "Who made your robot?"

Aviva said nothing.

"Say something!" Emil shouted.

"Emil, be more hospitable to our guest," Clara pleaded. She returned the breadbasket back to the table.

"Aviva, dear, please tell us about yourself," Clara urged. "You can imagine how you and your robot have bewildered us. We've not seen anyone like you before, so we don't know what to think. We need to know everything before we can decide whether to stay or leave."

"Okay, I'll talk if that will make you leave Germany," Aviva agreed. "My name is Aviva Loew, and I'm a lieutenant in the Israeli Defence Forces Robotics Corps..."

*

Aviva talked about the future in the past tense. For her, the next hundred and thirty years were history.

In 1939, Hitler's Germany started World War II, which was much more destructive than the Great War. In Europe, sixty million people died in six years.

Not only did Hitler fight a war, he also exterminated racial groups: Jews, Gypsies, and Slavs. The Jews lost the most people, six million dead. Only ten percent of German Jews lived to see the war end in 1945.

But in 1948, the Jews got their own country in Palestine. The Zionist dream came true. After over two thousand years, an independent Israel was reborn.

But Israel's existence was shaky. Surrounded and outnumbered by Arab enemies, it was always fighting for its survival. In the 1967 war, only nineteen years after its rebirth, Israel fell into the beginning of its end. The Arabs captured the city of Eilat in southern Israel. Without Eilat, Israeli ships could not sail through the Straits of Tiran, a vital sea route. Trade between Israel and other countries suffered, and the Israeli economy never recovered.

The impoverished state could not defend itself forever. Over the next hundred years, the Arabs used their foothold in the south to gradually conquer the rest of Israel. Despite foreign aid, Israel was reduced to a strip along the Mediterranean, north of Tel Aviv, by 2067.

To help Israel, the United States gave combat robots to the Israel Defence Forces. These included a tactical super-weapon with the English name "Military Expedition Land Offensive Giant" or "MELOG."

Aviva Loew could have lived a comfortable life in America. She had just graduated with a degree in architecture from New York University and had a job offer at a local firm. But instead, she went to Israel and joined the IDF Robotics Corps. Her first assignment: the MELOG Project.

MELOG robots were expensive, so Israel got only five of them, but they were enough to defeat an attack on Tel Aviv. But then the Arabs sent in their own super-robots, and the MELOGs could only fight them to a stalemate.

Then a time traveller, Mehmet Tasci, arrived by accident due to a power surge. He popped out of the air in front of a soldier in Tel Aviv in 2067...

*

"Mehmet Tasci said he was trying to prevent World War I, but he kept creating more problems as he tried to fix other ones," Clara continued.

"At first, we thought he was an Arab spy and arrested him. However, he looked so funny in a frock coat, a bow tie, and a fez. He also wore an Ottoman war medal. Not the most inconspicuous disguise for a spy.

"We questioned him for weeks, and he said that he had accidentally caused the 1929 Stock Market Crash and the abdication of King Edward VIII of Britain. We decided he wasn't a spy, but rather, a mentally ill person. But we couldn't explain what the witnesses said, that he had popped out of thin air.

"We finally believed his time travel story when we let him have his strange device, and he sent an intelligence officer one week into the future and back.

"This demonstration impressed the IDF, so we created a plan. We would send MELOG robots back to 1967 to defeat the Arabs and keep the south under Israeli control.

"Some scientists argued against the plan. They said that the butterfly effect would cause unpredictable changes in the past and in the future. But our present was desperate. We literally had our backs against the sea.

"Tasci agreed to help us. He too was worried of the butterfly effect, but he wanted to help the descendants of people he knew in the twentieth century. He thought the best way to do that was to prevent Israel's defeat in 1967.

"However, the space-time portal creation system had occasional power surges that could send time travellers to the wrong time and place. Nobody wanted to risk that accident with the robots. We gave him a lab to work out the problem.

"For testing purposes, he programmed the system to send objects to certain times and places. One of the space–time coordinates was Kleinheimat in 1937. He had lived here and hoped to revisit it.

"One day, I brought a MELOG to his lab so we could test whether the robot could go unaffected through a portal. A sudden power surge hit the system, a portal opened, and the MELOG and I got thrown to one of the programmed coordinates. That was Kleinheimat in 1937."

Aviva took another bread roll and resumed eating. Emil, Clara, and Otto stared at her in stunned silence.

Finally, Otto said, "I didn't see anything out of the ordinary in Tasci's shop. What does a time machine look like?"

"It's not like in the movies. It's not a chair, it's not a car, and it's not a telephone booth," said Aviva.

Emil didn't know why anyone would think that a time

machine would look like a chair, car, or telephone booth.

"It's a device that creates a space-time portal, and you walk into the portal," Aviva said. "It's not here and now. It's in Israel in 2067."

"If you don't have it, how will you get back home?" Clara asked.

Aviva held up her Star of David pendant. "Doctor Tasci created this emergency recall trigger. If I press this button, a portal will appear and send me back to the time and place from which I came."

"That necklace is a time machine?" Emil said in disbelief.

"No, not exactly. It only works once and in one direction. It's not programmable like a time machine is."

"How did he fit such a powerful device into such a small necklace?" said Clara.

"Nanoelectronics and power systems from the twenty-third century," Aviva replied.

"This is the most remarkable invention of all time!" Otto exclaimed. "Miss Loew, as a physicist, I'm extremely interested in the time travel system. I wish to ask for a favour."

Aviva looked wary. "What is it?"

"May I travel to the future with you?" Otto asked. "Don't worry about me getting trapped in the twenty-first century. I'm sure Doctor Tasci can send me back here."

Aviva smiled but shook her head. "I'm flattered that you want to travel with me, but you can't come. Only the robot and I can go back. The necklace is programmed to retrieve only matter that came from a different time. Even if you hold onto me, you'll be left behind here."

"Oh, well, that's too bad," Otto said. He leaned over the table and grasped the Star of David. "What technology! It's programmed to home in on you. What if someone presses the button while you're not wearing the necklace? Will you still be sent home?"

"Yes, so don't play with it!" Aviva pulled the pendant away from Otto's hand. "If you press the button, it will send me back to 2067."

"Speaking about going home," said Emil, "you're well enough to travel now. You could have gone home already, but you haven't left. Why are you staying?"

"I'm not leaving until *you* leave," said Aviva. "If I can save even a few Jews, my stay here will be worthwhile."

"But don't you have to go home to 2067, pick up more robots, and go to 1967 to save Israel from defeat?"

Aviva grinned. "That's the beauty of time travel. I can leave here anytime and still arrive in 1967 on time."

"How long will you be staying here?"

"I don't know. I'll stay as long as it takes to convince you to leave. Go to Israel or Britain. The United States and Canada are good places too, but they're not letting a lot of Jews in. Do *not* go to France, Poland, or Russia."

"None of those places really appeals to me."

"Then I'm going to stay here and pester you until you leave."

"I hadn't planned for a house guest—"

"Oh, Emil, let's not be so hasty," Clara broke in. "I'm sure we could have her stay for a while. God knows our number of Jewish friends is decreasing. Even our daughter has left."

Otto suggested, "I could find her work at the Catholic school. As you know, Father Bernhardt doesn't mind hiring Jews. We'll continue the ruse that she's your niece from Munich."

"I wouldn't be a burden on you," Aviva promised.

Emil sighed. "Well, okay, but only for a few weeks."

Clara went around the table and hugged Aviva.

Emil looked at his guest. "I'm letting you stay because you're an army officer, like me."

Aviva smiled and saluted.

*

August 31, 1937:

Aviva was still living with the Hirsches four months after her arrival. Pretending to be a niece from Munich, she wore Helena's clothes and blended into the town's Jewish community. Father Bernhardt hired her to work as a cleaner, to Mayor Wettig's disapproval. Aviva explored Kleinheimat and learned about the town.

In contrast, the MELOG stayed in the Hirsches' basement. Each night, Aviva went downstairs and ran the robot's diagnostics program to ensure that it would work if she ordered it into action.

The MELOG wasn't the only electronic device that Aviva had brought. She carried a "pocket computer" in her shoulder bag. The small device performed various tasks, including making math calculations and recording images and sounds.

To amuse Emil, she used the pocket computer to project a three-dimensional image of his house in the air. Emil could see through the walls and into the interior. He was amazed by the detailed images of the rooms, the stairs, and the basement.

"Why would the IDF put an architect in the Robotics Corps? To make holograms of buildings," said Aviva. "Our spies got the plans of the Arab Joint Military Headquarters in Eilat. I used the drawings to create a holographic model of the building.

"I downloaded the hologram into a MELOG and programmed it to break into the building, go to the computer server room, and destroy the mainframe computer system. Since the MELOG knew exactly where to go, it moved quickly, and the Arabs didn't have the time to fight back."

Emil put his hand through the image of his house. "This hologram, as you call it, is amazing. I use cardboard to make architectural models. You can use light."

"You can't find toys like this in 1937. Now do you believe that I'm from the future?"

"I don't know. You're from America. Americans invent all sorts of things. Is your equipment from secret military research?"

"Still a non-believer? My, you're stubborn, but that'll make you a good Zionist." Aviva turned off the hologram. "Let's talk about Israel. Even if you don't believe I'm from the future, will you still consider going to Israel?"

Emil shrugged. "How long will that country last? You say that Israel will lose a war in 1967, and the Arabs will conquer most of it. Why go to a doomed country?"

"Because we Israelis are fighters," Aviva replied. "All is not lost. A part of Israel survives to fight in the twenty-first century, and we have the chance to restore our country. You have a much better chance of survival in Israel than you do here, where the *Shoah* is coming."

*

As Aviva got to know and trust her hosts better, she revealed more about her times. She liked talking to Otto, who corresponded with the most famous German Jewish scientist of all time.

"Einstein's general theory of relativity says that gravity warps space-time so that light bends around an object of very high mass, like a black hole," Otto said. "Your robot can't possibly be so massive, though. How does it become transparent?"

Clara shook her head. "No, it's got nothing to do with that. The MELOG is covered with millions of plasmonic transceivers. Each transceiver receives ambient light that is then retransmitted at another transceiver on the opposite side of the robot, hereby producing the effect of semi-invisibility.

"The plasmonic transceivers can't cope with all the different wavelengths of electromagnetic radiation yet, and they do not uniformly cover the robot's body at a uniform density, which is why the robot is only semi-transparent and not completely invisible. But the engineers are working on both the wavelength and transceiver density problems."

"The problems didn't stop you from sending the robot into battle," Otto said.

"No," said Aviva. "We needed all the help we could get."

*

September 1, 1937:

Rumeder and his Brownshirts finally joined Wettig's campaign against the Jews. They carried signs reading "BOYCOTT JEWISH SHOPS" in front of Hoffman's tailor shop. Rumeder pasted a poster on the door. It showed a man with a gigantic nose, scraggly beard and hair, and the words "THE ETERNAL JEW."

When Hoffman came out to protest, they shoved and hit him until he retreated inside. From across the street, Emil and Aviva watched in dismay as customers approached the shop and turned away.

"Hoffman is a veteran of the Great War," Emil said. "Treating him like that is disgusting."

Emil and Aviva continued on their way to Father Bernhardt's church, where they had work. Five hours later, when they left the church, the Brownshirts were still at Hoffman's shop. The golden pheasants did not stay much longer, though.

"We've spent enough time in front of this Jew's door. Come on, boys, let's go to Schneider's Tavern," Rumeder suggested.

The Brownshirts cheered and shook their fists at Hoffman's window. As they left, Rumeder shouted, "Don't think you've escaped, Jew Hoffman! We'll be back tonight to smash your windows!"

Aviva said softly, "I'll be back tonight too."

"I don't know what you're planning, but I don't like it," Emil whispered.

Aviva gave him a sneaky smile.

*

That night, Aviva ordered the MELOG to come up from

the basement. Emil stared warily at them as they walked to the door.

"Don't go out," he pleaded. "You'll draw attention to us."

Aviva looked back at him. "Don't worry. We won't leave any evidence behind."

"What do you mean?"

"There won't be anything left of the Brownshirts to bury."

"Don't kill them! You'll get us all arrested!"

"No, we won't. If the police show up, we'll liquidate them too."

"Just like my daughter, never listening to me," Emil muttered.

He followed Aviva and the MELOG out of the house. The robot turned transparent. They walked to Hoffman's tailor shop in the dark.

"We'll get into trouble," Emil said. "Let's go home."

"Oh, stop arguing," Aviva snapped. "People will hear us."

Emil turned as quiet as the MELOG.

Since all the shops and offices surrounding Hoffman's were closed for the evening, nobody else was in the area. They hid in an alley across the street from the tailor shop. Emil looked out. The Eternal Jew poster stared back at him.

"No sign of the Brownshirts," he said. "Perhaps they're not coming."

"No, they're coming," Aviva assured him. "They never miss an opportunity to break windows at night. They'll be breaking windows all over Germany in November next year. You have to leave before then."

As Aviva had predicted, the Brownshirts returned. Two men, both carrying sledgehammers, approached Hoffman's shop.

Aviva whispered commands in Hebrew to the MELOG. The robot strode silently towards the shop.

One of the Brownshirts faced the window and raised his sledgehammer. "Take this, Jew dog!" he yelled.

He did not notice the MELOG coming behind him. The robot shot a white ray out of its head. The ray burst into a flash of light as it hit the Brownshirt's back. The man screamed, dropped his sledgehammer, and collapsed to the ground. The MELOG continued shooting the white ray at him.

The MELOG became visible again. The silver metal giant hovered over the man. The Brownshirt, lying on his back, writhed and howled in agony as the white ray drilled into his body. Blinding light engulfed him.

Both the Brownshirt and his sledgehammer disappeared, and the MELOG turned off its ray.

The other Brownshirt raised his sledgehammer against the MELOG, but the robot shot him with its ray. Again, a blaze of white light engulfed the man, and he screamed and vanished.

Emil rushed across the street. He found no trace of the Brownshirts: no body parts, no blood, no scraps of clothing, and no sledgehammers.

The MELOG turned transparent again when Aviva joined them. Emil pointed at the spot where the Brownshirts had stood.

"They've vanished, turned into thin air," he remarked.

"A successful field test," Aviva declared. "The disintegrator ray works.

"However, the plasmonic transceivers are faulty. The MELOG became visible when light from the disintegrator reflected off the Brownshirts, and the transceivers became saturated. An invisibility shield is useless if you become visible while using it. We need to fix it before 1967."

"Let's talk about the weapons testing later," Emil urged. "We should get out of here."

They went home with the MELOG. Aviva sent the robot down into the basement. Then she yawned and stretched.

"It's been a long day. I'm so tired, but we had a successful mission," she said. "If you don't mind, I'm going to take a shower now. I need to relax."

"Sure, go ahead," Emil replied. Aviva showered at night, a habit she developed when her barracks needed a whole day to heat its water tank.

Moments later, Emil heard the water spraying in the shower. Aviva had just killed two people with a super-robot, and now she was showering as if nothing had happened.

*

Three days later, the *Kleinheimat Zeitung* published the news:

SA Stormtroopers Missing

SA Stormtroopers Hans Hentschel and Johann Berghof have not been seen since September 1st. Police have found no trace of them or any evidence of foul play, not even at

*the Jewish tailor shop where they had been protesting.
Ortsgruppenleiter Joachim Rumeder does not know where
the men may have gone. They were last seen at Schneider's
Tavern...*

The police arrested and questioned Hoffman, but he had an alibi. That evening, he had been at Father Bernhardt's office to meet officials of Haavara Ltd. The priest had let visiting Haavara officials rent space in his church basement because nobody else in town would.

The Zionist Federation of Germany and the German Government signed the Haavara Agreement in 1933. Under its terms, Jews could immigrate to Palestine if they gave up their possessions before leaving. However, they could later obtain their assets by exchanging them for German goods to be exported to Palestine.

The new police chief thought all Jews were liars, so he kept Hoffman despite his alibi. But Father Bernhardt demanded that they release him.

"You have no proof that he did anything against the two stormtroopers," the priest argued. "Also, this man was making a new stole for me. I want to wear it for this Sunday's Mass."

"But Father, who else can we arrest?" the police chief argued.

"Why not the two men themselves?" Bernhardt suggested. "They were drunkards who never came to Mass or confession. Unrepentant sinners, though I pray for them. They're probably passed out drunk somewhere in the countryside."

The police released Hoffman, who promptly delivered the new stole to Father Bernhardt. Two days after the

Mass, Hoffman and the Haavara officials left town.

A month later, Emil received a letter from Hoffman in Tel Aviv:

Dear Emil,

I am sorry to have left our beloved Fatherland, for which we fought and bled in the Great War, but as you know, the situation for Jews is bad. After much deliberation, I decided to go to Palestine, at least while the National Socialists are in power. May sacred Germany become free again!

I set up a tailor shop here. Your daughter and Corporal Tannenbaum visited me yesterday. It was so nice to see people from our town...

I did not take my phonograph records with me because of limited luggage space. How I miss my records. The record shop here has only RCA Victor records, but I prefer German ones. Could you please send me the Deutsche Grammophon recording of George Frideric Handel's Keyboard Suite in D Minor? I love its fourth movement, the Sarabande.

Sincerely,
Artillery Sgt. Ernest Hoffman

*

October 17, 1937:
Emil and Clara listened to the news on the radio. Pro-German riots had broken out in Sudetenland, Czechoslovakia.

"Bolshevik-inspired Czech police are slaughtering peaceful Sudeten Germans," said the announcer. *"The* Führer *demands that Czechoslovakia allow Sudetenland to reunify with the German Fatherland..."*

After the news ended, the radio station played music by Beethoven. Emil sat back and listened. The radio was one of the few remaining ways that Jews could enjoy the great composers. Many concerts banned Jews from attending. On May 14, the government had forbidden German Jews from playing music by Beethoven and Mozart at Jewish cultural concerts.

"What do you think?" Clara asked.

"I have mixed feelings," said Emil. "I agree that German territory should be reunited, but I don't want it under the National Socialists."

"Elections are abolished. How can we remove the National Socialists from power?"

"I don't know," Emil said as he listened to Beethoven's Symphony No. 7 in A Major, op. 92.

Aviva came into the living room. She looked willowy in a light blue, short-sleeved dress with a high bodice and flared skirt. Helena had called it her "swing dress," named after the American dance music that the National Socialists despised. A silver barrette decorated her hair.

"You look beautiful," Clara remarked. "Where are you going?"

"I'm going to the church," said Aviva. "I got a waitress job today. Father Bernhardt asked me to serve tea and crumpets at a meeting with the Archbishop of Munich today."

"Wonderful. I'm glad that Bernhardt is meeting him," Emil remarked.

The Archbishop, Michael von Faulhaber, had written the only Papal Encyclical in German, *Mit Brennender Sorge*, "With Burning Anxiety," a criticism of National Socialism and racism. It condemned the exaltation of race and state above God, who has "issued commandments whose value is independent of time and space." Secret couriers had delivered it to all parish priests in Germany, who read it aloud at Mass on Palm Sunday. It infuriated Hitler.

"It'll be nice to meet the Archbishop," said Aviva. "I'll also earn a few reichsmarks."

Clara nodded. "Thank you. We appreciate your support. It's so hard for Jews to earn a living now."

"Anything I can do to help you."

"Take care, dear."

Emil stood up, went to Aviva, and glanced at her Star of David pendant.

"I know you're proud to be Jewish and Zionist, but I don't think it's a good idea to wear that necklace," Emil advised.

"Oh? I've worn it before. I don't think Father Bernhardt and Archbishop Faulhaber will mind."

"They won't mind, but Wettig and the Brownshirts are out there."

Aviva sighed. "Okay, if it makes you happy." She took off the necklace and put it in her purse. "I still need to keep it with me. It's my emergency recall back to the twenty-first century."

"Yes, the year 2067," said Emil. "When will you go back there?"

"I won't leave until you leave," said Aviva. She kissed him on the cheek and left the house.

Clara waited until Aviva was gone before speaking. "Do you believe her when she says that six million people will die in a pogrom?"

"I don't know," said Emil. "She seems sincere, but it's

hard to believe. This is Germany in the twentieth century. This is a civilized country and a civilized time."

"You've said that before, but how true is it, when each day, they take more rights away from us?"

"We've suffered prejudice before and always bounced back. Jews are part of the economy. When the economy suffers, the people will realize that they need us as much as we need them."

"But if no pogrom will occur, why would Aviva lie to us?" asked Clara.

Emil shrugged. "She's a Zionist. Maybe this is her way of encouraging us to go to Palestine."

"Maybe."

Beethoven's music continued playing on the radio.

*

October 18, 1937:

Aviva and Emil went to the farmers' market. Though Mayor Wettig had banned Jews from selling at the market, he allowed them to buy there as long as they paid their money to "Aryans."

As Emil bought some potatoes, he heard shouting. He saw *Ortsgruppenleiter* Rumeder and his SA stormtroopers pushing Doctor Berl. The doctor carried a chain of sausages.

"What have we here?" Rumeder said as he grabbed the sausages from Berl. "Aryan families starve because Jewish bankers have stolen their money, but a Jewish doctor stuffs his fat stomach with sausages. Is that fair?"

Rumeder was hardly starving. His uniform bulged more than Hermann Göring's.

"Please, I don't want trouble," Berl pleaded. "Let me have my sausages, and I'll go away."

Rumeder waved the sausages in front of Berl's face. "Jew, take your sausages back."

Berl raised his hand to take the sausages, but Rumeder whipped them across the doctor's face. The Brownshirts laughed.

Aviva moved forward, but Emil stopped her. "There are five of them and only three of us," he whispered.

Aviva nodded silently and grimaced.

Rumeder chanted, "*Hepp, hepp*, Jew! *Hepp, hepp*, Jew!"

Berl tried to grab his sausages, but the Brownshirts punched him repeatedly.

Finally, Berl muttered, "Just let me go."

Rumeder nodded, and the Brownshirts shoved Berl away. The doctor ran to Emil and Aviva.

Rumeder shouted, "Leave town, doctor! We're going to destroy your office tonight!"

"Yeah, don't go to work tomorrow!" a Brownshirt said.

Emil, Aviva, and Berl watched grim-faced as Rumeder swaggered past them. Then he turned to his men.

"Gentlemen, let's go to Schneider's Tavern," he said.

His men cheered and marched out of the market. The townspeople watched the small parade of brown uniforms.

The local SA had become more visible and violent recently. Rumeder, the lazy drunkard, must have realized Wettig was competing with him for the position of *Ortsgruppenleiter*.

Berl shook nervously. "That was no idle threat. He'll ransack my office."

Neither Emil nor Aviva said anything. What could they

say?

"Doctor, please take these," Emil said, breaking the silence. He gave some potatoes to Berl.

"No, you keep them," Berl said.

"I insist."

"How can you afford to give food away?"

"Father Bernhardt hired me to design and build a small chapel for the Virgin Mary," said Emil. "If I'm lucky, he'll get me to build shrines for a hundred Catholic saints. I'll get by. Take the potatoes."

"Well, in that case, thank you," Berl said. "God bless you, *Herr* Hirsch. I have few patients left. If it weren't for people like you, I would starve."

Emil nodded silently.

"We'll get through these troubled times, just like we did during the Great War, I'm sure," Berl said. His words were optimistic, but he sounded uncertain.

Berl raised his hat to Emil and Aviva. They watched him walk away.

"Doctor Berl treated soldiers in the trenches, and now the Brownshirts will vandalize his office," Emil said with disgust.

"The MELOG will protect the doctor," Aviva promised.

*

Aviva and Emil went to the Michel Building, where Doctor Berl had his office. The street was bright with lamps, so this time, Aviva did not want to hide the MELOG in an alley. She opted to send the MELOG inside Doctor Berl's office after the building's workers had gone home for the evening. If the local Brownshirts followed a pattern, they would arrive in the late evening, when the area was deserted. The MELOG would wait for them in darkness and kill them when they entered the office.

This time, Aviva would not accompany the MELOG and give it orders during the attack. Instead, she would program it to go directly to the killing zone, like in the attack on the Arab Joint Military Headquarters.

"You designed and built the Michel Building, didn't you?" Aviva asked.

"I did," Emil replied.

"Show me all the floor plans and working drawings for it. I need to build a holographic model of it."

"You're not seriously going through with this plan, are you?"

"Of course, I'm serious."

"What if you get caught?"

"Don't worry about getting caught. The MELOG works silently and leaves no evidence."

"But people will gossip about why another bunch of Brownshirts disappeared..."

They argued until Emil finally agreed to help Aviva.

"Okay, I'll help you only because I like Doctor Berl," Emil conceded, "but this is the last mission."

Emil gave Aviva the floor plans and other working drawings of the Michel Building. In less than an hour, she had created a hologram. Unlike the hologram of the house, this one lacked details of decor and colour, but otherwise, Emil thought it was an accurate model of the Michel Building.

"Michel hired me for minor renovations until the anti-Jewish boycott began," said Emil. "This model includes my renovations, but I don't know if other people have built additional ones since then."

"I'll take that risk," said Aviva. "If the MELOG runs into something that doesn't match the hologram, it'll stop briefly while it re-orients itself. We'll lose time, and it might destroy more property and people than planned, but it'll do its job."

Emil was shocked by how casually the young woman talked about killing people. However, he remembered that he and his generation of men had done the same during the Great War.

Aviva downloaded the hologram to the MELOG. Then they waited for nightfall before leaving the house.

As before, Emil accompanied Aviva and the MELOG. Although he was worried, he cooperated willingly this time. He had felt some grim satisfaction when the MELOG killed the two Brownshirts at Hoffman's tailor shop.

*

They arrived at the Michel Building. All its windows were dark. Emil was relieved; nobody was in there.

The MELOG shot its disintegrator ray at the front doors and melted their locks. The robot swung the doors open and silently entered the building. If all went as planned, the MELOG would climb the staircase to the fifth floor and go into Doctor Berl's office.

Emil and Aviva hid behind a newspaper kiosk across the street. An hour later, the Brownshirts arrived, singing "The Horst Wessel Song".

They sang out of unison. Someone was off-key. How much beer had they drunk in Schneider's Tavern? As a veteran army officer, Emil felt contempt for Rumeder's lack of discipline.

Emil counted five men. All the golden pheasants that had harassed Berl, including *Ortsgruppenleiter* Rumeder, were coming.

The Brownshirts entered the Michel Building, oblivious to the damaged lock on the front doors. Emil waited impatiently.

He didn't have to wait long. Flashes of light appeared in a window on the fifth floor. Next, the window glowed with white light for half a minute, followed by more flashes. Then the window went black again.

Several minutes later, the MELOG left through the front door and stood still. The robot shone like silver beside a streetlamp.

Aviva whispered commands in Hebrew to her pocket computer. The MELOG turned transparent again.

"Mission accomplished," Aviva said. "Let's get the MELOG and go home."

They ran across the street. Aviva spoke more orders, and the robot followed them through the empty streets.

When they got home, Aviva took a shower, as she did every night.

In the morning, Emil visited Doctor Berl. The doctor said that someone had broken the lock of his office, but nothing else was damaged or stolen.

*

The article in the *Kleinheimat Zeitung* read:

Ortsgruppenleiter *Disappeared Five Days Ago*

Ortsgruppenleiter Joachim Rumeder and four members of the local SA chapter have not been seen for five days. They were last seen at Schneider's Tavern, where they spent several hours celebrating the inevitable reunion of Sudetenland with Germany.
Mayor Karl Wettig said, "It's not unusual for Joachim to go missing for long periods, is it?"
Wettig has advised the police that foul play is unlikely and that further investigation is unnecessary since Rumeder and his men will probably return home.
When asked about Rumeder's absence, Gauleiter *Julius Streicher relieved Rumeder of his command in absentia.*
The Gauleiter *will appoint a new* Ortsgruppenleiter *with orders to recruit more Party and SA members in Kleinheimat...*

"Hah, hah, we got the *Ortsgruppenleiter* too!" Aviva gloated as she put the newspaper down.

"But who will be the next *Ortsgruppenleiter*?" said Emil. "Rumeder was lazy and incompetent. We might not be so lucky with his replacement."

"It doesn't matter. One dead Nazi, ten dead Nazis; we'll just kill them all as they come here."

"Aviva, your robot has killed seven people. You've changed your history, and thus, the future. Do you think it's safe to keep changing history?"

"But perhaps the unaltered timeline actually has me coming to this time and carrying out my operations."

"Are you sure of that? Who can be certain which timeline is the unaltered or altered history? Are you sure that you aren't making the future worse?"

"I don't know, but this is what I do know," said Aviva. "When I joined the army, I took an oath to protect Israel and its people. You and your wife count as my people. It's my duty to protect you, whatever happens."

*

November 1, 1937:

At the farmers' market, Emil heard that Wettig had killed Rumeder and his closest Brownshirts. Nobody thought anything unusual about the rumours. In power struggles between National Socialists, they destroyed their own kind, as Hitler did to Röhm in 1934.

Emil liked the rumours. Although false, they deflected attention away from Jews as suspects in Rumeder's disappearance.

But when he read the news in the *Kleinheimat Zeitung*, he wondered if killing Rumeder had been a good idea.

Wettig to Lead NSDAP and SA in Kleinheimat

Gauleiter *Julius Streicher has appointed Karl Wettig, our Mayor, to be both* Ortsgruppenleiter *and commander of the SA in Kleinheimat. Like his predecessor Joachim Rumeder, Wettig will perform both duties but will also retain his duties as Mayor.*

"By having Herr *Wettig act as Mayor,* Ortsgruppenleiter, *and commander of the SA, we will consolidate all local political power in one person. All Germany should be governed this way," said Streicher.*

Gauleiter *Streicher and the* Führer, *Adolf Hitler, will appoint Wettig as* Ortsgruppenleiter *in a ceremony at the*

Veterans Hall on November 7.
Wettig's appointment ceremony will be the first time that
the Führer *will visit Kleinheimat. The* Führer *will be*
touring in Bavaria for the fourteenth anniversary of the
Beer Hall Putsch. After visiting Kleinheimat, he will give his
annual speech to the Old Fighters in Munich on November
8...

"This is terrible," Emil told Aviva. "You got rid of Rumeder, but now, Julius Streicher and Adolf Hitler will be coming to our town. They're the two worst National Socialists!"

Aviva's eyes lit up. "I never expected this to happen! Oh, we're so lucky!"

"We're in luck?"

"This is our chance to kill Hitler."

"Shush! Don't say that aloud!" Emil warned, even though Clara was the only other person in the house. Plotting to assassinate Hitler was punishable by death.

"I can save sixty million people," Aviva declared. "Oh, this is too good to be true! Hitler will be here, and so will I."

She stood up and paced around the kitchen. "Security will be heavy, probably lots of SS. If Hitler realizes that someone is attacking the Veterans Hall, he'll have time to escape. The MELOG can't waste time looking for Hitler. It must know exactly where to go and who to kill."

She opened a newspaper, tore out a photo of Hitler, and rushed into the basement. Emil followed her downstairs, where she was holding the photo to the rectangular lens on the MELOG's head.

"What are you doing?" Emil asked.

"Getting the MELOG's facial recognition system to remember Hitler's face," Aviva said. "It will spot and target him in the crowd."

The lens glowed white briefly. Aviva's pocket computer clicked. She looked at it and frowned.

"Damn, the facial recognition software is corrupted, possibly by the space-time travel," she complained. "The MELOG won't be able to identify Hitler."

"Then the plan is off," said Emil.

"No. I can program the MELOG to shoot its disintegrator ray at a wide angle and sweep it across the room. Everyone will die, but Hitler will be one of them."

"You're crazy. You and your robot will never get past the guards. You're not aiming at Rumeder. You're aiming at Adolf Hitler, *Führer* and Chancellor, the head of state."

"The Nazi, anti-Jewish head of state."

"Also the best-protected head of state in Europe."

"The MELOG can kill Hitler and everyone around him in seconds. They won't know what hit them," Aviva said. "Emil, I need your help. I need all your plans, working drawings, and photographs of the Veterans Hall."

"So you can build a hologram of the Veterans Hall?" Emil said. "No, I won't help you this time."

"Huh? Why not?"

"I will not conspire to assassinate the head of state of Germany."

"Why not?"

"The heavy security is one reason."

"There's another reason?"

"Yes. No honourable officer would kill the head of state of his country. That would be treason."

"Treason? Hitler stripped the Jews of all their rights.

He abolished elections. He scrapped the Constitution. He imprisoned and executed people without trial. *He's* the traitor!"

"Even so, I won't help you assassinate him."

Aviva stormed out of the kitchen and marched into the study. "Where are the plans for the Veterans Hall?"

Emil followed her. "I'm drawing the line here. I won't help you this time."

Aviva opened a filing cabinet and searched it. After finding nothing useful, she went to the next filing cabinet.

"Where are the plans for the Veterans Hall?" she demanded.

"Think of the butterfly effect," Emil urged. "Who knows how much you have done already? By killing Hitler, you could make the future worse."

"What could be worse than six million Jews and over fifty million other Europeans dead?" Aviva argued. "Can there be anything worse? I won't know until I try."

She searched his desk, but again, found nothing.

"Give me the plans or the MELOG will find it by tearing your house apart," Aviva threatened.

Emil's blood boiled. "Would you do that to my wife and me after we have taken you into our home, given you food and shelter, and treated you like a daughter all these months?"

Aviva sighed. "One way or another, I'll find the plans."

She left the study by walking past the portrait of the Kaiser and the safe hidden behind it.

*

November 3, 1937:

Sometimes, Aviva would plead for the plans of the Veterans Hall. At other times, she would demand them. A few times, she threatened him.

Emil tried to reason with Aviva. "Let's say you do succeed in killing Hitler. You would change history. When you return to your own time, would your world exist? Would Israel exist? Would *you* exist? Or would you wipe yourself out of existence?"

"I need to take a risk on those uncertainties," said Aviva. "Future generations will wish someone had dealt with Hitler."

But Emil had his own way of opposing Hitler. He reconvened the local branch of the Reich Association of Jewish Frontline Soldiers at Doctor Berl's house.

"Doctor, did you get the leaflets from national headquarters?" Emil asked.

Berl nodded and opened a large envelope. "Lieutenant Hirsch and I will hand them out in front of the Veterans Hall tomorrow. Who will join us?"

Emil picked up a leaflet. It was addressed "TO ALL GERMAN MOTHERS" in bold, black letters.

A drawing showed a woman sitting in front of a gravestone with an Iron Cross at its top. The woman wore a black dress and held her hands to her face. Carved on the stone were the words:

12,000 German Jewish soldiers died on the field of honour for the Fatherland.

Emil took a deep breath as pride and sadness swelled within him. He continued reading the leaflet.

Christian and Jewish heroes fought together and lie together on foreign soil. 12,000 Jews fell in battle. Blind, enraged Party hatred does not stop at the graves of the dead.

German Women: Do not allow the suffering of Jewish mothers to be mocked!

"This is what we need to tell the people of Kleinheimat," Emil said. "Who will join us tomorrow morning?"

All six of Kleinheimat's remaining Jewish veterans agreed to hand out leaflets.

*

November 4, 1937:

The Jewish veterans wore their medals on their business suits and stood in front of the sign reading "NO JEWS ALLOWED INSIDE!" There they handed out leaflets to people walking by.

Today, Emil felt proud to be German. His medals showed his service to the nation in the Great War. He also felt defiant; for the first time, he openly opposed the National Socialists.

A few people stopped to take leaflets from them. Most, however, kept walking, ignoring the Jews.

But Wettig and the SA did not ignore them. Even before his appointment ceremony, he had recruited new men into the SA. The mayor led twenty Brownshirts towards the six Jewish veterans.

"Hey, Jews, what are you doing here?" Wettig asked.

"We're veterans of the Great War, and we demand to be heard as German soldiers," Emil said.

Wettig laughed. "Look at the war memorial behind you. Do you see any Jewish names on it?"

Thanks to Wettig, the bronze plaque had dents and creases where Goldstein's and Luxembourg's names had been.

A Brownshirt tussled with Doctor Berl. The doctor dropped all his leaflets, and they scattered over the ground. The Brownshirt laughed and pushed Berl backwards repeatedly.

Emil recognized the SA man.

"Gunther!" Emil cried. "What are you doing?"

Emil's former employee turned to him and growled, "Dirty Jew dog, what do you want?"

Emil's heart skipped a beat. Never before had Gunther talked to him with such hatred and disrespect. Emil had given Gunther an education and a career. Now his protégé was insulting and beating Jews.

"Gunther, there's no reason for unpleasantness," Emil said calmly.

Gunther stepped forward and spat into Emil's face. The Brownshirts laughed and chanted, "*Hepp*, *hepp*, Jew! *Hepp*, *hepp*, Jew!"

Another Brownshirt shoved Emil from behind. Emil turned to look at the man.

"I know you," Emil muttered. "Fritz Schultz."

Schultz had danced with Helena at a Christmas party in the Veterans Hall five years ago.

"Jews stabbed us in the back in the Great War," Schultz accused. "How dare you pretend to be a German soldier?"

"I *am* a German soldier," Emil said defiantly. "Fritz, you know that. You knew that when you danced with my daughter."

Schultz swung his fist at Emil. Emil dodged the blow, dropped his leaflets, and hit Schultz in the ribs.

Fighting broke out between the Brownshirts and the Jewish veterans. Though the Brownshirts outnumbered the Jews twenty to six, and though the Jews were older, the Jews fought rather than retreat.

"Stop it! Stop it!" a voice screamed. "Stop in the name of God!"

Father Bernhardt appeared and pulled a Brownshirt away from Emil. Next, he shoved himself between Gunther and a Jewish veteran.

The priest raised his arms and shouted, "Enough! Enough! In the name of God, I order you to stop fighting!"

The Brownshirts stopped and looked at him. The Jews picked themselves off the ground and stood up. All the Jews had bruises.

Wettig's face was red with anger. "Father, why are you here?"

Bernhardt pointed at the Veterans Hall. "Don't fight in front of the war memorial. The Veterans Hall is a sacred shrine to our glorious dead. Why do you always forget that I blessed it before God? You're desecrating it again."

"But Father, these Jews were handing out Zionist Bolshevik propaganda," Schultz complained. "It's our duty to beat them!"

Bernhardt picked up a leaflet and guffawed. "*Herr* Wettig, you call this Zionist Bolshevik propaganda?"

"All Jews are Zionist Bolsheviks," Schultz said.

"Have you ever fought in a war?" Bernhardt asked.

Schultz looked startled. "Uh, no, I've not had the

honour yet, sir."

Bernhardt grabbed Schultz by the arm and hauled him in front of Emil. The priest pointed at Emil's Iron Cross First Class.

"Look at the Iron Cross," Bernhardt ordered. "This man fought bravely in the Great War. Believe me, armed combat is not a child's game. I gave the Last Rites to so many men at the front. Show some respect to these German warriors."

Schultz, visibly shaken, darted to the other Brownshirts. Wettig scowled at the priest.

"Bernhardt, your collar can't protect you forever," Wettig warned. He turned to his men and said, "Come on, boys, we'll get them another day."

The mayor led the Brownshirts away. Bernhardt shook his head.

"None of them served in the army or fought in a war, but they call themselves stormtroopers," Bernhardt said. "What an insult to the real stormtroopers."

Emil felt his heart sink. One of the Brownshirts had been his loyal employee. Another had danced with his daughter. If men like these could change to hate him, what fate awaited him in the Third Reich?

Finally, Emil realized what he needed to do to save his sacred Germany.

*

When Emil returned home, he phoned Otto and asked, "Are you going to Wettig's appointment ceremony on November seventh?"

"Hah, no," said Otto. "Wettig didn't invite any Social

Democrats, not even war veterans like me."

Emil felt relieved. Otto would be nowhere near Hitler.

"Oh, sorry to hear that, but you don't want to be surrounded by golden pheasants," said Emil. "Isn't it terrible that our Veterans Hall will be used for a National Socialist rally?"

"You're right, it's terrible, an insult."

"Such a beautiful building put to such an ugly use. Do you know which room they'll be using?"

"The general manager told me it's the main dining room. It's the only room large enough to hold all the dignitaries."

"Ah, the main dining room, with the big painting of Hitler."

After the phone call, Emil swung aside the portrait of the Kaiser, opened the safe, and took out the plans of the Veterans Hall. He gave them to Aviva, who made a hologram quickly. She worked through the night to plan the attack and download its program and the hologram to the MELOG.

At nineteen hundred on November the seventh, the MELOG would crash through the front door, storm up the spiral staircase to the second floor, and run into the main dining room. The robot would sweep its disintegrator ray across the room and kill everyone.

After the assassination, the MELOG would run downstairs and exit through the front door, where Aviva would be waiting. She would press the recall trigger on her Star of David pendant. A time portal would open and whisk her and the MELOG to Tel Aviv in 2067.

Emil watched in fascination as an animated image of the MELOG ran through the hologram of the Veterans

Hall. In the computerized simulation, the attack lasted only ninety seconds.

Ninety seconds to change the future for eternity.

*

November 6, 1937:

An unexpected visitor appeared at Emil's door: Conrad von Seyfried, wearing his Army uniform.

"Colonel von Seyfried, what a pleasant surprise," said Emil. "Please come in."

"Thank you, Lieutenant Hirsch," Seyfried said. He took off his cap. "I've been away from Kleinheimat for too long."

"What brings you back?" Emil asked as he led Seyfried to the living room. He gestured at a couch, inviting his guest to sit down.

"I need to talk to you," said Seyfried.

Clara came into the room. "Ah, Colonel, welcome back. I didn't know you had come back."

Seyfried stood up. "It's a surprise for me too. I found out only yesterday that I had to return home."

"I wasn't expecting you. Will you stay for tea?"

"I suppose I could. Thank you."

Clara smiled and went to the kitchen. Emil sat down and asked, "What may I do for you?"

Seyfried gave three documents to Emil. They bore the Army's eagle emblem, the Colonel's signature, and the title "SAFE CONDUCT PASS – PORTS OF DEPARTURE" in large black letters.

"What are these?" Emil asked.

"They're safe conduct passes," Seyfried explained. "It's

getting harder and harder for Jews to travel without getting in trouble, so I signed three of them for you, Clara, and Helena. These will give you safe passage to any port, train station, or airport to leave the country."

"Conrad, you want me to leave. You, of all people."

"Please don't misunderstand me. It's because you're my friend that I want you to leave."

"But this is my country. I fought for our Kaiser."

Seyfried nodded sadly. "I know. Don't ever be ashamed of your service to Germany. But our country is changing. You should leave, at least while the National Socialists are in power."

Emil sighed. "So I'm an enemy to the country I defended."

"Emil, please consider it."

Clara returned, carrying a tray with a teapot, cups, and cookies. After she poured tea for Seyfried and Emil, she sat down and bit into a cookie.

"You came back on short notice," Clara said. "What brings you back?"

"The appointment of Karl Wettig as *Ortsgruppenleiter* and commander of the local SA," Seyfried replied. "I'll be attending the ceremony tomorrow night."

Emil stopped drinking his tea.

"Not everyone gets to go to important events, least of all, us," Clara said ruefully. "You must feel honoured."

"Is it an honour?" Seyfried shrugged. "Perhaps. Most of the people there will not be military officers or nobility. They'll be Party members and SA. Beer hall brawlers and golden pheasants."

"If they're not your crowd, why are you going?" Emil asked.

"The War Ministry ordered me to attend because I'm the highest-ranking officer who ever came from Kleinheimat," Seyfried said. "Hah, I guess I'm a local hero."

"Do you have any chance to skip the ceremony?" Emil asked hopefully.

Seyfried shook his head. "No. I have my orders."

"Isn't there something urgent that you need to do, like plan an invasion of Sudetenland?"

"Hah, hah, that's funny! But I think I can survive one night with Party members."

The front door opened, and Aviva walked in. She stopped and stared at Seyfried. Emil saw the fear in her eyes.

Emil had to assure Aviva that their guest was harmless. He smiled at her.

"Aviva, this is our friend Army Colonel Conrad Baron von Seyfried," said Emil. It was postwar practice to combine a nobleman's title with his family name.

Seyfried stood up, clicked his heels, and bowed to Aviva. He strode to the girl and kissed her hand. "I'm pleased to meet you, Miss Aviva."

Emil chuckled softly. Seyfried couldn't resist showing off like a Prussian cadet to a pretty girl.

Aviva looked warily at Seyfried and said, "Thank you."

"Aviva is my niece from Munich," Emil lied.

"Munich? That's a beautiful city," said Seyfried. "By the way, where's Helena?"

"She went to Palestine a while ago."

Seyfried nodded. "You should visit her. I gave you three passes. Why not hold a family reunion?"

"I'll consider it," Emil said.

"Okay." Seyfried grabbed his cap. "Unfortunately, I have some business at the Veterans Hall. Please excuse me."

"Please visit again," said Clara as she opened the door for Seyfried. The colonel bowed to his hosts and left.

*

Later, Clara went out to buy food. Finally, Emil was alone with Aviva.

"Aviva, we have to abort the mission," Emil said.

"Why?"

"Colonel Seyfried will be there. He'll get killed if the attack proceeds."

"We can't abort now. This is the best chance that anyone will get to kill Hitler."

"But we can't kill Seyfried. He's a good man, a real *mensch*."

Aviva looked shocked. "A *mensch*? Are you kidding?"

"Colonel Seyfried is a friend. He wants to help us. You can't kill him," Emil pleaded.

"Why shouldn't I?" Aviva demanded. "He's an army officer."

"So are you."

"He's a German."

"So am I," Emil declared.

"No, you're not," Aviva snapped. "You're a Jew."

"That's what a National Socialist would say."

Aviva scowled at him. "Damn it, how can you give up this chance? So what if we kill him? We'll be saving sixty million people. One man is a very small sacrifice."

"Jews don't sacrifice humans," Emil retorted. "Not

even Abraham had to do it."

"What about your comrades who died in the war?" Aviva said. "Wasn't that a human sacrifice?"

"That was war. This is murder," argued Emil.

Clara came in, carrying a bag of food.

"Is everything okay?" she asked, looking worried.

"Uh, yes, everything's fine," Emil said. Aviva nodded silently in agreement. They had kept the assassination plot secret from Clara because they knew she would disapprove of it.

"That's good. I thought I heard shouting when I came in," Clara said as she walked to the kitchen.

Without saying more, Aviva went upstairs to her room. Emil went down to the basement.

The MELOG stood there, still and silent. Emil waved his hand in front of its head. It did nothing. He tapped the robot's chest. Again, it did nothing. It was in sleep mode.

He went to a desk, opened its drawer, and pulled out a necklace with a Star of David pendant. It was the birthday present he had bought for Helena.

*

An hour later, Clara called them to dinner. Emil and Aviva talked only about mundane things, hiding the truth from Clara.

Aviva wore her Star of David necklace. The plotting against Hitler must have aroused her Zionist zeal, Emil guessed. He knew how well patriotism fuelled the urge to wear national symbols. He was German.

"That's a pretty pendant," Clara said. "Emil, you sent a

similar one to Helena for her birthday, didn't you?"

"Yes, from the same mould," said Emil.

After dinner, they listened to the news on the radio. The government was confiscating Jewish businesses across Germany. A program of music by Mozart followed the news.

"I'm going to take a shower now," Aviva said before going upstairs.

Emil listened for the sound of water. When he heard the shower, he slipped into Aviva's room and found her Star of David necklace on the dresser. He took the necklace and put the other one in its place. It had a fake button glued to its back.

Emil was not very religious, but now, he prayed silently: *Please, God, tell me if I am doing the right thing for the future of the world and our people. Speak to me or show me a sign.*

But God stayed silent and invisible that night.

*

November 7, 1937:

Emil looked at his watch. Eighteen hundred, forty-five: only fifteen minutes until Hitler and Seyfried would die.

Aviva had been calm all day, showing no excitement or anxiety. She was a good soldier, not letting fear or doubt stop her. The Israelis had trained her well.

Clara was away. Emil had urged Clara to visit Doctor Berl and his wife and discuss getting aid from a Jewish relief agency in Munich. He wanted her out of the house tonight.

Aviva came down the stairs. She wore all black: a

jacket, a blouse, and a straight skirt, all from Helena, and the boots of her Israeli Army uniform. Her dark clothes contrasted with the gold Star of David around her neck.

The MELOG came up from the basement. Unlike Aviva, the robot shone like polished silver.

"You're really going through with this," said Emil.

"Don't stop me," Aviva warned. "I like you. Don't make me hurt you."

The MELOG turned its head to Emil.

Aviva gave some commands in Hebrew. The MELOG marched to the door, opened it, and walked outside. Aviva followed the robot.

"Damn, some of the plasmonic transceivers aren't working," Aviva muttered.

"Then abort the mission," said Emil.

"No."

Emil followed Aviva and the MELOG. He watched them go down the street.

"Aviva, please forgive me," he said.

He took Aviva's necklace out of his pocket and pressed the button on the Star of David.

A flash of white light burst around Aviva and the MELOG. A second later, they were gone. Only Helena's black clothes and gold necklace remained on the street.

Emil returned inside the house and ran up to the girls' bedroom. He looked for the Israeli Army uniform but couldn't find it. It must have gone to the future too.

I hope I made the right decision, Emil thought.

*

November 11, 1937:

For the last time, Emil walked through his house. He could sell only a small fraction of his belongings and had to leave much behind. He saw a framed print of the famous drawing "Praying Hands," a Deutsche Grammophon record of Symphony No. 5 in C Minor, Helena's copy of *The Sorrows of Young Werther*, and a newspaper showing a Nobel Prize laureate.

Emil had been proud to belong to the nation of artist Albrecht Dürer, composer Ludwig van Beethoven, author Johann Wolfgang Goethe, scientist Max Planck, and countless other contributors to every area of human achievement. The German people were a great civilization.

But now their civilization had disowned him and was falling into barbarism. It was time for him to leave.

*

1937–1948: Jerusalem, Palestine:

Emil and Clara reunited with Helena. They also saw the Tannenbaums and Hoffman again. They formed a little community of Bavarian exiles in Jerusalem.

The news from Germany grew grimmer each day. On the night of November 9, 1938, the SA Stormtroopers ransacked Jewish businesses all across the country. They looted, burned, and demolished over seven thousand shops and two hundred synagogues. Glass from broken windows lay all over Germany on *Kristallnacht.*

The mass arrests of Jews began. The police imprisoned thirty thousand Jewish men during *Kristallnacht.* Two thousand died within three months.

Emil received a letter from Otto:

The police arrested Dr. Berl and his wife yesterday. I hear they are in a work camp in Dachau. I hope they are well.

Mayor Wettig has expelled all Jews from Kleinheimat. He gave the Jews forty-eight hours to leave for large cities, like Munich. He put a new sign in the town square. It reads, "WELCOME TO KLEINHEIMAT, A JEW-FREE TOWN."

The *Shoah* had begun.

Less than a year later, World War II began. The Haavara Agreement ended, Jews stopped arriving from Germany, and Emil never received another letter from Otto.

In 1942, Emil volunteered to join the British Army's Palestine Regiment. He was too old for combat, but he told the British that he spoke fluent German and could talk to prisoners. The British took him as an intelligence officer. The job suited Emil; as much as he hated the National Socialists, he did not want to take up arms against Germans. However, he agreed to interrogate them.

He surprised his commanding officer by wearing his German medal ribbons on his British uniform, but nobody complained. A captured Afrika Korps captain recognized the Iron Cross ribbon and accused Emil of treason. Emil simply continued questioning the officer.

*

In January 1945, as the Germans retreated from Russia, Emil monitored their radio broadcasts. He heard this news:

The Waffen SS executed Colonel Conrad Baron von Seyfried in Lublin yesterday. The Colonel found a nest of Jews hiding in the countryside but let them escape. A loyal soldier reported him to the SS, which promptly investigated the incident and found him guilty. Let this be a warning to soldiers about the importance of performing your duty to the Fatherland. The German people do not tolerate slackers!

Seyfried had joined the sixty million dead.

Devastated, Emil put his head down on his desk and wept. He had saved Seyfried's life for nothing.

*

Seyfried's death haunted Emil. He wondered if he should have let Aviva and the MELOG attack the Veterans Hall. If Seyfried were to die anyway, wouldn't it have been better to kill Hitler too?

"Don't think about it," Clara advised. "Would you have saved all those people? Maybe. Or would another man have taken Hitler's place and done the same things? Maybe. Hitler couldn't have done everything by himself. He had most of the country helping him."

Emil nodded. His mind told him his wife was right, but his heart felt guilt for sixty million dead.

*

After the war, he returned briefly to Kleinheimat. His old house had burned down during fighting against the Americans. The Veterans Hall was in ruins.

Doctor Berl and his wife never returned from Dachau.

In 1939, the SS arrested Otto Schmidt. They shot him and other Social Democrats at Dachau.

In 1940, the Gestapo arrested Father Bernhardt and beheaded him after a quick trial. His replacement never talked about *Mit Brennender Sorge*.

In 1941, the Army conscripted Fritz Schultz and gave him the honour of fighting in the war. He also had the honour of dying in Stalingrad in 1943.

Gunther Schloss did not die in combat. Instead, he froze to death in Leningrad in 1944.

In 1945, *Ortsgruppenleiter* Wettig put on his dress uniform and swallowed cyanide a day before the Americans arrived. He lacked the courage to fight an armed enemy.

Except for those who had escaped, everyone whom Emil had known was dead.

*

Emil travelled with the British to meet the Soviets in Poland. At a displaced persons camp near Lublin, he showed Seyfried's photo around, hoping someone would recognize him. He was lucky; he found a teenaged boy who had met the colonel.

Witold Kaminski was a fighter in the Polish Home Army when Seyfried's patrol found him and other young Jews hiding in a cabin. They had buried their weapons and Home Army armbands, so Seyfried did not know that they were partisans.

Kaminski recalled the incident. "When he saw us, he told his men, 'They're just kids, let them go.' Most of them agreed or didn't care, but one guy argued with him.

The officer told him, 'The war's almost over. Let's just go home.'

"Then he told us, 'Run away and don't let me catch you again. If I find you again, I'll shoot you.' We ran into the forest and never looked back. You say he's dead now?"

"So I heard on German radio," said Emil. "Thanks for telling me what happened. He was a good friend. I wanted to know what the Germans did not report in the news."

"He saved me and my friends. Isn't it odd? I owe my life to a German officer."

"Yeah, that's odd." Emil paused for a moment. "Where are you going now?"

Kaminski shrugged. "I don't know. My whole family is dead. My village never liked Jews, so I don't want to go back there. I don't think the Communists want me either."

"Kaminski, you've got military experience, you've got brains, and you've got guts. I know a place that could use your talents," Emil said. "Have you considered going to Palestine?"

"No. Why should I live in a desert?"

"Because it's *our* desert. We need people like you to build a new country. I'll tell the Jewish Agency for Palestine that you're here. They'll help you get there."

Kaminski nodded. "I'll think about it."

*

Emil returned to Palestine to find that he could not escape war. Now the Zionists were fighting the British for the independence of Palestine. He was too old and tired to fight for another country. Helena, however, joined the Haganah but quit when she became pregnant with Rachel and got married.

Then, as Aviva had told him would happen, the British Mandate of Palestine became the State of Israel, which the Arabs attacked on its first day of independence.

*

June 10, 1967, West Jerusalem, Israel:

"Aviva was very clear that Israel will lose the 1967 war," Emil remembered. "Our defeat was the reason why the Israelis will be experimenting with time travel a hundred years from now."

Rachel pointed to the TV, which showed Israeli tanks in the Sinai Peninsula. "Obviously, we were not defeated."

"I suspect Aviva or Tasci are here in Israel, at this time," Emil said.

"But would they come without the MELOG? Nobody has seen it," said Clara. "Maybe they didn't need to come back. Maybe they already did something in the past that caused this victory. The butterfly effect."

Rachel shook her head. "You're missing another possibility. Maybe we won on our own, without help from time travellers or robots."

Clara smiled. "Of course, dear. We shouldn't underestimate the IDF."

Rachel hugged her grandparents. "I have to go to work now. I'll visit again. Don't think about time travel and whether you made the right choices. You'll only torture yourself."

Emil ignored her advice. He muttered, "Poor Colonel Seyfried lived and died for nothing. Why did I bother saving him?"

*

As Rachel drove to work, she wondered what had really happened in Kleinheimat in 1937. When she was young, she thought that her grandparents invented the tales to entertain her. But as she grew up, they kept insisting that their stories were true. She refused to believe that people and robots could travel back and forth in time.

No time traveller had helped Israel win this war. The Israelis had won with their own boldness. They began the war by sending almost two hundred fighter jets to attack the enemy airfields. The Air Force held back only twelve planes to patrol Israeli airspace. It was a risky strategy because Jordan and Syria could have attacked by air from the east and easily overwhelmed the dozen planes and the missile batteries. Few countries would have taken the risk, but Israel did.

Rachel went to her desk at IDF Headquarters, where she worked for the Air Intelligence Directorate. As she stapled a note to a photo of an Egyptian airfield, her fellow officers began murmuring. She looked up and saw Major General Mordechai Hod, Commander of the Israeli Air Force.

The Major General walked through the room. The officers cheered as Hod shook hands with them.

Another man, in an Air Force captain's uniform, accompanied Hod. After greeting some officers, Hod stood in an open area among the desks.

"Thank you for your brilliant work," he announced. "Your intelligence analysis helped us defeat the enemy and save our country. Our strategy was risky. I had trouble getting the General Staff and the Prime Minister to agree to it, and even I was unsure it would work."

He looked at the captain. "But this man convinced me the plan would succeed. He convinced me that people who take risks will win. We owe him our gratitude."

Hod brought the captain to Rachel. She stood up, saluted, and said, "Second Lieutenant Rachel Pressburger, sirs."

The Air Force Captain returned the salute and introduced himself. "Captain Witold Kaminski, ma'am."

Rachel couldn't wait to tell her grandfather.

About "Kleinheimat"

Futurecon, founded by Canadian TV host Liana Kerzner, was a science fiction-themed New Year's Eve party run as a "relaxacon", a science fiction convention with limited formal programming and more oriented towards leisure activities. It was also a rather long New Year's Eve party; in its first two years, it began in the evening of December 30 and ended in the afternoon of January 1st. Futurecon ran from 2010 to 2013.

Futurecon spawned two cosplay calendars, which I edited, and a chapbook called *Klein*. My novella "Kleinheimat" was paired with J.M. Frey's story "On His Birthday, Reginald Got" in *Klein*.

Although I was born in Canada and lived here all my life, some people refuse to accept that I am Canadian. Chinese Canadians are especially prone to the perpetual foreigner syndrome, where the dominant society constantly stereotypes them as foreigners.

"Kleinheimat" was inspired by the true history of Jewish German veterans of World War I. Many Jewish Germans served in the German military. Like all soldiers, they loved their country and wanted their country to love them in return. However, less than two decades later, their country stripped them of their human rights and killed them with the rest of the Jews.

I later wrote a paper called "The Perpetual Foreigner Syndrome in Chinese North American Science Fiction and Fantasy". I presented it at the Academic Conference on Canadian Science Fiction and Fantasy (ACCSFF) in 2017, and *The New York Review of Science Fiction* published it in issue 348 (August 2018).

Thanks to Liana Kerzner for publishing "Kleinheimat".

Publishing credits

"Luck of the Irish"
Published in *The Ultimate Unknown*, issue 21, spring 2001, Streamwood, Illinois.

"The Polar Bear Carries the Mail"
Published in *The Dragon and the Stars*, edited by Derwin Mak and Eric Choi, DAW Books, 2010.

"Mecha-Jesus"
Published in *Wrestling With Gods* (*Tesseracts Eighteen*), edited by Liana Kerzner and Jerome Stueart, Edge Science Fiction and Fantasy Publishing, Calgary, Alberta, 2015.

"The Snow Aliens"
Published in *Tales From the Wonder Zone: Explorer*, edited by Julie Czerneda, Trifolium Books Inc., Toronto, Ontario, 2002.

"The Shepherd's Blessing"
Published in *The Chain Story*, developed by Michael Stackpole, 2011.

"Songbun"
Published in *Strangers Among Us: Tales of the Underdogs and Outcasts*, edited by Susan Forest and Lucas K. Law, Laksa Media Groups Inc., Calgary, Alberta, 2016.

"It Came to Eat Our Chicken Wings"
Published in *RicePaper*, winter (Dec.) 2002, Vancouver, British Columbia.

"The Faun and the Sylphide"
Published in *Tesseracts Sixteen: Parnassus Unbound*, edited by Mark Leslie, Edge Science Fiction and Fantasy Publishing, Calgary, Alberta, 2012.

"Seventy-Two Virgins"
Published in *Thou Shalt Not...*, edited by Lee Allan Howard, Dark Cloud Press, Monroeville, Pennsylvania, 2006.

"Cloned to Kill"
Published in *Infinite Space, Infinite God II*, edited by Karina and Robert Fabian, Twilight Times Books, Kingsport, Tennessee, 2010.

"Family Tradition"
Published in *Night to Dawn*, issue 17, March 2010.

"Kleinheimat"
Published in the chapbook *Klein*, by Futurecon 2 science fiction convention, Markham, Ontario, 2011.

Derwin Mak's story "Transubstantiation" won the 2006 Aurora Award for Best Short Fiction. *The Dragon and the Stars*, an anthology that he co-edited with Eric Choi, won the 2011 Aurora Award for Best Related Work. *Where the Stars Rise*, an anthology that he co-edited with Lucas Law, won the Alberta Book Publishing Award for Speculative Fiction Book of the Year in 2018. Derwin also founded the cosplay competition at Anime North, Canada's largest anime convention. He has degrees in accounting and military history and was the first person to capture a Pokémon inside the Royal Canadian Military Institute.